The
BELLES

The BELLES

A NOVEL

LACEY N. DUNHAM

ATRIA BOOKS

New York   Amsterdam/Antwerp   London
Toronto   Sydney/Melbourne   New Delhi

ATRIA
BOOKS

An Imprint of Simon & Schuster, LLC
1230 Avenue of the Americas
New York, NY 10020

This book is a work of fiction. Any references to historical events, real people,
or real places are used fictitiously. Other names, characters, places, and events
are products of the author's imagination, and any resemblance to actual
events or places or persons, living or dead, is entirely coincidental.

First Atria Books hardcover edition September 2025

ATRIA BOOKS and colophon are trademarks of Simon & Schuster, LLC

Simon & Schuster strongly believes in freedom of expression and stands against censorship in all
its forms. For more information, visit BooksBelong.com.

For information about special discounts for bulk purchases, please contact Simon & Schuster
Special Sales at 1-866-506-1949 or business@simonandschuster.com.

The Simon & Schuster Speakers Bureau can bring authors to your live event. For more
information or to book an event, contact the Simon & Schuster Speakers Bureau at 1-866-248-
3049 or visit our website at www.simonspeakers.com.

Interior design by Lexy East

Manufactured in the United States of America

1   3   5   7   9   10   8   6   4   2

Library of Congress Control Number: 2024061482

ISBN 978-1-6680-8486-1
ISBN 978-1-6680-8488-5 (ebook)

To Jan Finkbeiner, who first called me an author,
and to Anne Dunham, who first read me books

"Every old thing is plagued by secrets and ghosts,
real or imagined: the accumulation of buried stories
and the weight of the past."

—Rowan Butler Mandell,
*The History and Myth of the Kitsap and
Natthoghak Valleys of Southwest Virginia*

"The May Queen never fails to be perfect,
the court all shining and beautiful—
and everything tends toward fun."

—Hollins College Handbook
written by students, for students (1950)

The
BELLES

The MISSING GIRLS

BELLERTON COLLEGE, VIRGINIA

WE were Bellerton students once. We traversed the road that curled around one side of the mountain like a black ribbon, winding its way to the six hundred verdant acres of campus nestled in the valley below. The road ended at a spiked, twelve-foot-tall iron gate that reared up like a startled stallion. A painted wood sign sanded and refreshed every August announced BELLERTON COLLEGE in blocky letters, its base crowded by bruise-colored hydrangeas.

We are the girls who followed the road into Bellerton desperate to belong but never to come out.

We arrived on campus with proud parents for whom the very word Bellerton meant prestige and refinement. Bellerton implied family wealth and a surname of solid reputation—proof that we were a privileged class.

As future Bellerton graduates, we would be able to hold our own during conversations on both politics and literature, and we would also know how to arrange excellent charcuterie. We might be smarter than our husbands, but at Bellerton we would have learned the necessary tact to never point this out.

Bellerton was steeped in ritual and surrounded by rumors. Like a conjuring of the imagination, Bellerton was a place threaded with myth. The South as it wanted to be seen, not as it was.

As for us girls, the college wormed into our bodies, molded us into its likeness, created us the same. We were meant to give ourselves over to Bellerton completely. We were meant to heed the paths laid long before us.

But we were the unfavorable ones. The unlucky ones. We were the girls punished for our choices, our iconoclasm, our refusal to conform. We were either too much or not enough. We had not yet learned how to navigate our truest selves in reconciliation with the world.

Within Bellerton's walls, terrible accidents occurred. We went for a walk in the woods and disappeared. We followed mountain paths and were never seen again. We were devoured by a black bear, our remains never to be found. We hung from a library beam. We dropped from a window and broke our neck. When we fell gravely ill, no one believed it was poison. We were disposed of in shallow graves or flung into the creek. Dissolved into the college's maw.

With the start of each new academic year, we recalled how our eyes shone with hope and determination. How we once walked the campus's circular road, counted the ancient trees. Whether we went left or right didn't matter since the road curled back to its beginning, complete and whole.

And now, it's your turn.

Beware of who keeps secrets because appearances can be deceiving. We are not the only ones who will be watching.

Always remember that these grounds are haunted by girls who were once exactly like you.

Fall
1951

Welcome to Bellerton, where you are
now part of a very special group of women.
We hope you will find it easy to blend in and
to follow the rules. The boundaries are clear.
Stay within them, and you will thrive.

—BELLERTON STUDENT HANDBOOK, 1951–1952

Chapter 1
DEENA

SHE had done it: traveled five hours through three Virginia counties to arrive at Bellerton College as someone different than who she had been yesterday, or this morning, or even an hour earlier. She'd had no idea what new life she was embarking on when she climbed into the cab at the Greyhound station and the driver loaded her brand-new Chic Miss suitcases into the trunk. Now, with golden light flooding the campus and the air thick with humidity, she was eager for it all to begin. She was ready to fulfill the promise of attending Bellerton as Miss Deena Evangeline Williams.

She held tightly on to her pocketbook, which contained her acceptance letter, detailing her room and dormitory assignment, and her last three dollars. She considered the stately trio of dormitories flanking the center of campus, where enormous oaks with leaves of the deepest green she had ever seen cast wide gulfs of shade over a lush quad. The mountains lay beyond, ominous. The three-story brick buildings had shutters flayed wide in defiance of the day's heat. White columns held up porticos that jutted over porches painted a deep navy, dotted with white rockers. Deena imagined how lovely it would be to sit there, drinking sweet tea from a sweating glass pitcher with yellow lemon rinds floating at the top.

A shadow moved on the nearest porch, and a pale hand emerged from the gloam to grip the railing.

Someone was watching her.

"Hello?" Deena called.

She fumbled with her luggage, carrying it a few feet down the walkway before setting it down and calling out again.

A slim redhead appeared on the stone steps that led from the porch. The girl wore a tailored green-and-white seersucker dress, and her neck and earlobes were adorned with matching pearls. A wide-brimmed hat shaded her face.

"You're in South Hall?" The girl's honeyed voice sounded disbelieving. She carried herself with such self-assurance that Deena's tongue stuck to the roof of her mouth.

She at last stammered yes and reached for her bags.

"Darling, don't worry," the girl said in a pitying tone. "The help will take care of it."

Her words summoned an older man, whom Deena hadn't noticed standing nearby. He wore a porter's uniform with a tight cap and gold-buttoned jacket. He was grandfatherly but deferential, and he must have been hot wearing all those dark colors, the jacket buttoned to his neck. Deena swayed uncomfortably when he took up her suitcases, which had been expensive. She had even paid extra to have them monogrammed with her new initials, and she didn't want any scratches or dented corners.

"You can take those bags to—" The girl inclined her head at Deena. "What room?"

Deena retrieved the crumpled paper from her pocketbook. "Room 210."

"Take these to 218 and leave them beside the bed." Ignoring the man she'd just given orders to, she said to Deena, "That's a better room. You'll like it."

"Is that allowed?" Deena didn't know what to do with her empty hands—everything she owned was in the bags the man held. Nervously, she tucked her hair behind her ears, uncertain of everything, herself most of all.

"I'll see that it's sorted with all the right people. It will be our little secret."

The man was waiting expectantly. The girl cocked her head at Deena as if she was a child. Deena looked at the man and said thank you, yet he remained in place. The quiet was broken by the sharp crack of the girl's heels as she gracefully descended the stone steps, then unclasped her clutch. She reached in and passed the man a nickel tip.

He pocketed it and entered South Hall, where he could be heard clomping to the second floor.

"I see you're new here," the girl said, eyeing Deena up and down.

Deena flushed, embarrassed by her foible. The day was sweltering, the sidewalk in direct sun. She shielded her eyes, thinking she would have to buy a hat like the girl's once her next deposit came through. They might even go shopping together, and the girl could show her the fashionable places. Deena smoothed her dark skirt and righted the crooked seam of her hosiery. Her short-sleeved blouse was crumpled from hours of bus travel prior to the taxi, and sweat dampened the fabric at her armpits. The redhead was so pristine that Deena could imagine the girl's journey in contrast, riding in a large, air-conditioned white Ford with chrome teeth that gleamed viciously in the sun. Deena clutched her skirt, and tried not to feel like a drab, dirty speck beside this girl.

"It's a Bellerton tradition to dress up the staff in these silly costumes on freshmen welcome day, to help us girls settle in. First impressions are last impressions, my mother always says."

Deena wasn't sure what to say, already nervous of the first impression she was making.

"I'm Ada May Delacourt." The girl extended her hand delicately, palm down, fingers curled toward the ground. Deena grasped her powdery fingers with a quick shake. "My sister Caroline graduated from Bellerton class of 1949. She was crowned May Queen. That's how I know about the ritual with the staff."

"What's the May Queen?" Deena asked, her voice dampened by the humidity. Ada May continued as if Deena hadn't spoken.

"Your new room is a good size, middle of the hall, not too near the bathrooms." Ada May dropped her voice. "They make us first years share bathrooms, like we're in the army. My sister says it's not so bad, as long as everyone on your floor is clean."

Ada May smelled clean, of lye and a light perfume. Freckles dabbed her small nose, pleasant specks that made her appear refined. She was like a cat, Deena thought. One that would pounce when you thought it had been napping.

"Lovely to meet you." Ada May brushed past Deena and sailed across the grassy quadrangle before Deena could say goodbye. Only after she was out of view did Deena realize that Ada May hadn't asked for her name.

She was exactly the type of woman Grandmother had warned her about.

◆   ◆   ◆

Perched on her bed after unpacking, Deena considered how easy it had been to cross the threshold between her life before and the one she was just beginning. She tucked her room key on its string beneath her blouse and used the bathroom, where the light pulsed gray through the frosted windows, and she heard the rustle of distant whispered conversations. She was about to return to her room when a trio of cleaning women appeared on the stairs wearing crisp smocks the color of robin's eggs. They immediately went to work. Two women ran dust rags over the doorframes and wainscoting, while the third mopped the wood floors. Their movements were quick and efficient, and languid strings of conversation passed between them.

Deena thrilled in seeing them. They reminded her of her grandmother—except Grandmother was white and these women were Black. But they held the same stiffness in the joints as they bent over, the same easy handling of mops and polishing cream. All her life, Grandmother had scrubbed the floors and toilets of other people, washed their linens and made their beds. Collected their secrets. You could know a person from the hairs on their pillow and what you pulled from the pockets of their dirty laundry on washday. Pay attention, her grandmother often said. Things that were of no consequence to those who paid you might become useful to you. And hadn't she been right?

One of the women straightened and stretched her back, her movement labored, her joints cracking. Her gaze settled upon Deena, and she let out a choked shriek. Deena startled and rammed into the doorjamb, then dug her nails into her palms, worried she might say the wrong thing. The scent of lemon and bleach filled her nose. The oldest of the trio held up her hands.

"Miss, pardon us, miss. Alice is—" She bowed her head. "I mean we're sorry to disturb you, miss."

Deena understood what it could mean to become visible when you served others: accused of stealing jewelry or ruining a piece of delicate white tablecloth with careless ironing; subjected to fingers crawling over your body like you were a beautiful vase. An object meant for the pleasure of another. She understood because it was her mother's story. It was her story. If her mother had not been a vase, Deena would not exist.

She remembered Grandmother gripping her five-year-old wrist the day of her mother's funeral, her face bent to Deena's.

"The most important rule of cleaning houses is to stay unseen. Never let yourself be visible without an invitation." Deena would come to know her grandmother's words by heart: Never leave a smudge on the drinking glasses or silver. Check the linens and bedsheets for stray hairs. "You don't want nothing to show you was ever there. Me, I'm the quietest little ghost. No one sees me unless I want them to see me. Then, poof! There I am, neat and tidy in my uniform."

Deena's back throbbed from where she'd hit the doorjamb. The pain spoke to an inevitable bruise. She was about to wave them on and return to her dorm room, but then wondered how Ada May might respond.

The answer: firmly and without giving up any of her power. That's

what Bellerton girls did. Or so Deena had witnessed with the porter earlier. She would be kind about it; she would look the women in the eyes.

Deena drew herself taller and crossed her arms. "It's all right," she said
sternly. "I forgive you." The words sat heavy on her tongue.

The women took this as dismissal. They gave a stiff-kneed curtsey and
took the back staircase to the first floor. Deena waited until she heard
them leave, then descended the main stairs and paused at the bottom
when she caught a glimpse of herself in the mirror hanging in the entry.

Her face was a pale oval hovering in the glass, her features blurred and
smudged in the dust, all except for her eyes. She stepped closer, drawn
in by those eyes. If Deena hadn't known the reflection was her own, she
might have thought what she saw was an apparition. A spirit come to
haunt her.

Chapter 2
DEENA

DEENA soon learned she was one of only six freshmen granted permission to live in South Hall, and she felt chosen. The student rooms on the second floor were all singles. The third floor was the housemother's rooms and general storage, and the first contained formal spaces the college used for important gatherings, such as the annual trustees' lunch.

She had found out from a book on Bellerton history left in the dorm that South Hall was one of the school's original buildings, dating from the time when it was Belle Terre, an antebellum health spa offering water cures. Like its sister halls for sophomores, juniors, and seniors, South Hall was named for its compass direction; old and well tread, it was familiar with the wild ruckus of the new girls on arrival day.

Deena eavesdropped on the excited chatter, absently running her room key across her palm. Suddenly, her door was flung open. A girl who was a head taller than her, with proud shoulders and a commanding gait, blocked the entry, then pushed past, knocking into Deena.

"This is supposed to be my room!"

"There was a last-minute change," Deena stammered. She stuck out her hand, thinking to win over the complaining girl with friendship, then shrank back when the girl ignored her, making her feel the size of a dust mote. Deena tucked the key on its string beneath her blouse and flattened herself to the wall, hoping the hubbub would pass, yet at the same time disbelieving that *she* was the cause of it all. Never had anyone wanted what she had.

A man charged into the room and squeezed the girl's shoulder. "Sweetheart, be reasonable." His voice straddled patience and exasperation. The girl's father, Deena realized with a twinge of longing. He was also tall, his face broad and his expression disarming. "You still have four walls and a window, just like everyone else."

"She's hardly brought anything." The girl's eyes darted around the room, slipping past Deena as if she wasn't there. The girl wasn't whining; she was angry.

The father sounded pleading. "Now, I don't see what that has to do with—"

"I deserve the bigger room," the girl said obstinately.

Deena wanted to protest—she was certain the rooms were equal size because she had peeked inside each one earlier—but the girl's prickly irritation seemed likely to tip into a permanent grudge, and she didn't want that.

The knotted string at her neck snapped suddenly, and her room key clattered to the floor. The girl grabbed it triumphantly, a wad of chewing gum rolling on her tongue.

"Give that back!" Deena cried.

"Now, honey," the father said in a cajoling tone.

Ada May knocked. "What's the trouble?" Her voice was like rose water, sharpness cloaked in sweet.

The girl jerked her thumb at Deena. "She's taken my room."

"But I didn't," Deena said, swelling with frustration. "Ada May, you said—"

Ada May took the imposing girl's arm, an intimacy she had not extended to Deena. "There, there." She patted the girl's hand, leaning close.

"Sometimes accommodations are made for the benefit of all. The good news is that your new room is next to mine. We'll be marvelous friends. Come, I'll help move your things."

Ada May coaxed the key away and passed it to Deena without looking at her, then led the girl and her father from the room.

Deena slumped to the floor and drew her knees to her chest. What if her new classmates ended up hating her? Was that why Ada May had swapped the rooms—because already she didn't like Deena? But that was nonsense. They didn't even know one another. Grandmother had told her not to let the other girls bother her, that she was better than all of them put together. Deena thought about how far she had already come and the possibilities blooming before her after graduation: a large house boasting crisp linens and immaculate, polished silverware; lovely, fashionable dresses and felt hats with sprays of feathers. Everything Deena Williams deserved.

She fiddled with the string that was still looped through her room key, rolling the halves between her thumbs and forefingers, surprised to find that it hadn't frayed. The thread appeared to have been cut.

◆　◆　◆

THE NEXT DAY AT BREAKFAST, FORTY-ONE LIVELY FRESHMEN CHATtered on, everyone seeming to have found friends except for her. Deena asked for too much at the buffet, unable to refuse the gratuitous portions, and sat alone. Soon, guilt welled up when she realized that she would never finish it. Around her, waiters collected half-eaten plates abandoned by other girls: Whole slices of untouched toast and picked-at grapefruit. Glistening sausages and heaped scrambled eggs. The girls always drained their coffees, Deena noticed, then retreated to smoke on the porches. Already they had found their rhythms; already they knew exactly what to do. But hadn't they always known, just as Ada May knew to tip the porter for helping with the luggage?

Embarrassed to be the only girl sitting alone, she went to examine the portraits that lined the dining room walls—an unnerving ring of stern-faced men observing the girls—and was drawn to the largest and most richly detailed of the paintings. The man in it stood with one hand upon a desk and the other cocked at his hip. Various items were scattered on the desk's surface: gold coins and an eye patch; the skull of a small animal; a dried bundle of lavender tied with a navy ribbon. Over his shoulder, an idyllic scene unfolded beyond a window: rolling mountains in the distance and, nearer, a blotch of woods from which a sloughing creek emerged. She was intrigued by the painting's feeling of pretense, as if the man in his long coattails and cravat was in disguise.

Deena returned to her table, startled to find two girls sitting there. Her plate had been removed by a waiter while she had been beguiled by the portrait. She slid into her chair anyway, eager to finally have companions, and quickly introduced herself, remembering Ada May's words from the day before: first impressions are last impressions.

"I was worried I would be eating alone. I overslept," one of the girls said. "I'm Nell Lawton-Peters. It's nice to meet you." Nell's small eyes sank into her round, acne-scarred cheeks. Her skin was shiny and her hair flatly brown, pushed back from her face with a pink headband. She wasn't at all pretty and seemed talkative to make up for it. Deena felt a pang of pity for her.

Without waiting for the other girl to introduce herself, Nell indicated the portrait Deena had been scrutinizing. "That's Bellerton's founder, William Grayson Dickey. He was also the longest serving president. Someone told me," Nell admitted, pointing. "Her, over there."

Deena followed Nell's gesture and saw Ada May Delacourt, her copper hair glossy beneath the room's lights, her fingers delicately holding her coffee cup. A dozen girls crowded at Ada May's table, including the determined, bossy girl who had given Deena such trouble about her room yesterday. Her stomach knotted to think that she had missed out on a friendship with Ada May, who already appeared to be popular.

Nell gabbed on about setting up her room and the classes she planned to take, but Deena wasn't listening; she was too busy keeping an eye on

Ada May's table. When the group finished their breakfasts and rose in a flock of laughter, Deena vaulted to her feet, cutting Nell off mid-sentence. "I have to go." Nell looked startled, then offended, but Deena persisted, saying she remembered something she needed to do, and maneuvered past Nell and the silent girl whose clothes were all wrong for the season, thick woolens in winter colors. Whatever else she needed to learn to fit in, at least Deena knew to wear cottons until the first of October.

"Mary Burden," the girl said, introducing herself at last. "You should stay here with us, Deena Evangeline Williams."

Deena felt caught between Mary's invitation and the lure of Ada May's group, their faces radiant in the sunlight spilling from the open dining room door. Grandmother's advice rang in her ears. *Get in with the popular girls, and you'll blend in. Doors will open for you*, she had said. *But on your own, you'll stick out.* She needed the security of a group. Deena pretended she hadn't heard Mary and fell in behind the winsome girls as if she'd been with them all along.

• • •

AFTER BREAKFAST, DEENA AND THE SIX OTHER GIRLS IN HER DOR-mitory gathered in South Hall's drawing room for their official meet and greet, the first item on a typewritten agenda that had been slid under each girl's door early that morning.

The room was airy and light-filled, the French doors thrown open and a breeze ruffling the girls' hair. Unlike the dingy common room on the girls' floor with its banged-up furniture, the drawing room looked regal: the wallpaper washed, the wainscoting gleaming. Two oval mirrors inset in gilded frames hung opposite one another. Deena studied the intricate crown molding of vines and fruit, a delicious bounty she imagined plucking to eat. Were the freshmen assigned to other dormitories sitting in rooms as beautiful as this one?

It was nine-thirty. Another Bellerton year commenced like a sigh. A small circulating fan buzzed from atop the sideboard while the girls regarded one another in wary silence, unwilling to be the first to speak. Deena bit her cuticle but dropped her hand when Ada May caught her eye from across the circle and subtly shook her head. A creeping sense that she didn't belong at Bellerton stuck in Deena's throat for the second time that day.

Nell recited, "There are no happy accidents, only happy meetings." She blushed at her own earnestness and adjusted her pink headband. "My mother likes to say that. I miss her already."

She told them about herself, absently fiddling with a thin necklace chain on which hung a silver medallion. Nell Lawton-Peters was from Philadelphia and a Catholic. Strange, Deena thought, since even she knew that girls from the north rarely enrolled at Bellerton.

"Why do you have two last names?" interrupted a girl with bright red lipstick.

"My mother wanted to keep her name when she married, and my father insisted they hyphenate."

"Your mother's last name is Peters?"

"Lawton, actually."

"She put herself first." The lipsticked girl folded her arms over her chest.

The blonde who had barged into Deena's room introduced herself next, her hair swinging from its horsetail hairdo with her every gesture. She was gregarious and ready for fun. She was also the tallest of the South Hall girls and carried herself proudly. "I'm Sheba Wyatt. I went to boarding school at Kennewick in Albemarle County."

"Sheba's school and my school were rivals in equestrian competitions, and men. We sometimes took pity and let them win—with the men," Ada May said drolly.

Sheba spun to face her. "I knew you looked familiar. A Holloway girl!"

Deena bit the inside of her cheek, wondering if that explained why Ada May had swapped her room—not because Deena had favorably impressed her, but because she was already acquainted with Sheba and wanted to keep her close. Grandmother had warned her that the girls with common backgrounds always stuck together, even when they didn't like one another much, and that she'd need to find ways to stick with them, too.

Sheba slid a piece of gum into her mouth and pointed at the boyish brunette sharing her sofa. "You go next."

The girl hopped to her feet as if she had been called to recite her English theme to the class. Her bony limbs jutted from her torso. With no hips or breasts and very short hair, the girl, Deena thought, looked more like a boy. Despite her thin, angular frame, she was glamorous, and her androgyny felt mystifying, yet exciting. Deena had never met anyone like her. When the girl finally spoke, Deena noted her unapologetic and casual way of addressing them.

Her name was Fred Scott, but when she said where she was from, no one could understand her; she swallowed the word's interior, so it came across as a mumble. Fred repeated it, and still no one could make it out. "I said I'm from Bal-ti-more," she repeated, this time enunciating every syllable. This elicited sounds of approval.

"Isn't Fred a boy's name?" Nell asked. She had been slathering herself in sun lotion while the others spoke, and an unblended smear of it streaked across her nose.

Fred shoved a hand into her brunette bob, pushing it into disarray. "It's Winifred, but I hate that." She plunged into her seat, grumbling.

The lipsticked girl, to Deena's right, jumped in. Her name was Prissy Nicholson. She was from Texas, with family money from both oil and ranching. "All the best Texas has to offer," she said in a slight drawl, her vowels emerging as if they had been stuck in molasses.

Prissy was a slim girl with a rail-like body and curves in all the right places. Deena had overheard rumors in the bathroom that morning that Prissy rarely ate. In fact, she had seen Prissy at breakfast with a plate containing only a single salted egg.

Prissy continued. "My daddy's a Bellerton trustee, and I'm allowed a radio in my room. I hope y'all will come and enjoy it." She caught her reflection in the mirror and paused to adjust her hair. "I'm also permitted two horses in the barn. Dixie's all mine, but if anyone wants to borrow Dallas, just ask and he's yours."

Prissy's lipstick color reminded Deena of her grandmother's canned tomatoes, which she ate straight from the jar with a spoon, sprinkled with a pinch of salt and black pepper, the juice running down her chin and forearm.

Ada May's introductions came next. She held her elegant, pale limbs primly while she spoke, her back straight and her flute-like voice kind and inviting. Like Prissy, Ada May's father was a trustee, but unlike Prissy, she came from a long line of Bellerton girls and was descended from the founder. Deena was impressed by this fact, recalling the portrait hanging in the dining room. She studied Ada May more closely, taken by her patience and grace, the way she spoke with indulgence but never put others down.

Ada May was the type of Bellerton girl Deena longed to become. Prissy demanded that her new Texan money be seen, but Ada May was sure-footed concerning her place in the world. Ada May didn't share what kind of business the Delacourts were in, but Deena didn't doubt it was important. She wanted the warmth of Ada May's attention, the golden assurance of her recognition. And she noticed, too, how it wasn't just her that was enraptured by Ada May—it was all of them.

That summed up her dormmates, the other South Hall freshmen: Ada May (regal) and Prissy (spoiled) and Sheba (loud). Nell was nervous and overly earnest, and Fred was the confident misfit. What about Deena Williams? Who was she?

When it was finally her turn, Deena told the version of her story that she had practiced over these past few weeks: She was an orphan raised by her grandmother.

This much was not a lie.

What she would never tell them: She had left home as herself and stepped onto the Bellerton College grounds as Deena Williams. Her grandmother had told her often that being smart was recognizing when an opportunity presented itself, grabbing onto it, and never letting go.

As Deena Williams, she could take classes with girls like Ada May Delacourt. She could learn from the same books and study the same subjects, advance herself above her family's station and become better than a maid. She would learn to carry herself like the Delacourts did, and how to speak pleasantly. She would become refined and polished, indistinguishable from them.

The others might have been born with silver in their mouths and gold in their pockets, but as Deena Williams, she would prove that silver and gold could be fashioned from river pebbles if one paid attention to how it was done.

Chapter 3

DEENA

THE girls moved to the second item on the day's agenda, the campus tour, Deena still tingling with warmth from the others' approval of her story, especially Ada May's kindly squeeze of her arm. Perhaps she would fit in at Bellerton after all.

Several South Hall girls popped to their rooms for sunhats. Deena tore through her things, searching for her sunglasses, until she realized she must have left them in the taxicab. She had bought them with her new money and they were expensive. She was furious with herself for behaving so carelessly.

Then, a strange thing happened. The other girls had already left and Deena was about to join them when a door at the other end of the hall opened. A girl who wasn't at the meet and greet appeared, one Deena hadn't yet met, wobbling with the weight of two enormous suitcases.

"You're leaving?" Deena asked.

The girl wore white sheepskin traveling gloves and clutched her suitcase handles tighter. "I'm not staying." She sounded exasperated by the question. "You may help me by taking the rest." She indicated with a sharp nod toward her room. She spoke with condescension, and Deena rankled at being talked down to, especially by another freshman—treated like the girl she had once been. Did she look like an outsider? Or was this stranger simply used to ordering others around?

Deena raised her chin, thinking of the Bellerton girl she was supposed to be. "No, I don't think I will." She hurried downstairs and across the quad to the library where her dormmates gathered, burning with her own boldness.

She spotted the other South Hall girls, standing under the last ripples of morning shade and scuttled beside them. Already unspoken bonds were forming and she refused to be left out. The remaining freshmen, who had walked from the dorms at the far end of campus, were left exposed to the throbbing sunlight.

"Is Mary here?" Deena asked Nell, looking for her among the freshmen.

"Who?" Nell asked.

Deena was about to tell Nell about the student she had seen leaving, but just then a smartly dressed girl climbed the library steps, clapped her hands for attention, and introduced herself as senior class president Peggy Donovan.

"Welcome, future Bellerton graduates!" Peggy declared.

The girls applauded and cheered, her boisterous warmth putting them at ease. Already, Peggy felt like an encouraging big sister, popular and well liked by all. Deena thought her very pretty, with a friendly, open face and bright, confident smile.

"A few expectations before we begin the campus tour. At Bellerton, please don't pick the flowers, as tempting as they are. Be on time to your obligations. Dress with your self-worth and the college's reputation in mind. And finally, be ready to make friends that you'll have for the rest of your lives." The freshmen smiled shyly at one another when she said this. Deena stuck close to Ada May as Peggy ushered everyone into the library.

The sudden rush of darkness was exhilarating and momentarily disorienting. Deena braced herself against a wall, discombobulated. For a brief moment, she thought she saw a girl's bloated face, but it vanished with a shake of her head. The heat, she told herself, feeling light-headed. The valley trapped it. No one else seemed bothered, and she didn't want to call attention to herself. Peggy was already explaining library study hours and overdue fines. She told them about the two portable record players and records available for checkout, and the freshmen broke into excited chatter that she quieted with a finger to her lips.

"Are there any questions?"

Fred raised a hand. "I heard the library was haunted? Is it true?"

The girls all held their breath, waiting for Peggy's answer. Deena hadn't heard any ghost stories herself, but it was easy to look around the campus and know deep down that you were not alone walking the grounds.

Peggy dropped her voice, nervously looking around her. "There was a sad accident many years ago involving a girl who was deeply troubled. That's what you should concern yourselves with—the well-being of your fellow sisters, not fanciful ghost tales."

Prissy spoke up. "My father told me all about it. He's a trustee?" Her Texan lilt inflected upward on the last word. Deena thought Prissy's red lipstick looked garish in the library's half-light. "A girl hanged herself from a ceiling beam."

The freshmen collectively gasped, delighting in being afraid, whether they believed in the spectral or not, and though Deena played along, her gaze swept to the ceiling despite herself. The smooth plaster was dotted with light fixtures, no beams in sight. Yet she could not relax, seized by the idea of a girl her age choosing such violence against herself. Deena silently cursed Prissy for leading her into these dark thoughts.

"Her spirit is said to be trapped inside the library." Prissy calmly folded her hands over her skirt, clearly enjoying the attention, though by her smirk, Deena didn't think she truly believed the story she was telling. "She's often seen at night wandering the stacks."

Fred rounded her lips into ghostly moans. "Beware, beware." Sheba shrieked in mock fright, linking her arm with Fred's. Deena jealously watched the pair, longing for a fast friendship of her own. She noticed Ada May angling away from them, perhaps thinking the conversation was distasteful, even beneath her, and Deena mimicked Ada May's disapproving expression, hoping that would earn the girl's favor.

"There have been plenty of mysterious *accidents*." The last word dripped from Prissy's lips. "And lots of restless spirits at Bellerton."

"That's enough," Peggy said sternly. "Such nonsense. Ladies don't engage in gossip and rumors." The senior was on edge now, her indulgence of them wiped away. "Aren't you all seventeen? This is Bellerton, where we believe in rigorous study and moral integrity. And if you don't measure up, Mrs. Tibbert will hear about it, and then you'll have bigger problems. So, I'd worry less about made-up ghost stories and more about the academic year ahead." She dabbed her forehead with a handkerchief. Light traces of makeup materialized on the cloth.

Peggy led them back into the brightness of the outdoors with its suffocating heat. Deena lingered at the edge of the group; she couldn't help but feel drawn to the library and craned her neck to take in its sloping portico, struck by how it gave the impression of hooded eyes watching her. In the latticed window of the library's attic story, she was certain a shadow darkened the glass. They *were* being watched; she wasn't imagining it. She glanced at Peggy pushing the tour onward, then back at the library attic.

The shadow was gone.

♦ ♦ ♦

A BLACK ROAD CURVED AROUND THE CAMPUS LIKE A RIBBON, AND the tour followed its bend toward shaded barns ripe with the smell of hay and animal bodies. Peggy pointed to a dirt path that she said was perfect for walking in cooler weather. The path enclosed horse pastures bordered on one side by woods.

"The woods are off-limits." Peggy was firm on this point.

"Because of the bear attack," a girl with very thin eyebrows blurted out.

Peggy's look of sharp reproval squelched any further discussion. "Too many girls have lost their way in the woods. We don't want to risk that happening to any of you."

The trees whispered warnings that seemed just out of earshot. Deena shuddered, recalling the menace of hunched, gnarled trees at the end of the dirt road where she and Grandmother had lived. It went without saying that only a foolish girl would enter a forbidden wood when another path had been clearly laid for her to follow. Even from the pasture's edge, the somber trees seemed to warn the girls to keep away. Then, Deena remembered the founder's portrait and realized that there must be a lolling creek that cut through it. She smiled to herself, delighted that she had unearthed a Bellerton secret.

The whinny of a horse drew her back from her thoughts. It was midday now, the air dense with humidity. She shielded her eyes with one hand. Fred nudged her. "I have an extra pair of sunglasses in my room. You can have them." Before Deena could respond, Sheba stole Fred's attention away with her enormous laugh.

Peggy gestured to the stables. "Please remember that you cannot join the dressage team until your second Bellerton year, though you are welcome to go riding in your free time."

Deena stepped through the open stable door into the crepuscular light, drawn by the shuffle of hooves. She had never been near horses and hadn't expected the bulk of their muscular bodies, heavy as boulders. Beneath slick coats, they coursed with energy that yearned for release. The smell of sawdust and wild strength filled her with heady wonder. A black stallion stamped in its stall and turned toward her, wet eye rolling. The horse bucked its head and gibbered. She stumbled backward, tripping over the handle of a broom, and was caught by gentle, forgiving hands.

"I'm so very sorry," she said, her cheeks heating. She turned to see it was Ada May who held her, and her embarrassment deepened.

Ada May's touch on her shoulder was firm, a solid weight Deena hadn't expected. There was power behind it, a strength hidden beneath the surface. The gold ring on Ada May's left hand shimmered in the barn's dappled light: two bands connected with a striking green stone.

Deena dusted her skirt. "That was kind of you, thank you."

Ada May dispersed Deena's gratitude with a wave of her hand, reaching to tuck a strand of hair behind Deena's ear. "You had quite a start." She stepped back. "You sure you're all right?"

Deena's foot throbbed from having twisted at an angle when she tripped. "Oh yes, I'm fine." How silly she was to be frightened of an animal trained and tied. Yet she was, her body tense and humming, seeming to warn her she was in danger. "I've never been around horses. What's it like to ride one?"

"Freeing." Ada May gestured at the horse that had startled Deena. "That's my Brutus. He must have sensed I was near." The horse nuzzled his head into her palm. She cooed, "You're a good boy. Aren't you such a good boy, Brutus?" The stallion's muscles rippled beneath his shiny black coat. Deena was immediately jealous of their attachment. She wanted Ada May for herself.

◆ ◆ ◆

THE TOUR CONTINUED UP THE HILL, WHICH LEVELED ONTO A WIDE ridge where the professors and their wives lived in modest ranch-style houses hunched together like pigeons. Deena admired the homes' modest yards and quaint trees, the sturdy walkways demarcated by slabs of gray shale that led to a front door.

The girls neared a wide grassy lawn where a pig was being roasted on a spit. "The annual faculty barbeque," Peggy whispered, motioning them to stay close.

As the girls approached, the professors' talk fell away, replaced by the thrum of insects. Deena caught a glimpse of the faculty wives half-hidden by the shade of magnolias, their bodies as stiff as mannequins in a shop window. They were fitted to the nines in summer dresses, with bolero jackets for modesty, but their expressions were hidden beneath enormous sunhats and crater-like sunglasses. Most of the wives looked to be eight or ten years older than Deena, yet she felt like a child in her patent leather Mary Janes and pastel colors. The men's silent and intense gaze was unpleasant, the way their eyes crawled like ants over the girls. Their jowls made them look like catfish.

Peggy scuttled the group onto a short drive enclosed by poplar trees and mountain laurel grown to monstrous heights. "Well done, ladies. The men can sometimes be bawdy." Out came her handkerchief to daub the perspiration again. "Now, we visit Mrs. Tibbert, whose husband is the college president." A furrow appeared between Peggy's brows. "She's a very important person on campus. Best behavior is a must."

Deena wished Ada May would share what she'd heard from her older sister about Mrs. Tibbert—whether she was a hard nut to crack or a kind shoulder to cry on—but Ada May kept quiet, her blue silk fan trembling with short flicks of her wrist. A thin tendril of hair swept her cheek.

The walkway ended abruptly at a square two-story brick house simple in style, but that still awed Deena for its size. The sky peeked blue around it, and the bricks were whitewashed and pristine. She was far from the muck and grime of her childhood now. The shutters, hinged wide like jaws, were painted the same saturated navy as the porches. After a full afternoon of walking the Bellerton campus, the girls' tour ended here with the college president's wife.

Over the front door hung a metal decoration in the shape of two intertwined serpents. Deena swallowed hard. She had seen all manner of talismans meant to keep bad luck away, but nothing ornate like this, and she was glad when two freshmen she didn't know shouldered past her, jostling to be at the front.

Mrs. Tibbert stepped out onto the porch, wearing a navy dress with a high crisp collar, its creases sharp as razor blades and its sleeves clamped at her elbows like tourniquets. A string of pearls pressed against her collarbone, and for some reason they made Deena think of her grandmother's tumors. Matching pearls rimmed with gold weighted Mrs. Tibbert's earlobes. A few steps behind her stood a stately Black woman wearing a crisp white apron over her smock, a frilly white cap pinned atop her head. Deena recognized her as one of the women who had been cleaning the empty dormitory the day before. She wondered how many people Bellerton employed in service of keeping everyone comfortable.

Mrs. Tibbert took a platter from the housemaid and offered it to the freshmen. They surged forward, each taking a still-warm chocolate-chip cookie, Deena quick to snatch the biggest one before the others noticed. When the plate was empty, Mrs. Tibbert handed it to the woman and spoke while the girls ate their cookies. "I hope you have enjoyed your tour of the grounds. We are so proud of Bellerton's beauty."

There was a murmur of agreement from the girls, and Prissy with her mouth full of cookie wished out loud for a glass of milk. Suddenly, one appeared like magic, passed into Mrs. Tibbert's bony grasp from the servant hovering just inside the door. The girls parted as Mrs. Tibbert descended the porch steps with the glass in hand.

"There you are, my dear." She raised the large glass eye-level with Prissy, who took it silently and sipped. Deena's stomach tightened at the words, spoken in the same clipped tone as Ada May had used when she corrected Deena's faux pas with the porter yesterday. Mrs. Tibbert's voice dropped an octave. "My hospitality wasn't enough for you. You wanted more than your hostess offered." Prissy attempted to hand back the glass. Mrs. Tibbert's jaw twitched. "Drink all of it," she commanded.

"I can't." A white film ringed Prissy's mouth.

"You asked for milk, didn't you?" Her voice was syrup: a sweet, sticky trap. "A proper lady knows when requests are warranted and when they are inappropriate. We must learn to control our impulses."

"I really can't drink any more," Prissy said, tears forming. "Please. My father's a trustee."

Mrs. Tibbert put two fingers on the bottom of the glass and tipped it against Prissy's red-painted lips, holding it there until the girl opened her mouth and began to swallow the milk in large gulps. She tried to step back but Mrs. Tibbert was forceful, smoothly keeping the glass in place. Prissy spit up on the last swallow, a rivulet of milk staining her chin and dripping onto her blouse. The others averted their eyes, but Deena couldn't stop staring.

Mrs. Tibbert returned to the porch. The waiting housemaid took the empty glass, a smudge of crimson lipstick marring its rim.

"And what now, my dear?"

"Thank you, ma'am," Prissy croaked, tears falling down her cheeks.

Then, she lurched over her knees and sounded as if she was being garroted. A putrid smell curdled the air. Sour and acidic. Prissy's shoulders heaved helplessly.

Deena's limbs were leaden. She wanted to check on Prissy, but none of the others moved. They were all locked into place, fearful of becoming Mrs. Tibbert's next example of bad behavior. Prissy was exposed and alone, dangerously vulnerable because of her foible. And when one girl goes down, the others rise to prove themselves worthy.

"It is my pleasure to welcome you all." Mrs. Tibbert continued as if there had been no interruption to her speech. "You are now a Bellerton lady and a future Bellerton graduate. We are more than a college that educates women. We are a community composed of the *best* young women. You can expect to develop your mind but, more importantly, upon graduation, you will have developed what is required to enter the world as a lady who upholds our values of purity, honor, and beauty."

Deena straightened, drawing her shoulders back at Mrs. Tibbert's words. A smattering of applause rose from the freshmen, and the surrounding mountain laurel sweetened the air. Deena took a tiny step forward, feeling braver.

"You alone are responsible for your conduct. I expect that you will always be on your best behavior. You must think of your reputation and that of Bellerton. In the case of handbook infractions, punishments will be levied. If you see a girl about to run afoul of our rules, you are expected to remind her of her obligations to the greater community. There is strength in unity. We are Bellerton and Bellerton is us. Repeat this, please."

Deena parroted the words back, her voice lost in the chorus of the other freshmen. The glistening sea of faces promised acquiescence and obedience.

"Out there is the corrupting, vile world." Mrs. Tibbert pointed to the forest, to the mountains and beyond, her pupils enlarged by her own authority. "Here, we will build you into ladies strong enough to resist the allure of change. We expect you to adhere to our values. They are the ideals by which Bellerton lives."

In the corner of Deena's eye, Prissy rocked with sobs, marked by her grievous error. Sweat rolled across her neck, and her face was flushed with humiliation.

"When you return to your dorms, you'll find the college's handbook waiting for you. I expect you'll read it thoroughly. As senior class president, Miss Donovan can answer your questions as well." Mrs. Tibbert tapped her pearls, her welcome speech coming to an end. "And ladies, Bellerton turns one hundred this May. Our entire community—past and present—will come together in celebration of a century's worth of girls' education. This year, more than any other, you must adhere to our expectations so that Bellerton can shine."

The freshmen buzzed with excitement at the news. Deena exhaled, her shoulders unclenching, relieved it was over. She hadn't shamed or exposed herself. She planned to keep it that way. She wouldn't give her classmates any reason to think that she wasn't their equal.

There was no turning back now.

◆ ◆ ◆

With the promise of afternoon sweet tea, Peggy finished the tour by quickly leading the freshmen back to their dormitories, South Hall being the last stop. She stood with Deena and her dormmates beneath the shade of hangman's oak and offered her counsel like a big sister would.

"It may not always be easy, but be a good Bellerton girl and Bellerton will be good to you. That should be foremost in your mind, always."

Deena looked at Prissy, then at the others. Prissy hung her head, her lovely face still crushed with shame. Nell wound her gold necklace chain around her finger, turning the tip purple, and her small eyes blinked rapidly. Sheba pushed her shoulders forward, as if determined to show she was exactly the good Bellerton girl Peggy spoke of. Fred kept her gaze on her feet.

Would Deena find Prissy in the hallway tomorrow, also leaving? Girls were vanishing from Bellerton before ever getting a toehold, but to Deena's great surprise, Peggy folded the chastened Prissy into a hug.

"Lean on your sisters for support." Peggy squeezed her tightly, looking above Prissy's head at the other girls. "You can help each other be good."

"Yes," Prissy whispered, her voice breaking. "I will be good, yes. I will."

Her lipstick and mascara were smeared, her eyes puffy and red-rimmed. She was nothing like the strong-willed, boastful girl she had been in the drawing room an hour earlier. Even she, with all her privileges, was beholden to Bellerton's grip and the way it shaped each girl into its ideal.

Deena joined the press of bodies that enveloped Prissy in a group hug. Ada May's lavender scent rose above the choking humidity, above Prissy's unpleasant, vinegary throw-up smell. Prissy was a lesson to them all: Nothing short of perfection was acceptable. The realization made Deena shiver.

Chapter 4
DEENA

DEENA settled quickly into her Bellerton routines: meals and classes, daily walks to the stables and back. She had to write out papers by hand because she hadn't known to buy a typewriter. It was one small thing among many that made her feel like she wasn't the same as the other South Hall girls. Then again, living in South Hall made her different from the other forty or so freshmen who lived two to a room and far from the beauty of front quad. Deena had even overheard a girl from Jackson Hall complaining about the dung smell from living so close to the stables. She never discovered who the girl was that she'd seen leave on the first day. Her dorm room remained unoccupied and locked, and none of the others seemed bothered by it. Deena decided to forget the whole thing.

The other real difference she experienced was the way she struggled to stay on top of her schoolwork, though no one else seemed to have trouble with it. Grandmother had warned her one night that this was likely to happen, as Deena massaged her gnarled legs with a soothing balm. Her attendance at Bellerton had just been secured. It was mere weeks before Grandmother would die, and Deena tried to make her as comfortable as possible.

"Always be three steps ahead. Those girls'll have the best schooling and private tutors. But you got smarts, girl. Kinds they won't have. Do what you need. And don't think twice about it." Though it was the thick of summer, Grandmother pulled her quilt tighter.

Only fifty-two when she died, her grandmother had gotten cancer from all the chemicals and solvents she used to clean rich folks' homes.

At Bellerton, Deena kept Grandmother's words close. She made certain she enrolled in classes with at least one other girl from South Hall, someone she could pepper with questions or study with. Her one rule was never to ask Ada May for help, but to accept if she offered it. Deena found that both Sheba and Fred were liberal about sharing their rhetoric and British history homework, and left-handed Fred also made it easy to copy from the next desk over. Nell eagerly partnered with her for their speech and elocution assignments.

English literature was a boondoggle. Deena found the readings obtuse, and when asked to analyze passages for assignments, she had no idea what to do. When the professor handed back her second paper with its failing red mark, his unyielding stare made her want to disappear. Afterward, Deena followed Prissy back to her room and stood on the threshold, her arms squeezing her literature textbook. "What do you say we partner on assignments? Double-check each other's work?" Prissy was the only other South Hall girl in the class.

"I don't need anyone's help." Prissy's nose crinkled, as if the mere suggestion carried a distasteful smell.

Deena considered shutting the door behind her and telling Prissy the truth, that she was failing, but she didn't trust her enough yet. She refused to panic, and she wasn't a beggar. If Prissy wouldn't give her what she wanted, Deena would find another way to get by.

◆　◆　◆

HER OPPORTUNITY CAME TWO DAYS LATER. DEENA WAS LEAVING the library with Prissy and Ada May when there was a sudden downpour, and the wind kicked up.

"We can make it to the dorm if we run," Ada May said.

Shrieking, the girls dashed down the library steps and into the storm. Deena was behind the other two when she saw Prissy's English lit homework flutter to the wet ground. She snatched it before the water could soak through and shoved the pages into her textbook, then tucked the book under her blouse.

"Ugh, my hair!" Prissy moaned, fingering her damp locks as the trio climbed the stairs. The lamps at either end of the hallway flickered with each boom of thunder.

Sheba stomped out of her room in a dressing gown, her blonde hair loose around her shoulders, her irritation even more intimidating given her height. "Does someone have extra soap I can borrow? I can't find mine. I mean, it's gone."

"You lost it?" Deena paused at her doorway.

"It's missing." Sheba's tone was accusing and Deena, startled, took a step back.

"I'm sure it's only misplaced," Ada May said gently. "I have an extra. Wait just a moment." A soft, warm glow flooded from her doorway. She re-emerged with a small bar wrapped in waxy brown paper. Sheba snatched it up without even a thank-you and slammed her door.

Deena gripped her rain-splattered textbook that concealed the purloined assignment. "Have any of your things gone missing?"

Ada May squeezed her shoulder firmly. "You mean misplaced. I don't believe so." She regarded Deena curiously. "There's no reason to make Sheba feel badly about her absentmindedness."

Deena blushed. "I'm not. I wasn't—"

The chapel bell announced the three-quarter hour.

"Best hurry to freshen up. The lunch bell will come soon."

Deena lay Prissy's damp homework pages on her radiator to dry, listening to Sheba grumble about the missing soap on her way to the bathroom. She repeated Ada May's assurances that Sheba had only misplaced it, but quickly checked her few possessions to ensure they were still there: Grandmother's quilt and Bible; the photograph of them, hidden in the desk drawer; pencils in a shiny tin case; and her broken glass jar filled with silly odds and ends. The closet with its few items of clothing and her second pair of shoes. All of it pitiful to her now that she'd seen the quality of what the others tramped about in.

♦ ♦ ♦

AFTER SUPPER THAT NIGHT, THERE WAS A RAP ON DEENA'S DOOR, and she hurriedly slid Prissy's homework beneath her own, managing to hide it just as Nell entered, shaking a tin of rock candy. Deena welcomed the break and piled onto the bed with Nell.

"What's on your necklace?" Deena pointed.

Nell fidgeted with the necklace constantly, sliding the medallion back and forth along its silver chain. "My St. Christopher's medal. For protection."

"Protection from what?"

Before Nell could explain, Fred knocked politely at Deena's door, wearing a pilled wool sweater with long sleeves, her bob disarrayed. Deena thought how Prissy worked hard to cultivate her look, but Fred was glamorous because she didn't try at all.

Sheba flounced past Fred with a smirk, tugging her into the room by the hand. "What are you two up to?" She perched on Deena's desk and patted the spot beside her for Fred to sit. Fred hesitated, looking to Deena for confirmation that it was okay. Deena felt helpless to do anything but give an encouraging smile. At least Fred was polite about it. Though Sheba never brought up the swapped rooms, she was possessive around Deena's things, behaving as if it all belonged rightfully to her. Sheba leaned back into her hands, almost knocking the pile of homework papers—Deena's and Prissy's—to the floor.

Deena stiffened with fear. What would happen if she was caught? Academic probation, suspension, or even expulsion seemed likely. If the punishment of asking for milk was to be drowned in it, she didn't want to think about the consequences of stealing homework.

"Let me move those out of your way." Deferential, thoughtful. She had learned how to feign both, had seen Grandmother do it a thousand times. Deena hurriedly tucked the papers into her desk drawer. She would finish the assignment the second the girls left, changing things just enough to avoid the professor's suspicions, then get rid of Prissy's papers by dropping them near the front door, as if they had been there all along.

"Your room is so plain, Deena," Sheba said. "So empty."

Deena mumbled with embarrassment, "I wanted things simple."

"I think simple is sophisticated," Fred said.

Deena hadn't anticipated how homey and personalized each girl would make her room, hanging curtains and laying rugs over the hardwood floor. Desks turned into vanities crowded with glass bottles of perfumes, tins of creams and lotions, and makeup. Corkboards were pinned with family photos and magazine cutouts of dreamy Montgomery Clift. Deena's room held only the furniture the school provided; the one thing pinned to her bulletin board was the typewritten Bellerton admissions letter.

But she was tired of Sheba's judgments. She had a growing collection of banking deposit slips tucked into a plain envelope hidden under her mattress, evidence of money slowly accumulating in a bank account, proof that her father was upholding his end of the deal. Soon enough, she would buy whatever she desired.

Deena straightened the quilt draped on her bed. She felt emboldened by Fred's kind words. "Fred, do you think I can have your sunglasses later?" It had been several weeks since Fred had promised them to her during the campus tour.

Fred was quizzical, but Sheba didn't miss a beat.

"Why would you think you're entitled to her things?"

"I—I'm not." Deena swallowed, her cheeks hot. "She offered them."

Nell moved to the opposite end of the bed. A pit opened in Deena's stomach, her embarrassment as wide as a lake. Had she done something wrong? Perhaps Fred had changed her mind? Maybe Deena had confused mere politeness with a sincere offer. She shrank inside the knife-sharp silence.

But why did Sheba care? She was always touching Deena's things, as she had done earlier when she came into the room without asking and claimed Deena's desk as her seat.

Fred bent over her elbow to pick at a scab. "I saw someone walking the quad last night after curfew. Already breaking the rules. She was wearing a cloak and disappeared behind the library."

"A cloak?" Sheba repeated. "It's only October."

Sheba's feet swung from the edge of the desk. She opened the middle drawer where the homework papers were—Deena sucked in a nervous breath—closed it, then picked up one of Deena's pencils and twirled it around her fingers. "Probably just an upperclassman. They get away with all sorts of things."

Deena said, "Maybe it was Mary?" She had seen Mary walking around campus but was never able to catch up to her. She's just shy, Deena told herself, remembering Nell hadn't bothered to greet Mary in the dining hall that first day. She's just like me, deciding who she can trust and trying hard to fit in.

"There was definitely something moving out there." Seemingly satisfied with her work on the scab, Fred propped her foot on the desk and tucked a piece of rock candy into her cheek.

"Wait. Some*thing* or some*one*?" The candy tin rattled in Nell's nervous hands. Deena had noticed how quick-fingered she was, whether popping her zits in the bathroom mirror or picking up things others had dropped. Only yesterday, she had watched Nell pluck a late-season cherry tomato from Prissy's plate and pop it into her mouth while talking to her, all without Prissy catching on. If Nell's hands were trembling, then Fred's talk genuinely frightened her. Deena nudged the candy tin from Nell and set it on the desk.

Fred shrugged. "We've *all* heard those stories about missing girls. And we all know how strange it gets around here after dark."

Sheba turned playfully to Fred and put on a dramatic, booming mimicry of Boris Karloff—one that Deena had to admit was quite good. "Maybe you saw the girl who hanged herself in the library, rising with the moonlight to take her revenge!"

Deena didn't know how she felt about ghosts, though her grand-mother had been a believer. She had to agree, that once night slid over the valley and the fog bore down, Bellerton changed. Fall leaves that crunched like glass underfoot in the daytime were muffled into a preter-natural silence at night. She sensed darting movements among the giant trees anchoring the quad. It was quite possible that what Fred had seen wasn't a student at all.

Fred accidentally knocked the candy tin to the floor. Deena scram-bled to pick it up, setting aside the pieces covered in dust and hair, but dropping the ones that had landed cleanly on the desk chair back into the tin.

"Stupid of me to have set it there," she mumbled.

"Look." Fred had twisted toward the window and was pointing to the quad below. *"He* shouldn't be down here."

The front quad and adjoining dormitories were off-limits to profes-sors, but when Deena peered over Fred's shoulder with Nell close behind, she saw Bellerton's youngest and newest English professor slinking along the buildings, a cigarette burning between his fingers, oblivious to the girls at Deena's window. He was from New England and fancied himself a poet. Girls swooned in his presence, and suddenly all the poetry books had been checked out of the library.

Even the South Hall girls were drawn to him. Last week Sheba had galloped around the dorm like Paul Revere, crying, "He's twenty-six and a bachelor!" before confiding that whenever she saw him, she felt a stir-ring in her soul, to which Fred had joked, "That's not your soul," and Ada May had clucked her tongue at the implied vulgarity. Not to be outdone, Prissy had announced that she was declaring English as her major. The others clamored to agree. Deena thought he seemed full of himself, but Grandmother's advice echoed in her mind: *You get a Bellerton degree, find a man, and marry him. That's the full ticket. That's how you survive.*

"Why doesn't he use the sidewalk?" Deena muttered. He carried no umbrella, and the wet grass might ruin his shoes if he wasn't careful—but then, he was a professor and probably had a closet full of shoes.

"He often comes this way. I've seen him before," Fred said. "Though he wasn't who I saw last night. I'm certain of that."

"Should we tell Mrs. Tibbert?" Deena asked. "He really isn't supposed to be here."

Fred opened the window and shouted, "Hey there, Prof!"

The poet-professor stopped short. Fred ducked out of view, burying her face in Sheba's lap while Deena resisted the urge to duck. Luckily, the professor, skinny and awkward as a foal, moved on indifferently, disappearing behind the senior dormitory, a haze of cigarette smoke lingering in his wake.

Sheba picked up the bric-a-brac jar on Deena's desk, nose wrinkling. "This is cracked."

Deena snatched it away protectively and shoved it under her pillow. She knew it was cracked, but she was fond of all the useless junk she'd crammed into it over the years.

The rain came down harder. Briefly, the sun emerged, painting the quad golden.

"The devil's beating his wife," Sheba said.

Nell startled. "What did you say?"

A breeze brought rain through the window Fred had left open. Deena rushed to close it. She slammed the sash, and the girls jumped. "Sorry," she called. "Usually it sticks."

The front door banged below. Nell ran to meet Ada May and Prissy, who had just returned to South Hall, dusty and sweaty from the exertion of equestrian practice in the riding ring.

"Fred saw something on the lawn last night," Nell blurted. "Do you think there are actually ghosts?" Prissy stopped short, her lip curling at the question, but Ada May shook out her lovely red hair from its braid and considered it, her boots coated in dirt. The smell of it reminded Deena of her childhood.

Thunder cracked. The lights blinked, their puce haloes wobbling, then steady.

Ada May said, "One never knows about these things, dear Nell. There are all sorts of surprises at Bellerton."

"Spirits, ghosts—it's all fakery." Prissy marched toward her room, imprinting dusty boot marks on the hall rug.

"I saw a hooded figure wearing black." Fred picked at her cuticles. "So maybe not, since ghosts wear white."

"And glide, as if they're wearing roller skates!" Sheba exclaimed. She teasingly pinched Nell. "Oh, come on, Nellie. Plenty of girls wear cloaks. Ada May herself owns one. Isn't that so?"

Ada May gave an exaggerated curtsey. "Naturally, there have been rumors. Misbehaving girls who have disappeared."

Nell gave a squeak, her fingers tugging at the medallion on her necklace. Sheba mocked Nell, and Fred swatted at her, mouthing silently for her to stop.

"But one of the ghost stories might be true," Ada May said. The girls stopped fooling around, all eyes now on her. "Years ago, during my mother's time at Bellerton, a girl who wasn't very well liked climbed from her window onto the porch roof. Not unusual in those days, according to Mother."

The girls were silent, waiting for Ada May to continue. "The girl tumbled off the roof and broke her neck. Some say she was pushed." She combed her ivory fingers through her copper hair. "Her ghost is said to haunt the campus, her neck bent at a permanent angle."

Nell backed away from the others. "That's horrible."

"What made her so disliked?" Fred asked.

"She refused to follow the rules and was arrogant. Or so my mother says."

Footsteps thundered above. Prissy pointed to the housemother's rooms on the third floor. "Maybe Fred saw *her*." Hired to keep tabs on the girls, the housemother enforced curfew and quiet hours, ran daily inspections, and collected and distributed linens from the washerwomen. Though alcohol was strictly forbidden on campus, the girls saw enough to know that she was a drunk.

"Then, the figure wasn't wearing a cloak at all," Nell said, stumbling over her next words. "She was just—"

"Fat," Prissy finished. The other girls laughed.

Deena tensed. If the cleaning women were a reminder of her grandmother, the housemother was more so: white and poor, someone easily disdained. Though in other ways, she was nothing like Grandmother, who had taken pride in her appearance, even while on hands and knees scrubbing another woman's kitchen floor. Deena twitched in revulsion whenever she thought of the housemother's bunched stockings and stained smocks and the beads of sweat that collected in the trough beneath her nose.

"What if we played a game on her?" Sheba suggested.

Deena didn't like the housemother but it didn't feel right to make fun of the woman. Her eyes met Ada May's. "She's just minding her own business."

Sheba ignored Deena and clapped her hands eagerly together. "We make the housemother believe South Hall is haunted."

"South Hall *is* haunted," Nell insisted. She gripped Deena's arm, her fingers like claws. "Does no one else feel it?"

"Toying with the housemother." Ada May regarded Sheba approvingly, and Deena felt a twinge of regret in publicly sticking up for the undignified woman. "What fun that could be."

Chapter 5
DEENA

IT wasn't difficult to convince the housemother that Bellerton was visited by spirits. The October days became foreshortened; the nights drew long breaths. When the sun sank behind the mountains, Bellerton hardened into a living ruin, the grounds solemn.

Sheba suggested they trick her by moving things ever so slightly, and Deena seconded the idea, not wanting to be overly cruel in their games. They started by shifting her matted slippers that smelled of onions from the right side of her door to the left. The table lamp in the first-floor hall slid from front to back. Then, Sheba escalated things by proposing they rearrange the common room furniture: sofa near the door instead of the window; chaise half-propped on the cold hearth and the end table shoved to the wall. How the housemother shrieked when she went in to clean the next morning! Deena's stomach knotted; they were successfully getting under the housemother's skin. This must have been what boarding school was like, full of playful bedevilment, and Deena began to warm to the games. None of it was serious; there was no real harm.

After they switched the furniture, they began to slide small objects beneath her door: sticks and pebbles, leaves and petals. A black-and-white photograph cut from a magazine that, loosened from its text, became a monstrous, disembodied face. A spidery typewriter ribbon. The housemother's caterwauling quaked the walls. Deena didn't know which girl left which item, but it didn't matter; with every prank, they were becoming one ghostly presence.

"Stop with these messes!" the housemother shouted from the landing of the floor above. The small items had accumulated, first one week's worth, then two. She thundered down to make her indictment known. "Youse did this." Her finger jabbed the air.

The girls gathered in the corridor: eyes wide, lips pouted.

"Ma'am, what are we being accused of?" Sheba tilted her blonde head. Innocence embodied.

What a terror Sheba must have been as a child, Deena thought. Gregarious one minute, pitching a tantrum the next, her moods and manipulation forgiven because her hair was the color of corn silk.

"Youse are tugging my goat." The housemother dumped the objects onto the hall carpet, where they formed an odd, depressing array.

"Why would we bother with *this*?" Prissy asked derisively.

"I was a girl once and I liked my fun. This isn't a spot of fun? You would swear it?"

Rather than confess their deeds, they crossed their fingers behind their backs, and crooned, "No, ma'am. Not us."

The housemother harrumphed back to her rooms.

The next night after curfew, as an obliterating fog crept onto campus, they amassed in the hallway outside her door. They rapped their knuckles along the plaster walls, the sounds echoing eerily, until the housemother howled, torn from her sleep with fright. Deena was giddy with exhilaration, her reservations having long ago melted away. She clamped her teeth to keep from laughing, especially after she spied Nell on the stairs, illuminated by faint light from the floor below, poised to run for cover in case they met with any actual ghosts.

Grandmother had often shared her thoughts about ghosts. Deena remembered her once saying, "Spirits can't hurt you. You got no reason to fear them. It's only the living who inflict true harm."

There was nothing to be afraid of; they were just girls playing frivolous games. At least, that's what Deena believed.

◆ ◆ ◆

BY MID-OCTOBER, NIGHTS WERE COLD AND A FEET-NUMBING draft skittered down the hallway. Initially, the girls made a game of chasing it, having tired of nightly tricking the housemother. They posted themselves along the corridor and stuffed the gaps under their doors with rolled sheets, but the draft eluded them. As soon as Sheba cried out that she'd found the source and Deena rushed to plug the hole with rags, Fred heard hollow drumming at the hall's other end, and her face was blasted with a ripple of cold air that hadn't been there before.

"It's useless. Don't bother," Prissy said distractedly from where she lounged on her bed, flipping pages in *Mademoiselle*. Deena thought the clothes in its pages were chic and terribly expensive. Prissy's door was wide open, and a lemon rind was curled behind her teeth; she often did this when she skipped a meal, as she had earlier that night.

The girls gave up eventually on trying to corral the draft, and it went away on its own.

Days later, Sheba reported that she'd heard faint crying at night and—certain it was not the housemother's wailing—tracked the noise to Nell across the hall. She confronted her as they settled in at breakfast.

Nell insisted it wasn't her. She fidgeted with her silverware, her leg bouncing. "I heard the crying, too," she said. "But I thought it was you." She pointed at Prissy, whose room was catty-corner to hers.

Prissy rolled her eyes. "I'm not homesick," she said, even though she talked too much about her mother and the family dog for Deena to believe her.

Ada May unfolded her napkin in her lap. "I hear tapping on my window at night," she said, her face grave. "When I look out, I don't see anything. There's only darkness staring back."

"I've heard it, too"—Sheba's room was beside Ada May's—"though we're on the second floor. It's very odd."

Ada May pointed at Prissy. "You stay up later than all of us, night owl."

Prissy's eyes were hard. "It isn't me."

Deena bit at her thumbnail. She could not tell the others the truth, which was that at Bellerton, she slept better than she had in all her years. Fed and washed, dry and warm, each night she succumbed to a deep and dreamless sleep, leaving the world behind. She felt truly safe for the first time in her life, secure in the cocoon of their sisterhood. Even still, she couldn't shake the disquieting feeling that their games had set something in motion that could not be stopped.

Chapter 6

PEGGY

JUNE 2002
BELLERTON'S 150th ANNIVERSARY

WHAT Peggy Donovan most remembered was how things at Bellerton could vanish without a trace. When thick, gray fog settled in the valley, eclipsing the grounds, Bellerton disappeared into the swirl of mist and blackness. It was possible to lose your way, convinced you were steps from your dormitory only to feel the scratch of tree branches at the wood's edge against your cheek. Sounds deadened as if swallowed by hungry, unseen mouths that lived off such clatter. Girls huddled close, fall and winter a paranoid time, the grounds alive in strange ways. Anything could go missing.

Peggy remembered how, once the fog settled in, Lucille Whittier lost her sense of propriety. Ada May Delacourt, that elusive, slippery girl, lost her balance on her horse. Peggy lost her friend Ann Goodchild. They had been walking with arms linked until they arrived on the library steps. Peggy turned to see Ann wasn't there, her arm crooked for empty air, though she swore she had just felt the weight of fingers pressing through her coat.

"Ann!" she'd called, fog swallowing the name. "Yoo-hoo, Ann! I'm at the library!" She waited in the chill before going inside, intending that she should meet Ann at their usual study carrel on the second floor, surprised as she approached to see Ann raise her head, hair shining under the lights.

"What did you think you were doing, running off like that?" Ann squeezed Peggy's arm in the exact spot she had felt the hand, the fabric of her wool sweater damp beneath the touch.

"But I didn't run off," Peggy said. "*You* left me. I got to the steps, and you simply weren't there anymore!"

Ann brushed a stray hair from her friend's coat. "Oh, Peggy. You're such a jokester."

Peggy started to disagree, but she noted Ann's pale face and the tremble in her hands, and decided to go along with her. "I *am* silly, aren't I?" she said, embracing her friend tightly.

Five decades later, Peggy told this story with Ann sitting beside her, a gaggle of septuagenarian alumnae squished beneath a white tent on the Bellerton lawn. Swamped by late-June humidity, the day felt tender and portentous.

The campus was buzzy, their class's fiftieth reunion overlapping with the one hundred and fiftieth anniversary celebrations of Bellerton's founding. The weekend was structured to get alumnae drunk on wine and nostalgia. Later, there would be a campus tour and yet another pitch for donations. A new recruitment tagline claimed that Bellerton was *leading women to their bright futures.* New, new, new—the predominant word of the weekend, strange to the ears and disorienting, like an air raid siren. The slogan ignored the incontrovertible fact that the future was always waiting; it was unavoidable. It was the past that trapped you, with its bewitching comfort.

Back when she was a senior and Bellerton was celebrating its centennial, Peggy had been excited by the idea of a century of prestige and tradition braiding together in the year of her graduation. She had been proud to join an esteemed lineage of Bellerton graduates. Now, with another half century behind her, she felt tired.

Peggy found it impossible not to remember the last Bellerton celebration she attended in her senior year: the sun bright on the white dresses of the May Queen and her court, the shy buds peeking from the green tresses of bushes. Beside her at the alumnae anniversary weekend, Ann was still talking about the amorphous Bellerton fog.

"There was something spooky about it," Ann was saying. "It stole things and rearranged them. It liked to play little games. You know"— she leaned forward, lightly touching Peggy's arm but speaking to the group gathered around the table, where gnats hovered over the remains of lunch—"I've always believed the rumors that Bellerton was haunted. We all know girls who witnessed strange occurrences." She sat back with finality, the folding chair creaking under her weight.

Peggy patted Ann's knee. The gesture was intended to calm, but Ann only grew more strident. "We aren't the only ones either," she continued. "I was talking with young ladies who graduated only a few years ago who told me that when they were students, they often saw two figures walking near the woods late at night. And how trinkets went missing from their rooms, just small things. They blamed the cleaning staff but, of course, it isn't that. We all know it isn't them."

When she had returned to campus after all this time, Peggy was shaken by how much Bellerton felt the same—haunted by the trappings of its past. She wasn't sure why a young woman would pick Bellerton today. Was the pull of tradition and legacy that strong? Or did Bellerton provide a sense of refuge from a rapidly changing world? A way for young women of the twenty-first century to indulge certain nostalgic longings?

Earlier, Peggy had taken her café au lait to a rocking chair on South Hall's porch, enjoying the cool morning that would soon become soggy with humidity. Nearby, three students interning for the admissions office that summer gathered around a card table and chatted breezily. She paid them no attention at first, until one of them said, "Can you believe that Bess doesn't want to get married? Who says that?"

Peggy's gaze drifted in the girls' direction. Their youth made them beautiful. Each girl wore her hair pulled back in a ponytail that was adorned with a ribbon the color of cotton candy; each one had donned pearl earrings. Their lips were glossy, their smooth skin unblemished and sculpted by makeup to make their cheekbones sharp, their noses pert, their eyebrows perfect arches. They reminded her too much of the Bellerton women in her own time.

A girl wearing Kelly green shorts cinched by a white belt dropped a stack of envelopes into a small box. "She said she doesn't want kids either."

"Oh my stars, she did not!" The original speaker, polished-looking in her summery linen dress, hung her mouth wide in shock. "Who's going to take care of her when she's old?"

"Who's going to take care of her *now*?"

A third girl, until then silent, shrugged off her seersucker jacket and fanned herself uselessly with her hand. "Bess has always been so odd though. It sounds just like her, don't you agree?"

The day warmed up and the girls moved back inside to complete their work. Peggy had been stunned by how much they sounded like the girls in her own Bellerton class, those intelligent, ambitious young women who had funneled all their dreams into propping up a man.

Thinking now of the women she had overheard that morning, Peggy asked the table, "Do you still have your mask from the Senior Serenade?" She turned to Ann. "Remember that old tradition?"

Ann shook her head. "Lost in a move."

Peggy was disappointed. Her Bellerton pieces were tucked inside an attic trunk along with other mementos from her life, the only things she still owned that were a tangible reminder of those shared days. And yet, she couldn't say exactly how she felt about Bellerton. Even if it represented the best years of her life, Bellerton had always been a hard thing to love. And how could she feel fondness for it with the way her senior year had ended?

Peggy squeezed Ann's arm. "Save some chardonnay for when I return," she said. "I need a walk."

• • •

PEGGY STRODE PAST THE OLD GYMNASIUM AND SUNBATHING court, the latter paved into a faculty parking lot. Nearby squatted a brick structure with halls jutting from its center like octopus arms. A paved path led to the modernized, state-of-the-art stables atop the hill where once there had been faculty houses. The old pastures had been paved over into yet another parking lot.

The woods, that impenetrable thicket of danger that had given her such fright as a student, had been sliced in half. When the wind was right, the shush of traffic from a nearby highway drifted across campus, a sound like the ocean. Earlier that weekend, Peggy had met a woman, class of '71, who mentioned it; the highway hadn't yet existed when Peggy was a student.

"I had never left Oklahoma before coming to Bellerton. I believed there was an actual sea just past the woods. I thought the Atlantic Ocean rolled against our door."

Peggy asked, "You came all the way from Oklahoma?" What an ignorant question. The world had grown smaller over the past fifty years, and she smaller within it.

The campus was not so isolated now. Cloistered in its own way, it was a glass bubble that kept girls inside with weekend concerts on the quad, theatrical and dance performances, and endless clubs to join—but the wider world was encroaching.

And yet the past loomed closer than ever for Peggy. She had felt the tug of it all weekend, the splitting. Bellerton clung tightly onto tradition, with no clear sense of the way forward.

At the edge of the woods she stopped, the old fears rising. Ann was coming down the path, sun hat held firmly to her head with one hand. Tied around its crown was a long navy ribbon with gold tassels. Ann waved her unencumbered hand, and Peggy, relieved that she wasn't alone, waited for her friend to catch up.

• ◆ •

"Why, these woods aren't scary at all!" Ann exclaimed as they picked a path through the trees. The underbrush had been cleared away and sunlight pierced the ground in thin shafts. They paused amid the rustling of small animals and the cackle of birds, the light somnambulant. Bellerton had vanished from view.

Peggy inhaled the fragrant June air. "I smell the creek." She gestured toward a bevy of rhododendrons buffeting the bank. She had believed the creek escaped through the campus wall, but it must have bent back and returned somewhere farther along, drawn to the Bellerton grounds the way she was: unable to fully leave, called again and again to return.

Peggy and Ann pushed through rhododendrons and found themselves staring into the creek's sluggish, silty water, though Peggy heard its merry tinkle downstream as it bounded over stony rapids. Tadpoles and silvery creek minnows darted in a pool formed by erosion beneath the roots of a large hickory. She measured the water's depth with a stick, stirring up mud. "There's a huge rock down here," she said.

"The minnows look like my box of tangled Christmas lights." Ann balanced against the tree and peered over Peggy's shoulder. "I wish I hadn't been so afraid of these woods when we were at Bellerton. It's beautiful here."

"I think the path has been cleaned up, made accessible." Peggy gathered pebbles near the toe of her sandal and rolled them in her hand like dice, then let them tumble from her fingers into the water, where they sunk with a gulp. "Maybe we had reason to be afraid back then. You said yourself that Bellerton always felt off."

Ann was firm. "I said I believed Bellerton was haunted. Remember the scratches we woke to on our arms and legs? From the demon ghost cat?" Peggy said nothing. Ann leaned into the hickory's ridged bark. "Even the Senior Serenade. Peg, who does that? We were raised to be polite, well-bred girls. What on earth were we thinking?"

"Oh, Ann, it was just a silly children's game." Peggy wasn't sure she believed her own words. "We were innocent then. We probably still are."

A shadow fell over them as a large woodpecker swooped silently past, its red crest raised. "There's something wrong about Bellerton." Ann appeared troubled. "Those terrible things that happened, and not just for the disobedient girls."

Peggy rolled her shoulders, sore from sitting in cheap folding chairs all weekend. "Remember the expectations heaped upon us? Remember that ridiculous handbook? Behave like this, say these exact things, dress in this manner. Be perfect or you'll let everyone down. All that pressure to perform, to represent a certain ideal. Told we were responsible for keeping others in line. The constant judgments." Peggy heaved a stone into the creek. "Maybe we were what was wrong."

Ann pulled her hand from the tree trunk and examined the marks left on her palm. "The younger girls are as obsessed with Bellerton traditions as we were. I heard someone already asking about who would be the next May Queen."

Peggy said, "Imagine being a young woman today and caring about something so silly as a May Queen."

"Oh, Peg. Girls should be allowed some fun."

Ann's response disappointed her, but instead of sharing her thoughts, Peggy found a thick branch with limbs like a divining rod. She swished it back and forth through the water.

"You were always steady, Peggy. Even when we were Bellerton girls. Steady, sturdy, and true. The best of us all." Ann squeezed Peggy's shoulder. "We should make our way back."

Peggy stretched her stick deeper into the creek, distracted.

"What are you up to, Peg? Come on, let's go."

"There's something here." Peggy trawled the muddy bottom. "I keep hitting it."

Ann peered at the turbid water. "Just a rock."

Peggy's palms sweated. A rock, she repeated to herself, tracing its contours with the stick, desperate now to confirm for herself that's what it was.

The past rose like mist. She pushed at the silt, attempting to loosen the rock from the muck. The woods fell quiet. She grunted, heard the sucking depths exhale. With a gurgle, it came free. She waited. Of course, a weight heavier than water. It wouldn't rise on its own. She grabbed another stick and plunged both down, using the V-like prongs of one and the guide of the other to nudge the thing toward the surface. When it was close, she scooped a hand into the water and grabbed it, falling backward onto the damp, sandy earth. She cursed, fearing a mud stain on the back of her slacks.

"Oh, my lord," Ann whispered.

Peggy looked at the smooth, bald rock nestled between her knees, stained the color of the creek bed. The dirty brown of cold tea.

"Ann, help me up." She reached out, but Ann stumbled back. Like an old, irritated cow, Peggy rolled onto her knees and pushed herself to her feet, bracing against the hickory until her equilibrium returned.

Ann was several yards away, her hands held up as if to stop Peggy from coming closer. Peggy lifted the thing she had dug up. Not a rock at all, she realized, staring at the depressions in the hard bone. The dark, starving cavities. Not a rock, but a human skull.

She thought then, as she hadn't in years, of the girl who went missing in their senior year.

"Peg," Ann whispered. She was trembling. "Peg, what have you done?"

Fall
1951

It is advantageous to be friendly, nice, and
well liked always. Gum chewing and complaining
are unladylike habits, so don't indulge your temptations.
Finally, you would do your best to steer clear of
asocial attitudes and perverse thoughts.

—Bellerton Student Handbook, 1951–1952

Chapter 7

DEENA

IN the waning days of fall, when the known world is tipped sideways and loosened, endings and beginnings jumble together, and the membrane between the world of the living and the dead is thinned. After weeks of trying to fit in, Deena found herself at ease, sitting in the shade of South Hall's front porch the last Saturday in October, inhaling the scent of cinnamon and hot apple cider from a hand-painted porcelain cup she was holding. Around her, the clack of rocking chairs was pleasant, otherworldly.

By three o'clock, the morning's clinging mist had burned off into a warm ocher light and chatter bubbled from all sides of the quad as the dormitory porches filled with students gathering for the Senior Serenade, a Bellerton tradition. Ada May had explained it to the others earlier that day: the seniors would show their allegiance to one another with a ritual that sealed their loyalty. It was a rite that dated back to her great-grandmother's time, in the days of Bellerton's founding.

Deena didn't notice at first that the serving and cleaning staff were given the day off, and the dormitory housemothers made themselves scarce. Even Dr. and Mrs. Tibbert overnighted elsewhere for the weekend. Only later did she realize why the girls had been purposefully left alone.

Deena searched without luck for Mary in the amassing crowds on the porches of East and West Halls, curious to know how she had fared these past two months. She was oddly drawn to the peculiar girl. Did she belong to a group like Deena did? Or did she plan to leave like the girl Deena had seen on her first day—the one who couldn't handle it and returned home.

Prissy fluffed the pin curls she had spent the prior evening rolling, her shoulders draped with a mink stole, the weather too warm to justify it. They had done one another's makeup that morning, squealing over Sheba's tube of Hazel Bishop no-smear lipstick and testing it by kissing each other's hands and cheeks and lips. Deena hadn't been able to tear away from her own reflection, stunned by how much she was starting to look like the others. "Hazel Bishop's a chemist, you know," Prissy had said. "She's used her brains for us girls."

Now, in the amber light of afternoon, with gold and maroon leaves dotting the grounds, Deena was gripped by feelings of both anticipation and foreboding. Beside her, Fred flicked cigarette ash into her saucer, her feet kicked over the arm of her rocker.

Sheba nudged Fred's dangling foot with her elbow. She had trussed up her usual horsetail with a braid and tied an elaborate bow around the end. "I'll take one." She leaned forward for Fred to light it.

"I do say, you're an elegant lady." Fred attempted her best Virginian accent, but the vowels dropped heavy as anchors. Sheba pushed a long stream of smoke in Fred's direction, her fingers trailing along Fred's arm.

Deena rested her elbows on her knees and watched the seniors begin to assemble below, spinning one another like coins, their moods buoyant. Peggy Donovan stood out among them in a lovely pale-yellow dress, its hem flicking her calves, and several girls embraced her. Deena wondered what it might take to be adored like Peggy. She yearned to be part of such open affection and was jealous of the seniors' loving abandonment to one another. Since her arrival at Bellerton, she had seen how different cliques of girls stuck together. They disappeared inside their mutual affection and scorned everyone else.

Suddenly the girls on the porches stilled, their faces turned toward the quad. A hush fell over the gathered crowd. Deena slid to the edge of her rocker, tingling with nerves. The ritual was about to begin.

The seniors slid into formation with their hands clasped and heads bowed.

Peggy withdrew a mask from a wicker basket and slipped it over her face, then hoisted the basket before each senior, who also selected and donned a mask. One by one, they melded into anonymity, and when Peggy stepped back into the circle, Deena strained to pick her out despite her yellow dress. The day shifted into a portentous mood.

The seniors began chanting, the words too faint to distinguish, until a sharp clap propelled them apart. They dropped their hands, linked pinkies, and marched one step forward in unison. Another clap resounded. Another step, the circle drawing tighter, cinching like a noose. A trajectory locked into place. Deena leaned forward to see more clearly.

A pair of hands hoisted a doll toward the graying sky. The doll's pigtails dangled, her dainty fingers crooked in delight. Black shoes and white socks adorned her feet, and she wore a black velvet dress over her cloth body. The doll's rouged cheeks rendered her young, but the dress was a wife's garment, one she might wear after she had tucked the children away and was playing hostess. Was it a mother doll or a baby doll? The most unsettling thing was that Deena couldn't tell.

The senior who held the doll nestled her into the crook of her arm and tenderly kissed her forehead. In her other hand, Deena saw the glint of metal blades—a pair of scissors. The doll's merry face winked. The senior drew back her arm and plunged the blades deep into the doll's soft body.

Deena recoiled into her rocker as if struck.

The doll changed hands; the scissors trundled from girl to girl. The blades sucked at the air, slashing the doll's face and body; small chunks fell away, swallowed inside tight fists. Deena covered her face with her hands, watching between slatted fingers until nothing was left of the doll but a bodiless, gutted head.

Light rain began to fall, and the masked seniors scattered like seeds. The dispersal was swift; Deena questioned whether what she had seen was real. It made her sick to her stomach and reminded her of things from her old life that she preferred to forget. The seniors were well-bred girls, yet the disturbing scene had been senseless cruelty. The opposite of the restraint they were meant to exemplify.

The others seemed to be just as shaken—all except for Ada May.

"What was that?" Deena whispered to her. "What did we just see?"

Ada May smiled like a cat, the tips of her hair flickering. "Tradition is a funny thing."

Deena ground her palms into her eyes: The Bellerton girls had been meant to witness the ritual. The blades, the violence, the anonymity—the longer she remained on the grounds, the more she felt its tightening. Her, the other freshmen, the upperclassmen. They were all becoming part of the wild creature that was Bellerton. It was not just about conformity. Bellerton was teaching them how to take and keep the modicum of power allowed to them. Did Mrs. Tibbert approve this vicious tradition? Or did she leave because she wanted no part?

The rain opened into a downpour and the day's golden color washed away. The other porches emptied, but at the end of South Hall's porch, where the railings bent into elaborate finials, Peggy Donovan tarried, watching them. Droplets knocked from the gutters, spraying onto her hair and shoulders. Deena sensed, though she couldn't say for certain, that Peggy had been standing there for a while. That it was another Peggy, an imposter Peggy, who had dashed onto the quad and impaled the helpless doll.

The chapel bell resounded, and Deena's head whipped toward the sound. When she looked back around, Peggy had moved closer, walking in a steady pace toward them and morphing back into the warmhearted senior they all knew. She gestured to another girl who trailed on her heels.

"This is my best friend, Ann Goodchild."

Deena grabbed for Peggy's yellow dress, the fabric scratchy against her palm—proof that Peggy wasn't a chimera or a ghost. Smoothly, Peggy pinched her skirt free.

"Hello, then." Ann was stout, her hair mussed, one side pinned up crookedly. She dropped into a rocker, slumping for a moment before she arranged her limbs in the usual Bellerton style: legs crossed at the ankles, back straight, hands folded in her lap. "This rain is a disappointment!"

Peggy poured cups of cider from the silver carafe and settled gracefully beside Ann. "This will keep us warm." She sipped. "How are you ladies finding Bellerton?"

An afterimage of what Deena had witnessed still hovered above the empty quad, the violence of the ritual lingering.

"Cat's got the tongue," Ann said to Peggy. The rain kept up its low, persistent drum.

Deena wanted to say, *It's the doll—it's* you—*who's got all our tongues.*

"Like the wicked cat that sneaks about our dormitory," Peggy said playfully.

"There's a cat in the senior dorm?" Nell asked. The sudden clinking of her cup and saucer jolted the girls. Deena loosened her grip on the arms of her rocker. Fred lit another cigarette with a shaking hand.

"A phantom cat," Peggy kindly explained. "Long ago, guests came to Bellerton to take the waters of the healing springs. A guest who hated animals locked the groundskeeper's cat out one night, and the poor thing was eaten by varmint."

"They found its remains the next morning," Ann chimed in. Her hair frizzed in the humidity. "Ever since, the cat has sought revenge. Its spirit knocks our things to the floor. It's cracked two hand mirrors of mine already this year."

"It scratches girls it doesn't like," Peggy added. She and Ann exchanged devilish grins. "We won't say who. That would be rude." She slipped a half-eaten molasses cookie onto her saucer. "One might say the demon cat is a Bellerton tradition."

Ann's cup rattled as she set it aside. "Like the Senior Serenade. Or the May Queen."

Deena glanced at Ada May, sister to a former May Queen. Tradition was strength, for the right sort. A tie that binds. A way to keep some people in—and others out.

A gust swept the porch and Deena caught sight of a figure outside the library: Mary. She nearly jumped up, eager to say hello to the elusive girl. But she remembered her manners in the presence of their guests and waved instead.

"What is it?" Fred asked.

"A girl I know."

Fred squinted into the rain. "Where?"

The downpour blurred the trees and Deena didn't see Mary any longer.

Peggy pressed her palms into her thighs and stood. "It's too wet. Ann, let's go."

Ann deposited her cup on a table. "We've been watching you ladies, and we're very impressed. You're acclimating well to Bellerton."

"You've been watching us?" Deena asked. The others appeared just as shocked.

Ann rested a hand on Deena's arm, her engagement ring flashing with largesse on her bald fingers. "Bellerton always has eyes on you."

Peggy said, "I'll let Mrs. Tibbert know how wonderfully you all are adapting. Good behavior comes with its rewards."

The graying light, the spraying mist from the rain: Deena couldn't be certain, but she thought Peggy winked.

Chapter 8
MRS. TIBBERT

WHILE Mrs. Tibbert waited in the stuffy South Hall foyer, she gripped her umbrella and examined the entry, satisfied with its cleanness and sense of order. She had heard good things from the senior class president about the freshmen housed here and felt it was time to see for herself. In the hall mirror she adjusted the sprig of dried, straw-colored flowers pinned to her felt hat, a seasonal necessity imparted to her by her mother. She had arrived early with the intent of eavesdropping on the girls—it was her duty—but the dormitory was unnaturally quiet.

From morning until late afternoon, Mrs. Tibbert monitored her Bellerton girls from a concealed perch in the library attic, keeping meticulous notes in a fastidious hand. She strode from window to window, and soon she knew them better than they knew themselves: their sweet young faces and soft, trembling limbs, their nubile bodies as ripe as peaches. She was a woman who knew how to bare her teeth. How to suckle the juice and when to bite.

She familiarized herself with their movements: how they chased the porch's shade from one end to the other; how they broke into chants and songs that passed among them in waves of unfettered enthusiasm. If they spent time apart, they ran into each other's arms like exuberant kittens, crashing and tumbling together. They threw wide their window sashes in warm months and drew gauzy curtains against the sharp light. She saw their lips move, overheard them caution one another against entering the woods. Older girls warned the younger ones about the thickness of the gate's iron bars and the height of the brick wall enclosing campus. Reminded them that the rules were meant to keep them safe.

At four o'clock each day, she descended to supervise supper preparations, otherwise Edith, their cook, grew overly imaginative and served ostentatious meals. Whoever heard of orange sauce on chicken or greens tossed with fruit? Mrs. Tibbert preferred the simple and straightforward. Give her a bowl of lemon-flavored Jell-O and get on with it.

Between these markers of her day, she needed only her binoculars, a thermos of water, a tin of saltines, and a block of cheese she pared into slices with a sharp pointed blade. She abhorred caffeine outside of breakfast and had been gifted an iron bladder. She was carved from flint, and the discomforts that bothered others did not concern her—except when any of the professors called her by her first name, to which she sharply rebuked them. She was *Mrs. Tibbert* to everyone. Her goal was simple: protect her girls. She'd rather a girl was dead than dishonored, though the goal, of course, was to prevent the dishonor from ever happening in the first place.

From the foyer, she finally heard whispers above; in a low voice, someone snapped, "Shut up, won't you?" The South Hall girls descended the stairs and clotted together. She enjoyed their fidgeting as she inspected their appearance and rigid postures before moving on to pluck at their seams, note their individualisms: the red lipstick, the blonde horsetail hairdo, the necklace with its bauble, the dime-store novel tucked into the waistband (curiosity momentarily gripped her, for she had an irrepressible taste for low-brow reading), the pair of scuffed shoes that stood out among the rest—strange, since the family certainly had money. She landed finally on the self-assured Delacourt girl, her red hair aglow with her family's legacy.

Mrs. Tibbert gave a short speech referencing Bellerton's values of purity, honor, and beauty. She remarked upon how they were all flourishing as ladies. She had delivered this speech only occasionally throughout the years—too much praise risked bolstering girls with overconfidence in a world that ultimately did not care about them—and concluded by saying that she had heard excellent things about their progress.

She knew her stern countenance did not match the enthusiasm of her words, but that was for the best. She had made her presence known. Time would tell if they were made of strong stuff. Life did not flatter, so why should she? They could learn a thing or two by navigating black waters. She was prepared to test their mettle.

Mrs. Tibbert snapped her fingers and pointed at the girl in red lipstick. She remembered her greediness that first day, demanding milk. "What are the consequences for a girl who strays from the approved lip colors?"

"Ma'am," the girl said in her thick Texan accent. "That girl would be instructed to scrub her face thoroughly. She would receive a failing mark in her classes for the day."

"That's correct." Mrs. Tibbert pointed at the tall girl to the left, whose predilection for gregariousness threatened her otherwise compliant demeanor. "When are quiet hours?"

The girl reached behind her head to tighten her horsetail, reciting the handbook rules verbatim. "Ma'am, Residence Hall quiet hours are from nine p.m. until seven a.m. and ladies are not permitted to receive phone calls after eight p.m. Violation of these rules results in two demerits."

"Very good." Her tone was not at all encouraging. She moved to the next girl, whose right hand flew up to stroke the necklace at her collarbone, her drab-colored eyes widening with nerves. "What are considered acceptable patterns for items of clothing?"

The girl squinted and looked beyond her, as if the answer were written in the sloping branches of the rain-soaked oaks. "Plaid. Tartan." She hesitated, then finished quickly. "Polka dot and floral in demure colors."

The girl beside her brushed her arm in a measure of support. Mrs. Tibbert wheeled to face this girl next, the dried flower in her hat seeming to wilt at the sight of the girl's over-worn shoes. The family was strange, retreating from all contact as soon as the girl had enrolled and the full year's payment was made. The girl was also odd, though Mrs. Tibbert supposed it was a family trait. She didn't quite appear to fit in, yet the others had welcomed her. Mrs. Tibbert narrowed her eyes.

"Describe your responsibility to maintain a clean room."

The girl swallowed. "Beds must be made daily. The housemother will do weekly room inspections. No Bellerton girl may call upon the staff to perform personal services, such as laundry, shoe polishing, dusting, or pick-up of a messy room."

Mrs. Tibbert was disappointed in the girl's correct response. She had wanted her to fail. She snapped her fingers and pointed. "Your shoes are filthy. Have them cleaned before I see you next." The girl rubbed her feet together, flushing at the rebuke. This satisfied Mrs. Tibbert.

She arrived last to the Delacourt girl, the obvious leader of this group. She knew well the Delacourts' place within the college.

"Miss Delacourt, please share the reasoning for these guidelines."

The girl was self-assured and calm, and the others turned their dewy faces toward her. "The guidelines, when applied diligently and consistently, weed out undesirable behaviors, identify opportunities for correction, and determine those undeserving of becoming a future Bellerton graduate. Finally, the guidelines allow for an ideal self to flourish within the college's loving bosom."

"Excellent, Miss Delacourt, thank you."

She was rather pleased. The girls were being perfected into better versions of themselves. Their behavior was uniform, and they respected the group's leader. Fine specimens indeed, Mrs. Tibbert determined. Perhaps the best Bellerton had to offer. Peggy Donovan was right—these six held promise. But she knew appearances could be deceiving.

When she herself was still merely a girl, naïve, unmarried, and young, she had been eager to leave home, where her father's brother lived with them, a frightening man consumed by deliriums, his body mangled by shrapnel during the Great War. Mrs. Tibbert, though she was just Agnes back then, enrolled in 1917, and Wesleyan's rules and structure had given her comfort in a period of chaos.

She met her best friend Ginger Comstock at orientation. She was lively and charming—everything Agnes was not—and yet the girls became fast friends. Ginger bound them with a blood oath that had left Agnes's pricked fingertip throbbing for days. Together they planned their futures: The bridal parties they would throw before their weddings. The children they would raise side by side. In the spring of their senior year, everything changed when Ginger became pregnant out of wedlock. Agnes did not understand how a nice girl from a good respectable family could let such a thing happen. Their every plan was upended because Ginger could not keep her knees together. The betrayal cut into Agnes's heart like a blade, and her endless, immoderate affection slipped into disgust. There was no restitution for a girl like that.

Ever since her husband Reginald had accepted the position as Bellerton's president, her life had been entirely devoted to her Bellerton girls, and she had thrown herself into the task of surveilling them. She would keep these girls pristine.

When she looked at the South Hall freshmen in front of her now, their cheeks flush and their hearts open, she was reminded of her promise never to allow another girl to fall as Ginger had fallen. Never allow small misdeeds to go unchecked, because the accumulation of transgressions was magnified by a matter of degrees. A girl might stumble in myriad ways. Vigilance was constant. Swift reprisal for infractions was necessary if a girl was to be polished into a diamond gleam. Let one girl get away with rule breaking and soon the others would follow.

Mrs. Tibbert extended her arm, and one by one the girls detached from the group to shake her hand, squeezing it limply before they rejoined the cluster, where she continued to pin them with her stare.

"I am impressed by what I've seen today. You are precisely what it means to be a Bellerton lady. I have decided that you are true Bellerton Belles—an honor I am conferring to only the six of you." She felt their pride rising and worked quickly to tamp it down. "But that does not mean I can't take it away." She drew her sharpened gaze across them. "If I find your virtue lacking, or if I learn you have behaved in a way unworthy of the designation, I will take the necessary action." She thumped her umbrella against the floor. "Am I understood?"

"Yes, ma'am," the Belles said in a single voice. They curtsied. "Thank you, ma'am."

"Now on with you." She flicked her hand, and they scrambled up the stairs.

Humidity stubbornly stuck the front door, requiring her to kick it twice with the toe of her boot to open it. She departed the hall's stifling heat and, under the shield of the porch roof, steadied herself for the walk home. A senior named Lucille Whittier flounced by on the sidewalk below, avoiding puddles and giggling to herself.

Mrs. Tibbert clucked her tongue disapprovingly. Thank goodness the Belles would not disappoint. She wouldn't allow it. She knotted her hair scarf under her chin, raised her umbrella high, and stepped into the driving rain.

Chapter 9
DEENA

WITH Mrs. Tibbert's blessing, they began calling themselves the Belles, a word sweet like cotton candy. The thin lines separating the six of them smudged. They moved together with proprietary ease, rarely alone, the lilt of their soft voices pulling envious gazes in their direction, their carriage graceful and swanlike.

Prissy pressed a Sears catalog into Deena's hands soon after Mrs. Tibbert had visited them, the pages of shoe options marked with paper ripped from her composition notebook.

"Oooh, let me see." Sheba wrestled the thick catalog from Deena. "They sell fun little things."

The others filtered into the hallway and peered around Sheba.

"How do I order?" Deena asked. She had never shopped in the catalog. Grandmother had sewn all their clothes on a beat-up manual Singer, and for shoes they went to the church charity troves twice a year, at Christmas and Easter.

Prissy examined her fingernails. "How should I know? I thought it would help."

Nell patted Deena's arm. "My family shops at Wanamaker's."

Sheba pointed to an open catalog page. "Let's buy a baby chicken."

"Name it after me? And keep it in your room?" Fred asked. Deena blushed at the question's strange sensuality.

Ada May grasped Deena's elbow, her fingers digging in. "I'll show you what to do." Over her shoulder, Ada May said to the others, "My family, of course, shops at Woodward & Lothrop, among others." With Ada May's guidance Deena ordered two pairs of new shoes—two because she couldn't decide on which one before realizing that she didn't have to limit herself. She had money now, all her own, and she could buy whatever she desired. The world was opening to her. She would never have what the other Belles did, that she knew, but having her pick of things from the catalog was an entirely new pleasure.

◆   ◆   ◆

The Belles found that teasing the housemother was almost too easy, and they soon grew tired of their game. She became jumpy at the tiniest sounds. She avoided them suspiciously, and muttered prayers under her breath when she collected their bedding for washing. Deena was glad they stopped; it was becoming cruel, and she had enough trouble managing her studies without the additional late nights.

"We need a new game," Prissy declared, looking up from her latest issue of *Mademoiselle*. "One that's for us."

They were all gathered in the common room one evening, Deena's eyes just starting to blur from the lengthy British history class readings.

Ada May wasted no time. "I have an idea," she said. "Line up."

They scrambled to obey, with Sheba at the front, always eager to prove herself by being first to play along.

Ada May tapped her head. "You're it." She pushed Sheba toward a hardback chair. "Now, sit." Sheba did as she was told, and the girls circled around while Ada May explained the rules. "We each pluck a single strand of hair. Just one. The it girl—that's you, Sheba—will win the game only if she does not move when her hair is pulled. No wincing, no flinching. Not a single inhale or fidget."

"What happens if I lose?" Sheba asked.

"You're awfully confident," Deena joked.

"You must stand in the unlit bathroom for thirty seconds."

The Belles tittered at this rule. They had all heard the superstition that the ghost of a dead girl reached through the glass to strangle those who dared linger in the bathroom too long. They acknowledged it was silly, but what if it was true?

"These are the rules for everyone. We'll each take a turn being it." Ada May's blue eyes sparkled with glee. "All set? Everyone ready?"

The Belles grew solemn, the game a serious matter. Sheba lasted only three strands; Deena didn't even get a chance to pull a hair. They locked Sheba in the unlit bathroom and had Prissy do the counting, her Texan drawl slowing time: "*One Mississippi . . . Two Mississippi . . .*"

Sheba emerged looking dazed. "There are strange sounds in there," she said vaguely. "Very odd noises." She tapped Nell's shoulder. "You're it."

Nell flinched the moment the first hair was pulled, and they ignored her pleas, blocking the bathroom door while Prissy counted. When the time was up, she didn't come out. Deena flicked on the lights. Nell was flattened into a corner, hiccupping and sobbing. A scratch bled along her jaw, and Deena was flooded with guilt. She wondered if they'd been too rough shoving Nell into the bathroom when she refused to go.

Deena wetted her thumb and dabbed at the scratch, but Nell fled to her room, slamming the door.

Prissy's hand shot into the air. "My turn. I won't be such a baby."

She sneezed after two pulls, stomping her foot and screeching for a do-over. Fred managed to go four. Ada May reached four also; Deena felt smug that it was her pluck that had caused Ada May to squirm.

When it was Deena's turn to be it, she drew in a breath and clenched her eyes shut, listening as the others arranged themselves behind her. She decided this was her moment, and she clamped her teeth. One pluck, then two. She squeezed her jaw harder. Three, four. A long pause followed. If she opened her eyes, they would say she had moved, so Deena imagined she was a body frozen in a river, protected by a wall of ice. The fifth hair snapped.

"I'll be damned," Prissy said, her voice thick on the cuss word. "It's like she's not alive. Honey, you can move now."

Deena waited a beat longer, afraid it was a trick, before bounding from her chair. She was tougher than any of them, and she had proven it.

The front door opened, and the housemother's heavy tread labored across the checkerboard tiles and up the carpeted stairs. The girls quieted, listening to her mumble about the cold nights aching her bones. She climbed the stairs slowly, pausing every few steps to catch her breath, and when she reached the second floor, her hand flapped in greeting.

"I didn't know youse was here. I thought you were on the nature walk with the other freshmen." She wheezed and gripped the railing.

We must seem like dolls to her, Deena thought, when no one replied to her friendly banter. Shiny haired, our mouths stitched with thread. Pretty but mindless.

◆　◆　◆

By midterms, Deena floundered less in her studies and had earned high marks on several assignments in various courses, and although she continued to struggle in her English class, she had decided never again to steal Prissy's papers. Then, class rankings were posted and Deena was at the bottom, just above the half-dozen freshmen who had gone home.

She decided to ask Fred, who always had a book with her, for help. Fred offered to write her English assignments in exchange for Deena cleaning her room. The bargain made Deena dizzy—just when she thought she had escaped the humiliating limitations of her past, she was being asked to sweep another person's floors. She almost refused, then decided that the only thing worse than her hurt pride was being forced from Bellerton for academic failure. Reluctantly, Deena accepted the deal.

Now that English was handled, Deena could focus on getting her grade up in British history, her second hardest class. She studied routinely and paid close attention to the lectures, rushing to get down every word in her notebook. Whenever she looked around, she was the only girl bothering to do so. The others spoke fluently on historical events, but it was all new to Deena.

"I suppose it's better to be one of Henry VIII's wives who loses her head than never to have been queen at all," Prissy said, filing her nails as she often did during class. Her name had appeared first in the freshmen academic rankings posted at midterms, which surprised Deena.

"Why is that better?" Sheba asked. The desks barely accommodated her height. She sat awkwardly, her body rotated in her seat. The six Belles clustered in the middle two rows of desks where the polish had worn from the floor.

"It's better than being poor."

Deena stiffened, the ceiling a weight pressing down, flattening her.

"At least as queen you would have fine clothes and quality food before—" Prissy drew her finger across her neck, then picked up her nail file again.

"But your choices were so limited, and you'd have eyes on you all the time, judging what you do," Nell responded, pushing up her sleeves in the stuffy room. "Like Princess Elizabeth when she met with President Truman last week."

Prissy's emery board slapped the desk. "All I'm saying is that I would rather be well fed, wrapped with furs and jewels, than live by dragging my feet through the gutter for scraps, and queens were the richest of anyone."

"That isn't very kind," Ada May said. "We are duty bound to look lovingly upon the less fortunate and help them whenever we can. Isn't that so, Deena?"

The tip of Deena's pencil snapped. "What?" Grandmother had said malice was most dangerous when it shone like pearls.

Ada May passed her a new one, its point sharpened to a spear. Deena shook the tension from her shoulders, a puff of air escaping her lips. Ada

May wanted only to engage her in the conversation. She couldn't know about Deena's past. In the corner, the radiator hissed.

"Testing the valves today." The history professor nodded gravely to the metal contraption before barreling onward with the lecture. "Ladies, you must remember that Henry led a period of great change for the betterment of his people, freeing England from papal supremacy." He coughed, then spat a sticky globule of phlegm into his handkerchief. Nell, the sole Catholic among them, received a pointed look as he did so. "Without the Reformation, England might have become a more fearful, superstitious country, one under the thumb of the Pope."

Fred flung a balled-up paper that skittered across Sheba's desk. Sheba covered it quickly with her hand, then peeked at it, her Mary Janes scuffing the floor. She had fumed all that morning to discover her pair of black kitten heels missing from her closet, and Deena had watched Fred rub Sheba's arms to calm her down, the gesture both firm and intimate, so that Deena felt as if she had come upon two people kissing. Now in class, she craned her neck to glimpse the note, but Fred's scrawls were difficult to read even up close.

Ada May squeezed behind Prissy on her way to the pencil sharpener, tugging a strand of her hair as she went. Prissy yelped and whirled to swat back, but Ada May glided smoothly away.

The history professor peeked at his pocket watch, his shirt damp with sweat. He continued the lecture with seeming reluctance. "Becoming queen was an enormous opportunity for oneself and one's family, especially for women with fertile wombs."

Prissy went back to filing her nails, and he raised his voice above the persistent grating.

"Henry adored women. He was by all accounts sweet and exceedingly generous, giving them jewels and land and their every desire. And when they were with child, he treated them exceptionally well."

"Some generous king. When they couldn't produce a male heir, it was chop-chop," Fred mumbled.

The history professor sat up. "You," he pointed. "There will be none of that." The air in the classroom turned suddenly brittle. He leered across the row of empty desks toward Fred. "Two demerits. A woman should think before she runs her mouth."

Fred crossed her arms defiantly.

He banged the desk, shouting, "I don't know why your type is even allowed at Bellerton."

Sheba leapt to her feet and stood with her shoulders back, drawing up to her full height. "Exactly what are you saying, sir?"

Deena saw that the professor was not about to be intimidated by a student. Rage bloomed on his face. "So you're sympathetic to her kind."

Deena fidgeted and kept her head down, uncertain how she might stick up for Fred.

Prissy raised her hand, and the professor's gaze slid in her direction. "I had a question, sir," she said, her voice deep with the richness of oil, her Southern drawl just as slick. She made a show of pushing her bust forward and taking her time with her words, intentionally drawing his eyes away from Fred. Deena was impressed by Prissy's quick thinking and how she turned the professor's leering to her advantage. Prissy reached into her purse for cigarettes, giving the pack a shake. "Do you mind?" She lit one without waiting for his approval, blowing a gray plume, then slung her chin into her other hand. "Sir, what about Catherine Howard?"

Prissy's distraction worked; the history professor's chalk clattered at the board as he wrote the disgraced queen's name, entirely forgetting his anger. Fred crumpled in her seat, tears in her eyes. Sheba scooted her desk closer, but Fred refused to make eye contact with anyone.

"Catherine Howard made a mockery of herself, tromping about like a common harlot. She ensnared a grief-stricken man, and any historian worth his weight agrees that she deserved what she got: stripped of her title and beheaded, along with her lady in waiting and two courtiers. A pity, as Culpepper was one of the king's favorites." The chalk snapped in his fingers. "Write all that down. It's likely to show on next week's exam."

When class was dismissed, Deena gathered her things quickly and hurried after the other Belles, bumping at the door into Prissy, who looped her thin arm through Deena's and whisked her away.

Outside, the cold was bracing. Dead leaves clumped in low spots and flattened across the latticework girding the porches. Fred shot ahead of them like an arrow, clearly bruised by the history professor's cruelty, and came to an abrupt stop outside their dorm. The girls surged around her, their movements like a tide. Fred opened her arms and let her books crash to the ground.

"He's a vile man," Sheba said, lightly touching Fred's elbow.

Fred was crying and wiped her hand indelicately across her nose. "I'm not the way he was implying."

Deena twisted her toe against the grass. She knew what Fred had said wasn't true. Nell gathered Fred's books and papers, stacking them with her own.

"Even so . . ." Prissy trailed off, lighting another cigarette. "He shouldn't be allowed to speak to us that way. I heard from my father that he's estranged from his wife and daughters. Hasn't seen them in years, apparently."

"Lucky them," Nell said earnestly.

Fred smiled weakly. They surrounded her in a group hug.

At the threshold to the dorm, Ada May paused, looking at the girls, one by one. "We're the Belles now. We stick together."

The command crackled between them. Deena recalled the seniors and their queer doll ritual; alone, the girls were exposed, but together they were powerful. The world might fail them, but they could rely on each other. They could be one another's shield.

Together, there was no telling what they might be capable of.

Chapter 10
DEENA

AFTER the incident with Fred, the Belles would not be separated. Their insularity was protection, and they moved as one sweeping entity. They tied scarves around their necks in the European style. They wore identical wool stockings beneath calf-length wool skirts. Bound by their uniformity, they drifted across Bellerton like a perfumed cloud.

One morning Ada May donned a velvet ribbon, its color like the mouth of a forest, a shade eerily similar to the navy hue of Bellerton's porches. Soon, the Belles all trussed their hair with dark velvet ribbons, or knotted one around their wrists, the looped bows dripping. The ribbons made them prettier and further signaled that they belonged to each other. When Prissy raised a hand to her face at the same moment as Ada May, they were mirrors. Even angular, bony Fred chose to wear one. When other students begged to know from where the ribbons had come, the Belles were coy, drawing an X across their lips with the tip of a finger.

Only Deena did not have a ribbon to lovingly call her own, as she had no mother to send her one from a shop near home. A week after the others began wearing one, Prissy pulled her aside on the walk to supper, lowering her voice to a whisper. "Honey, you must get a ribbon." Prissy's ribbon circled her neck, cinched with a cameo broach. "You're a Belle now and shouldn't stand out."

Deena felt her closeness to the others fizzle. She saw for the first time how tenuous their acceptance was and wondered whether everything she had been through was worth the risks. But it would be foolish to give up now. *You got to fight tooth and claw*, Grandmother liked to say.

Deena squared her shoulders. "My ribbon's in the mail. I'll have it soon." She had let the other girls think hers had been lost by the post office. "You'll see. It's made of delicate French lace. It's being shipped directly from Paris." She wanted them to imagine it was better than anything they owned.

Prissy tugged a hair from Deena's head—a reminder of their game and constant testing of each other. Deena winced at the pain, and Prissy flounced away.

After supper that night, Deena pulled a snatch of puce-colored scrap from her bric-a-brac jar—too short for use, too ugly to wear—and set it on her bureau. The Sears catalog ribbons were cheap-looking and hideous; she threw the booklet across the room in frustration. Tears stung her eyes. She had already learned to navigate this new life by mimicking the way the other girls wore their hair and picking up on their words and phrases, but it seemed to be of no use. All week, she'd felt different, separate from the other Belles, and all because of a stupid ribbon.

Deena eyed the two shirts of Fred's she needed to iron to keep up her part of their deal. She had solved the problem of her studies; she would find a solution to the matter of the ribbon. She couldn't let her grandmother down. No matter what, she would fulfill their plan.

She was about to heat up the iron when she heard a shout from Sheba's room. Deena ran across the hall just as a plane flew into the mountain and exploded. South Hall's windows rattled, and a boom ruptured the night. Where the mountains should have been, a ball of fire ran straight up the sky, consuming the forest along the slopes, fifteen miles away but terrifying in its hunger. For the first time since her grandmother's death, Deena felt truly afraid.

The hall fractured into chaos as girls scrambled to dress, memories of air raid sirens and dim-outs throbbing in their limbs. Deena thundered downstairs, hugging her grandmother's quilt. The others' hauled blankets, too, and Prissy had tucked her hair curlers and a cigarette pack under her arm.

"Is it the Soviets?" Deena cried. "Should we go to an air raid shelter?"

"Is there one?" Fred gripped Deena's arm, her voice breaking with fear.

Bomb threats had hovered over their childhoods, and although the war with the Germans and the Japanese seemed far in the past, Deena recalled the choking uncertainty that had smothered her adolescence. Until now, she hadn't really believed the Communists' atomic weapons might reach them. She'd occasionally heard news bulletins on Prissy's radio but hadn't paid much attention—an easy thing when Bellerton kept the outside world at bay, and the other girls rarely spoke about matters distant and foreign.

They spilled outside, joining the upperclassmen from East and West Halls to stand in the shapeless place between horse pastures and the back side of South Hall. The housemothers for the upperclassmen dorms circled like anxious sheepdogs, and although it was her job to watch out for the girls in South Hall, Deena realized their housemother was nowhere to be seen. The night was pierced by buzzing disquiet, rumors that the plane had been shot down by the Reds. The Belles clung to one another, scanning the woolly dark for other aircraft, waiting for warplanes to materialize. In the distance, the freshmen who were relegated to the farthest dorm at the back of campus staggered into the night. The air was heavy with the smells of burning diesel and wood, the stars obliterated by a billow of black smoke. Deena began to cough uncontrollably from the dirtied air. Alongside the others, she waited.

No additional explosions cracked the stillness. No missiles whistled past.

A voice called into the darkness. "The radio station is saying it was an accident." Deena detected the low rumble of an announcer's voice. "An air force plane on a training mission. We're okay."

Deena sank with relief onto the grass, her muscles aching. Peggy's friend Ann raised up a prayer for the men who had undoubtedly died in the plane crash. Around the lawn, girls' heads bowed solemnly. Deena's heart ached with the tragedy of it all. Ann's prayer concluded with a hushed "Amen" from the girls scattered across the back lawn.

Nell pulled Deena to her feet and hugged her. Prissy offered the Belles cigarettes, passing the pack along with her lighter to Fred and Sheba, who each took one. Deena watched a circle of seniors sip bottles of Coca-Cola from the newly installed vending machine outside the mailroom. She had heard they were all recently engaged to men from VMI or William & Mary.

Prissy saw her staring at the seniors and said, "What I wouldn't do for a nickel right now."

Excitement over the evening's novelty took hold. Deena sensed the tragedy was kept at arm's length by Ann's prayer and the simple fact that the girls did not yet know the full extent of what had happened. The realization that they weren't under attack ballooned into giddiness that they were outdoors after curfew. The distant burning airplane was almost like a bonfire, and a singalong kicked up, with different classes trying to outdo one another. Deena didn't know any of the words and stood awkwardly to the side while the Belles sang along with the other freshmen. Even Prissy joined in earnestly. When the tune finished, Deena leaned close to her. "How do you know the songs?"

"The Bellerton Songbook. I'll lend you mine sometime. Uh-oh." Prissy made a sour face and pointed. Deena turned to see Mrs. Tibbert marching down the hill from the president's house, her chunky galoshes sliding across the wet grass, her expression twisted with fury. Her poplin robe peeked from beneath her drab coat.

Mrs. Tibbert began waving her arms and shouting, "Inside, now!" She looked considerably less formidable in her nightclothes and coat, even silly.

One of the housemothers spoke up. "Ma'am, we heard the boom and we thought—"

Mrs. Tibbert cut her off with a sharp clap that startled the crowd into silence. Her hair scarf came unknotted and floated to the grass, where it lay with solemn grace.

"Ladies, return indoors at once. I will not have you roaming the night like heathens."

The students groaned. Mrs. Tibbert cut off their complaints with a sharp gesture for silence. Slowly, a procession of students trudged back toward the dorms. Mrs. Tibbert herded the stragglers, her voice as piercing as a cattle prod. She commanded the Belles to hurry up and get indoors, leaving them alone on the back lawn while she followed the upperclassmen to front quad.

South Hall was menacing now that the lawn had emptied. A preternatural stillness cloaked the night. Deena coughed again, her throat gummy with the ash drifting across the air. She climbed the porch steps and turned the knob; the door was locked. In the rushed chaos of leaving, no one had thought to prop it open, and only the housemother had a key. Before she could react to the predicament, Ada May grinned mischievously at the Belles.

"We've been overlooked," Ada May said. The fire from the crash glowed with intensity behind her. "No one is paying us any mind. We can do whatever we want." She paused, taking each of them in. "Perhaps we can stay out and explore."

Deena was startled by Ada May's suggestion, but none of the other Belles flinched. The gloom chittered with anticipation. The night had begun in terror, but now blossomed with possibilities.

If anyone knew when the rules could be broken, Deena trusted that it was Ada May, and she suspected the others did, too. Ignoring Mrs. Tibbert and staying out past curfew was one way of pushing back against the restrictions confining them during the day. The way Ada May flicked a suggestion into the air, then waited for the others to seize it, was evidence of her influence over them. Deena couldn't help but feel a spark of admiration.

The idea warmed in the Belles' imaginations as it was passed between them: They would stay out. Race through the night. Sleep in the filth of the stables like guttersnipes, seek the nearness of the horses. It would be another thing to set them apart. And besides, what choice did they have since the housemother had locked them out?

Sirens caterwauled at the base of the mountain, and the starry pinpricks of vehicle lights zigzagged up the slope toward the burning airplane.

They tied their blankets around their shoulders. They gripped one another's hands and ran through the pastures while the mountain burned.

◆ ◆ ◆

LATER, IN THE STABLES, THE BELLES PETTED EACH HORSE, THOUGH Deena hung back, afraid of the mammoth animals. They cooed over Brutus, then settled into an empty stall and told ghost stories. Hours passed and they enjoyed having more freedom than they had ever known.

The others eventually slept, but Deena was too charged up by the evening's drama to rest. She paced along the row of stalls in the stable, staying clear of the lumbering horses. When she returned finally to where the other girls were, Nell was wide awake, small eyes blinking rapidly at Deena's approach. Deena sat beside her, and Nell snuggled against her shoulder.

"I can't wait to write my sister about this," she whispered.

Deena was surprised; for all her endless talk, Nell had never mentioned her sister. "She's at home still?"

Nell hesitated, pushing her pink headband off and sliding it back on, then tugging her St. Christopher's medallion. She said reluctantly, "My sister has polio. She's been bedridden for nearly a year, and the doctor said she might never walk again. Bellerton won't take her if that happens." She dropped her head wearily against the wall. "Father Lewis says it's God's punishment for my parents' divorce. He's been urging my mother to return to my father, but she doesn't want to and anyway, he's remarried. The worst of it was when a group of Baptists prayed for two whole days under my sister's window. They said she got polio because God hates Catholics."

Deena had never met a Catholic before Nell—but then, she had never met someone who had grown up so far from Virginia either. She thought of what Grandmother might say. "They're all wrong, you know. None of that makes any sense."

Nell snatched Deena's wrist, her small eyes flaring wide. "Don't you dare tell anyone."

Deena swore she wouldn't say a word. She understood the need to hide parts of yourself. She had suffocated the person she had been, an annihilation necessary to enter Bellerton. The smothering had been worth it. By casting aside the girl she was, she had moved nearer to who she was truly meant to be.

She had stayed out all night with the others, breaking the very basis of Bellerton's rules; she was in possession of Nell's secret. With both things, Deena was gripped by her own expanding power. She fell asleep reveling in the knowledge of how far she'd come.

Chapter 11
THE HOUSEMOTHER

WHEN she discovered the girls were missing after the airplane crash, her first thought was ghosts. After everything she had seen at Bellerton, it was a natural assumption. More than once from her window she had seen a girl-ghost crossing the quad, her effortless movement identifying her as not of this world.

The morning the housemother's charges weren't there, she'd known because of the building's eerie quiet. She walked carefully down the girls' hallway. Doors to the rooms flung wide. Beds in disarray. A radio had been left on, and music slithered across the walls, "Claire de lune" playing to an emptied room. What else could be responsible but spirits? She was damp with perspiration, her breath foul from too much drink the night before.

She thumped downstairs, where the table lamp struggled to illuminate the entryway, and shadows skipped across the parquet tiles. The porch rockers clicked like judgmental tongues. She wobbled down the back steps, the air sagging with the smell of fuel and woodsmoke, and howled when the girls stepped out from the fog like phantoms. She ushered them frantically indoors before anyone saw them.

They reeked of hay and manure and the fumes of an electric heater they must have run the whole night. A miracle they didn't burn down the barn. Back inside they all went, trundling behind her like ducklings and wiping at their runny noses with the backs of their hands. The skin beneath their eyes was puffy and bruised-looking, and their faces drooped with exhaustion. At the second-floor landing, she stopped dead in her tracks and blocked the girls' passage, determined to lay down her version of what had happened.

"Last night, youse getting left outside, that was an accident." She scratched her thigh through her skirt with its crooked hem, cheaper than anything they would ever wear. The girls regarded her stonily.

She had not accepted the Bellerton position out of tenderness, nor out of any false notions about the importance of girls' education. She had, of course, heard all the rumors about the school. She had accepted the position because the role was easy and she had an old woman's body: sore and used, with no dignity or attraction clinging to it. She was a widow and unlikely to find another husband; her two boys were married and slothful, with no interest in helping her. She had taken a cleaning job at the bottling factory downtown but left after a few months when the chemicals and the stretches of time on her knees dizzied her and left large bruises. She did not last long at the yarn factory either, her stiff fingers slow and inefficient. On her last day, she hurried past the bent heads and slumped shoulders of the young women who would soon be old, then punched her time card, marched to the foreman's office, and resigned.

"Too much for you, eh?" he said from behind his massive desk. His sausage fingers counted what she was owed, slid it toward her. He lumbered to his feet, a hand gliding to his belt buckle, his fingers dipping to the buttons on his fly. "For a little extra, I could give you a little extra." He leaned close, his breath smelling of onions and tobacco. "What do you say?" He had a minister's mouth: bleached teeth that promised, *trust me.*

The Bellerton opportunity was a miracle: The college gave her a place to live in a heated apartment above the girls' rooms. They gave her a radio, and on Sundays she was entitled to any leftover dessert. The pay was low, but the duties fair. There were few men to bother her. She was in a position for the first time in her life at nearly sixty years old to order someone else around. Here among the swaying oaks and stately brick buildings, she imagined herself the mistress of a large estate; she was, in the hierarchy of her life, almost a queen.

Not that they respected her. She was convinced all the Bellerton girls were wicked. Sick and rotten to their core. This new group coursed with energy, powerful with their own knowledge and daring. She hadn't seen harm in letting the Carter Family's gentle harmonies sway her into sleep last night after a few too many drinks. Now that it was morning, she realized her misstep: The girls had the power to get her fired. If they set their minds to it, there would be no stopping them—unless she could threaten them first.

She gripped the handrail sternly, attempted a commanding voice. "Breaking curfew, that's expulsion. You misses might not think it, but I read. I know what the handbook says. The old crow might want to know youse was out all night like a pack of wild dogs."

Six pairs of eyes looked at her as she taunted them with her authority. She had their attention, felt the ripple of disbelief pass between them.

A girl with acne-reddened cheeks rose onto her tiptoes inches from the housemother's face. "You're a drunk."

She drew back, startled that they knew about her nightcaps, and tried to explain herself. "Come fall, my joints hurt. My knees flame. I take my own medicine."

A bubbling disgust went around the group. "You locked us *out*," the Texan snapped.

"You're young. It's harder for youse to understand." It wasn't only that they were young. The substitute of booze for medicine was the cheapest solution available to her and not such an unusual thing, at least not down in the valley where she came from.

The girls stepped closer, tightening their circle. The wall pushed at her back. Her eyes skipped across them in calculation, weighing what she knew against the power they held over her—a computation she understood well because she had been making it all her life. Who would be punished with dismissal: her or the ladies? The answer plainly was her. That is what happened when you weren't a true queen, or even a lady-in-waiting, when you weren't pretty and wealthy: You had to fight for your place, protect it all costs. She hadn't meant for them to be locked out, but they hadn't tried very hard to get back in. They might have pounded on the door; they might have walked to the president's house for help—though lucky for her they had not.

Her determination to stand up to them was leeching away, replaced by a new idea. If they didn't get caught breaking the rules, then neither would she. She might detest them, but she was smart when it came to her own survival. "Misses, I'll keep your secret. That is, if you keep mine."

An unspoken exchange passed among them, an energy she remembered well from her youth before men and children destroyed it. She and the girls were wading together into new waters.

"How interesting."

They parted to let the redhead through. She clamped her fingers around the housemother's arm, her emerald ring sparking. All light had a source, and this redheaded girl was theirs.

A shadow moved on the floor above—or perhaps the housemother imagined it, since who else could be in the building? Though sometimes she wondered if the girls saw what she did. The whole of Bellerton was like a house with too many dark corners that daylight never reached. Girls disappeared overnight; more than one of her charges had gone missing over the years. Usually, they went home to Mommy and Daddy, who were more apt to spoil them. A girl once ran away with a beau who had got her up the pole, only to be abandoned at a motel in Tennessee. Just this semester, a girl had left the day after she moved in. But sometimes, unexplainable things happened. A rustling in the night like leaves. A scritch-scratch of claws inside the walls. When she tasted the tang of rust in her tap water, she knew a girl was about to vanish without a trace. It had happened three times now.

The redhead's grip tightened on the housemother's wrist. "We'll each have a secret. And we'll keep it, won't we?" The group answered with a collective *yes*.

Yesterday, there had been only rule-following, and now they were writing their own rules. Despite the danger of an undertow that might suck everyone under, her desire to challenge them was swept away by their collective will. "Yes," she echoed, wincing in pain when the redhead dropped her wrist.

"Ma'am." The girl's voice was satin. "You have our word."

She hiccupped. "Silent as nuns, we'll be." Whatever happened now would be a secret held just between them.

That same night, after the girls' curfew, the housemother hunkered inside her apartment, drinking from a glass brimming with gin, carried elsewhere by the music of Hank Williams and the Grand Ole Opry. She could not help but feel paranoid that she had made a deal with six devils that she was going to regret.

Maybe it was the girls' futures taunting her: their shiny, perfect lives in newly created suburban neighborhoods, insulated inside beautiful homes and with husbands who earned a good keep. She resented them, though they didn't know about the smallness of marriage, the tedium of child-rearing. Their minds would soon be swept by domestication into a shape like a horizon: flat, stark.

Alone in her apartment on the floor above the girls' rooms, she poured vermouth—its bitterness matched her mood. Girls were like fish: flashing and beautiful when the sun sparked the water, but they had the same seething, bloody insides of anything else. Oh, how quickly the patterns for being a woman would slide down and lock them into place.

They had no idea what awaited.

Chapter 12
SHEBA

June 2002

THE cream-colored envelope appeared that winter in the mailbox of her home in the Northern Virginia suburbs. Distracted by a lingering quarrel with her husband, she turned it over without thinking. On the back was an embossed Bellerton logo. Usually she discarded Bellerton mail immediately, but a strange compulsion led her to open this one.

Inside was an invitation for the college's one hundred and fiftieth anniversary. Sheba flicked the corner of the envelope, considering for a moment what it might mean to return after nearly fifty years when she had barely made it out. She shoved the envelope deep in the trash, but later dug it out, her hands smeared with coffee grinds and marinara sauce, though the invitation itself was only damp and frayed around the edges. She taped it to the calendar page for June, as if she might actually attend, when she knew deep down that there was no way in hell she was ever going back.

All that spring, after the envelope's arrival, a stone of anxiety sat in her stomach. The feeling spread across her body as the celebration dates approached. Sheba tried to stave off her growing dread by focusing on her routines: Therapy once a week, yoga twice a week. Daily five-mile walks. Saturday was laundry. Sundays she read for long stretches, losing whole days inside novels. In the warm months, she swam weekday mornings at the neighborhood pool.

Sheba had changed since Bellerton. She moved through her uninteresting life with a serious demeanor, her youthful gregariousness gone. Others often mistook her for Scandinavian because she was tall and blonde and reserved. Despite the solid build of her body, she often felt ungrounded, a woman floating down a river. There was plenty she withheld or didn't say. Because of Bellerton, she had practice keeping secrets.

The weekend for the Bellerton event came, and Sheba did her best to ignore it. This time, she threw away the invitation for good. She kept busy with a deep clean of her house, then she and her husband drove into the city with last-minute opera tickets at the Kennedy Center. It had been a while since she'd seen any kind of performance, and she told herself she was looking forward to it, but she continued to be trailed by a sense of unease. The show was merely okay and not the distraction she had wanted. She drank too much white wine at dinner after the show.

Monday arrived, and still Sheba was uneasy. She came home from yoga class and poured a tall glass of iced tea with a lemon wedge and generous splash of vodka. She was hungry, but the apple from the fruit bowl tasted mealy, and she tossed it. Nothing seemed capable of righting the day.

Sheba swallowed two aspirin for the headache coming on and ran hot water for a bubble bath, unable to shake her Bellerton memories. She sank down into the water, thinking of how she and Fred had frequently shared a bathtub and none of the other girls cared. No one really seemed to mind what she and Fred ever got up to, and only once did anyone try and confront her about it.

Though Sheba had been married to her husband for fifty-one years—they had met shortly after her graduation—she could still hear the alto of

Fred's voice and the huskiness of her laughter. Sheba realized at last what had been bothering her these past few months: There was no remembering Bellerton without thinking of Fred. The two were entwined.

The unshakable truth was Sheba was still in love with Fred, all these years later. Back then, she hadn't called what they shared a relationship. Such labels were not the way of the time. Even so, she and Fred had shared something special that had indelibly marked her in ways she still hadn't reconciled with. Back then, Sheba had resented Fred for breaking up with her after freshman year—and now it was too late for reconciliation. What the others never knew, or never cared to know, was that Fred had broken her heart.

Sheba twisted the tap with her foot and turned it to the hot water. She had never grieved her relationship with Fred, the fact of losing her, she understood that now. She reached for her eye mask and neck pillow and settled in, letting the water work out the tightness she'd been carrying. Sheba told herself that what happened was not her fault. What the Belles had done, and what had been done to her. It was a sentiment she clung to, the thing she used to try and smother her guilt with.

Sheba woke to her husband shaking her arm. The bathwater had gone cold, the bubbles had dissipated. He looked at her with such loving concern that she felt terrible about all of the secrets she'd kept from him. He kissed her forehead, slipping out of the room as quietly as he had entered.

Sheba drained the water and towel-dried off. He'd left a note on the bathroom counter about a call she'd missed while she was in the bath. She picked it up, her fingers dampening the paper. The name written there made Sheba's heart rate spike, even after all these years.

URGENT BELLERTON MATTER. CALL ASAP.
— ADA MAY

Fall
1951

How you present yourself is important
to the impression others will have of you.
Plan your primping to allow enough time for
careful grooming each morning. Keep your loafers
cleaned and your clothing pressed. Be sure to smile!
When in doubt, seek the advice of another to
set you on the path to looking your best.

—BELLERTON STUDENT HANDBOOK, 1951–1952

Chapter 13

DEENA

TWO days had passed since they made a pact with the housemother. Two days during which they gathered, weeping, around Prissy's radio, listening to news of the airplane crash and the three young men who had died. The hours that autumn were long, and the Belles fought like sisters, bickering and squabbling over the tiniest things. They elbowed each other at the bathroom sinks, flicking water in one another's faces. Deena felt their hunger rising and converging, its edges sharp. The Belles had broken curfew, testing the limits of Bellerton's allowances, and they had emerged stronger. More united. Girls reborn.

On the third night, they rose from their beds as if they were beads strung on the same invisible thread, and they wore the darkness like a cloak. They met in the hallway, where Sheba looked statuesque, and Fred's teeth glowed eerily. Nell's skin shone slickly like the caul-covered eyes of a newborn pup. Prissy, eternally vain, wore her favorite lipstick and was as striking as Barbara Stanwyck in a noir film. Ada May emerged wearing a black hooded cape that hid her face, and Deena envied it. Ada May stashed the South Hall dorm key in her palm—swiped, she said, fair and square. No one questioned her because a key was good to have.

They floated in pairs to the South Hall foyer. Deena marveled when the checkerboard tiles seemed to disappear beneath her feet. A trick of the murky half-light that was both deceptive and freeing. At the front door, they clasped hands and tiptoed onto the porch. They pressed their bodies into the night, leaning toward an invisible precipice where, if they abandoned the girls they were in daylight, they might discover who they really were.

By unspoken agreement, the Belles stampeded onto the quad, leaping beneath leafless trees and swinging in each other's arms. No one could stop them now. Deena delighted in the thrill of movement without purpose, existence for its own sake. She didn't have to sit tall, cross her legs, or listen politely. She wasn't being told to soften her voice, speak less, eat less, smile more, dress properly. In the dark, Deena could turn herself inside out if she wished and didn't need anyone's permission; she could just be. This was her first taste of true independence. And what was freedom if you never used it?

Prissy knocked into Fred and sent her toppling to the ground. Fred shouted, and her outburst shattered the delicate spun glass of the night.

The Belles froze, suspended in fear. Deena scanned the dormitories for a snap of light. Every sound was amplified: the screech of rubbing fabric, the explosion of a cough, the burst of a breath. Minutes passed. Bellerton continued to slumber. They had not been caught; they would not be punished.

Fred collapsed where she had fallen, breathing hard. Prissy towered above, smirking, and Deena's arms pricked with desire. If the seniors could tear apart a doll in broad daylight, what might be possible for them under the mask of night?

How much stronger could the Belles become?

As if she had heard Deena's thoughts, Fred tackled Prissy's legs and slammed her to the ground. Prissy lay panting, her lipstick smeared. She reached for Deena's hand as if to ask for help getting up, only to tug her to the ground with an ogre-like grunt. Deena squealed in surprise and quickly righted herself, her fist closing around a chunk of Prissy's hair.

"Truce! Truce!" Prissy cried. Deena let go. Prissy pushed her hair out of her sweaty face. "I feel as alive as I've ever been."

Deena dug her fingers into the earth, let dirt cake under her nails. She would have to scrub hard to erase the remnants of this night, and the thought was satisfying.

Sheba wedged herself beside Fred on the ground, and Nell joined, too, chattering until Prissy told her to shut up. After a moment of indecision standing over them, her long hair aflame, Ada May dropped to her knees, then lay back in a snow-angel pose. The Belles giggled. They were exceptional together. They had been marked.

"Hush, listen," Sheba said. Thunder rolled in a continuous, distant drumbeat. She whispered, "It sounds like the wild clapping of my father's congregations before he hung up his collar."

She had once described to them how her father, prior to dumping her in a boarding school, had dragged her across the South, where he preached the gospel beneath white canvas revival tents. When Sheba's mother died, her father's faith had fled him. Now he hawked miracle cures for any ailment under the sun. Sheba had relayed his change of heart in his own logic: that there was no difference between selling snake oil and selling Jesus. She had mimicked his voice: "Folks are just lookin' for answers, sweetie. If you can give 'em one and charge the right price, you'll never have to worry about a thing."

On the darkened quad, fat drops of rain found their skin. The Belles crossed the lawn in a contemplative march, bodies lit with pleasure: cheeks flushed, lips glistening. They had created their own Bellerton tradition.

There were only three bathtubs, so they shared, a few of the girls shyly covering with towels. They didn't worry about waking the housemother, who had by then taken her medicine of gin and drifted into a deep slumber. Their feet and ankles bumped as the water absorbed their imperfections, leaching the dirt and sweat off their skin. They drew washcloths over their limbs and scrubbed their faces pink. Deena saw how Fred was careful not to stare, her eyes darting to the window lattice, the corner of the mirror, the chipped tile, the white baseboards. Sheba dipped her toe into Fred's tub.

"Make room?" Sheba said, letting her towel fall. Deena was impressed by Sheba's boldness, the way she was unafraid of Fred's eccentricities—her room decorated with colorful draped fabrics, her tomboyish style, the way she carried on reading while the others painted their nails and chatted about their diets and their hometown crushes.

Thunder cracked overhead, close and terrifying, the noise rattling inside Deena's chest. Fred said jokingly, "Not another plane crash." Ada May hushed them with an index finger to her lips.

The girls dried off, drew hearts and wrote their initials in the fogged-over mirrors. Prissy emerged from the tub, a thin-legged fawn, water sliding down her goose-pimpled flesh in rivulets. Purpling discolorations speckled her shoulders, floated against her skin.

"Good god." Deena backed up against the sink, pressed her damp fingertips to her cheeks. This is what they had done: bruised one another, left their marks. Claimed one another in a physical way. She asked, "Does it hurt?"

Rain battered the high narrow windows, the dorm lights weakening with the storm. Water gurgled in the bathroom pipes. Prissy shook her head no, and casually reached for her robe, placing her delicate feet into pink slippers. The bruises moved with her, rising with her shoulders, climbing the back of a thigh. A spike of jealousy hit Deena's gut. She wondered what pressing her thumb into the aubergine mark near Prissy's clavicle might feel like for them both. Would it erupt with pain, or would it engender a flinching desire?

Prissy unknotted her hair wrap, humming tunelessly. She rolled her wrists, tapped the bruised flesh of her inner arm, and grinned.

Here at last was proof that they were more than the surface they presented. The Belles looked at one another with a thrill. They had found a new game to play.

◆　◆　◆

THEY DRESSED HURRIEDLY IN PAJAMAS BEFORE CRAMMING INTO Prissy's room, where she had her curtains drawn against the rain that sounded like pebbles being thrown against the glass. The lamplight emitted a warm glow, and the radio fizzled to static, the signal broken by the weather. It was past midnight—Deena had counted only a single tolling of the chapel bells while toweling off in her room.

"We need to be careful," Ada May said, demure in her white cotton nightgown with its ruffles and bow at the collar. "We don't want to be seen."

We don't want Mrs. Tibbert catching us breaking the rules, Deena thought, flushing at the bloom of danger. She had done what she needed to get into Bellerton and had assumed it would be enough, but hunger for more, for belonging, gnawed in her belly.

Fred pulled lint from her flannel pajamas and said in a dismissive singsong voice, "Little old Mrs. Tibbert can't handle the tiniest fibbert."

"Precisely," Ada May said. "We must take an oath. Keep this between us." Her copper hair shimmered in the dim lamplight.

"Like a secret club," Sheba added, grinning.

Deena fiddled with the white strands of Prissy's rug and recalled how she and a neighbor boy had sworn a childhood pact: linking their pinkies, biting their thumbs, then scrawling nonsense words in the dirt. The Band of Bandits, they had called themselves, but they were a band of two and their escapades mostly involved chasing the chickens in Mrs. Sampson's yard and then running like hell to evade the jabbing beaks.

"I'm in." Prissy reached for her tin of lotion. She loved deciding who was in and who was out. The radiators up and down the hall clanged in approval.

"Of course you are," Fred grumbled.

Deena thought Fred was like a wolf: able to travel in a pack, but ultimately alone. No one wanted to be singled out, however—not even Fred—and after another moment, she declared, "Me, too."

"Me, three!" Nell rose up earnestly onto her knees, seeming to tumble headlong into her decision.

"Count me in," Deena said. Like the seniors with their masks, agreeing was anonymity. "What happens if we break the oath?"

"We act," Ada May said simply.

"We drown you in the creek," Prissy said jokingly. Sheba barked with laughter.

Ada May spread her hands open before her. "Are we all agreed then? We swear never to tell on each other? When one of us falls, we all fall."

Sheba walked from girl to girl with a seriousness that belied her usual convivial nature. Her hand cupped a pot of India ink from her room. She dipped in a finger, motioned for each girl to turn her wrists outward like a supplicant, and traced an X across both palms.

"What if it doesn't wash off?" Nell asked.

"It's just paint, you dummy," Prissy scoffed.

The marks entranced Deena: a symbol of belonging. Her acceptance was written on her skin. Water would wash it away, but she would know it had been there.

"Repeat after me." Sheba cleared her throat. The girls came to attention. "Upon my heart and my grave, I swear to secrecy. I seal this oath."

The Belles formed a circle and held hands. Deena's palms tingled, the ink smearing.

"I seal this oath," the chorus of girls repeated.

Prissy's lamp flickered.

Sheba said, "We are bound and united into one."

Her fingers folded with Ada May's, Deena felt it: a unified, beating pulse. Astonished, her eyes drew wide.

What was this fearsome power moving through them like a heartbeat?

Had it been there all along?

The light quavered, and the air thickened into a beast that licked Deena's skin as she repeated the chant in unison with the other girls: "We are bound and united into one. We are bound. We are united. We are one."

The lightbulb hissed then cracked, and the room plunged into darkness. The Belles shrieked and clung together until Deena shook herself free.

"The bulb's burnt out." She unscrewed it, pricking her finger on an exposed shard. She set her finger on her tongue and tasted the bitter rust of blood.

◆ ◆ ◆

BACK IN HER OWN ROOM AFTER THE OATH, DEENA LISTENED TO the rain drum in the trees. A knock sounded on her door. Ada May slipped into her room and perched on her bed.

"I brought you a gift." She opened her hands and a dark ribbon spilled forth like a tongue. "I saw you didn't have one."

"Thank you." Deena held the ribbon carefully, afraid of Ada May's generosity because, as she knew from her grandmother, kindness was a debt to be repaid. But how lovely the slim, black velvet ribbon was, a slash across her palms.

"My great-grandmother believed ribbons were quintessential to a girl's self-presentation. Only after marriage should one forgo them. Let's see how it looks." Ada May swept her hands through Deena's hair, nimbly braiding it. Deena felt a tingle stir her body, a long-ago memory of her mother. "Oh my, yes," Ada May whispered.

She retrieved the mirror from the bureau, her eyes passing across the cracked glass and the dull tarnish of the cheap handle as she handed it over.

The ribbon was knotted into an elaborate double bow, elegant and feminine, the ends dangling down her back. Deena rubbed its beauty between her thumb and forefinger. She sensed her own allure rising.

Ada May smoothed Deena's hair. Then, she said what Deena had longed to hear. "You're one of us now." She placed her hands on Deena's shoulders, their eyes meeting in the mirror. "I knew you deserved the better room. You've really proven yourself."

Deena clutched the ribbon, evidence of Ada May's approval, though a note in her tone, or perhaps the way her pale fingers dug into Deena's shoulders as she gave them a squeeze, warned her not to fully trust the words.

Lightning dabbed the sky with a bluish tint: the burst of a match. Deena glimpsed in its half second of illumination a figure on the lawn, black hair billowing. She crossed to the window, certain it was Mary in her black hooded cloak, her curls tied back with her own velvet ribbon. Deena waited for another flash, but there was only the thunder echoing across the valley and the heavy, beating rain against the roof.

Chapter 14
SAUL

THE cemetery overlooked the campus but was invisible from below. Absent from maps and Peggy Donovan's tour, it sat on the highest piece of ground, higher even than the faculty housing. If genius, as the professors said, rolls downhill, then one might say the same about death.

Inside the walls were thirty-odd graves of so-called important folks in the school's history, marked by granite stones and box tombs that jutted like teeth. While the haze burned off the mountains and the sun worked its way up the sky like a balloon, Saul used a hand broom to sweep debris from the gravestones, then trimmed the grass and collected leaves.

Saul hated the place, but each visit was an opportunity to touch individual bricks in the wall that formed the cemetery's borders—a benediction for his ancestors who had laid them. If he looked closely enough, he could find indentations of their thumbprints in the mortar. The invocation drew him closer to those of the past, so even if their names were unknown, they were not forgotten.

Spring was his preferred time to be at the cemetery, when he could pick the colorful wildflowers dotting the surrounding fields, and give them to his wife.

"The dead don't like you taking their pretties," Netty teased, inhaling the blooms: vincas and marigolds; skullcaps and king devils; even a few mauve-green hydrangeas with thick, woody stems. The vincas especially cheered up the main room of their small home with their bright petals and flat leaves pointed in four directions like a compass, gesturing to roads untraveled.

"They grow there just for my love."

Netty nestled the bouquets in an old canning jar that sparkled with sunlight atop the table carved by his grandad, where generations of his family had taken their meals. She guffawed. "They grow there because the dead feed them."

Saul nuzzled her neck, and her fingers rubbed the smooth baby tenderness of his balding head.

Netty spoke the truth: The flowers and grass in the cemetery grew brighter and greener without tending or fertilizer than elsewhere on the Bellerton grounds. Saul took care to describe it as a peaceful place full of birdsong; in reality, the enormous sycamores and cedars cast a chilling pall. How might the young ladies feel knowing the dead were so close? Though, as Netty put it, the dead were always close.

His people were buried down the lane, the markers unengraved fieldstone. He visited on Sundays after worship and sat conversating with his ma and pa, his little brother Orville dead at thirty-six, and the baby that never made it to a year, talking with his grands and his great-grands, aunts and cousins and even a couple of family dogs lying worm food beneath the earth. He appreciated being near his ancestors' bones, the dirt that was sweet and sorrowful with their sweat and blood and labor, proud to have his family gathered in one place. Netty didn't. Her ma was buried in the colored cemetery by the railroad tracks in Prestonville, but she didn't know where her father or any others lay to rest, and it broke his heart that she was cut apart from her people.

If he didn't mind spring for tending the graves, fall and winter were his least favorite times. Saul worked fast, clearing the area in sixty, maybe seventy minutes, and in all the years he had marched up the hill to face the dead, no one living had ever met him. Then, one chilly morning in late November, weeks shy of Bellerton's centennial year, he whistled as he always did while making his way between the graves—for both the company and to quell the nerves buzzing in his stomach. He looked up and was surprised to see a copper dot bobbing up the hill, surprised more so when the dot resolved into a girl's bowed head. Her face was serene as she delicately climbed the grassy slope. He stood taller and whistled louder, not wanting to startle her into a scream, but she didn't look at him until her milky fingers reached out to unlatch the cemetery gate.

"Morning, miss," he said, pulling his hat from his head. She responded politely, the gate clanging shut behind her. Though he oiled those hinges every few months, the gate never closed on its own for him as it had for her. He squinted, sweat beading onto his brow.

She gestured for him to carry on with his work, waiting until he resumed sweeping the founder's stone before she stepped between the graves, reading each inscription. She had sharp blue eyes and a back so straight you could build the walls of your house by it. He couldn't figure out why she was up here; more importantly, he couldn't decide whether she would make trouble for him. She moved at an easy pace, calm among the surrounding dead. She was pretty and feminine, a Bellerton lady through and through. Be careful around her, his gut said. Watch her, his bones echoed. He felt the trees gathering as witnesses at his back.

She came gradually closer to where he bent with the trimmer to nip at the grass grown around the headstones. When he straightened, she was staring right at him. Her eyebrows faded against the cream of her skin.

"Can I help with anything, miss?"

Like a cat, she was. Still and watchful, mischievousness on her face.

"Do you often tend the plots here?"

Was she trying to catch him out in his scheme of putting distance between visits? "Yes, miss. I'm here as often as I can manage. It don't do to have the places of the dead in disarray." He hesitated, drawing up slightly. "I don't think they like that much."

She tilted her head but didn't speak, her fingers lightly caressing the name on a stone. Her silence unnerved him.

"Not many of the ladies come up here, miss," he said carefully. "It's not on the maps." He felt the tingling warning of danger throughout his body. The seasons were between, not quite fall or winter, and the day golden. The Bellerton ladies might pretend ease, but he'd gone once or twice to the county fair. He'd seen how the tigers in their cages grinned.

She moved closer, two arm lengths away. "It's not on any map, you're right," she said. "But I know about it anyhow. My sister told me, and my mother told her." She tapped the headstone beside her. "Do you know who this is?"

"That's the wife of the school founder, miss."

She raised a finger in stern correction. "The *first* wife of the school founder. Her children were all stillborn. She herself died suddenly."

Saul knew this story, the lore of it in his family, too. Saul's life and Bellerton were knitted together; the stories of his childhood were also the stories of Bellerton's past, and he knew that after the first wife's death, soon came the founder's second marriage. He did not speak these things to the copper-headed girl, however, even as she watched him with those blue marble eyes.

She read the inscription on the gravestone. "'Her gracious spirit yet outweighs, the measure of her earthly days.'" She pointed to the next one over. "And this?"

"The second wife of the school founder, miss." She was testing him, he saw that now, as if she needed to be certain he was worthy of his work clearing the cemetery. Yet what did she know about him or his people?

Again, the copper-haired girl read aloud the engraving. "'She had the intelligence to know her duty and the courage to perform. Hers are the ways of pleasantness, and all her paths are peace.'" A chill stirred the air. "That is my favorite."

From the stories he had heard about the founder's second wife, he would have thought her paths were anything but peace. Where the school's founder was a charlatan who had invented himself, his second wife was a devil.

The copper-haired girl went on down the row and to the next one, asking him to name the dead, testing what he knew, and he played along because he had no choice, though he felt his politeness increasingly strained. Grave after grave she went, pivoting in place and pointing with her long, delicate finger. After the last headstone, she stood in a corner where the grass resisted growth, the patch brittle and yellow, the ground sagged by a slight depression. A small stone marked the spot.

"I don't know that one, miss." He hoped he sounded contrite enough.

She bent her head, swaying on her feet like a wisp of delicate cattail. But he knew that delicate could also be sharp. Delicate could pierce clean through a thumb.

"That's the only stone without a grave," she said.

His arms itched. "No body there, miss?" His back sweated.

"That's the grave of a girl who went missing and was never found. The first girl from Bellerton to disappear." She regarded him, her face smooth and expressionless. "Why did they mark her here?"

He did not know whether she expected him to answer, so he waited, hoping she would think him slow rather than stubborn. He knew from his grandad about the missing girl, how her absence had poked holes in the holy shroud of the school's safety, and revealed the extent of the rottenness at the heart of this place.

Grandad Jack had been part of Bellerton since the beginning, bought from a man in Richmond and dragged over hill and yonder. When Grandad spoke, Saul and Orville settled in, listening ears ready for his stories, though they'd heard them a thousand times.

Saul remembered one evening in particular. The fire had popped. His fingers, sticky from cornbread smothered with honey and milk, kissed his cheeks. Orville had a blunder across his face, a light patch like bone pulsing across his skin, and he tapped his fingers impatiently against it.

"Go ahead, Grandad. We're listening." Orville rocked his feet against Saul's.

Grandad stared over their heads, seeing only the past. He spoke in long, unbroken sentences as if he had only one breath to say all he needed to say. Without preamble, Grandad launched into the story of the missing girl. "Oh, yes. The college president, that man with more names than money, he tells me to search the woods for her, and I found nothing except animals that should be found in the woods, but boys, I seen right off there wasn't a hope of getting to the bottom of what happened to her because the truth back in those days, and still is, a shapeshifter."

Grandad had only four digits on each hand—three fingers and a thumb. The skin sewn over the stumps of the missing fingers was smooth and shiny, as if they had simply failed to grow beside their siblings. He rubbed his chin, then groped for their heads, patting Saul and Orville in turn. How Saul missed the closeness of family and a belly full of sweets. "That girl was never found. Some said she got tired and quit here, but it smelt sour, the whole of it, because everyone liked her, thought she was nice as a chickadee, and she didn't leave no note, no sign of going, said no words to anyone—nothing, just weren't here one day and that was that."

"What happened to her?" Orville asked, unable to hold back.

Grandad scratched his brow, massaged his sore knees. His voice rasped, and his hands twitched. "I speculate she was poisoned by another girl, or maybe two or perhaps three, you never can separate the wheat from the chaff with white folks, and those girls were put to it by Mr. and Mrs. Dickey, but it weren't the only time Mrs. Dickey did it; she had a glass vial and tap, tap, in goes the additive to a dish or two. The girl was only the first student it happened to, but all them travelers passing through went missing by the same methods because no one would suspect a woman of tainting the body's nourishment. I tell you boys, don't go trusting that family, the whole lot of them smell worse than five-day-old fish. Did I ever tell you how Mr. Dickey went partially blind to avoid the war, only to turn out not blind after it? He spread his arms wide like Christ and tells me, 'Behold, the water cures work!' Water cures weren't nothing but a humbug."

"Jack, you hush now. Stop telling those boys stories keep them up at night," Grandmama Dotty called from the other room, ears sharp. Saul remembered her silhouette crawling up the wall, the tingling on his arms the same as he felt now when the redheaded girl stepped closer, enacting an innocence he knew better than to believe.

"But why?" Saul had asked, staring into his grandad's face. If Orville wanted to know what had happened, Saul was determined to unknot the reasons.

"Oh yes," Grandad mumbled, readying for another tale. But Saul wasn't finished with this one. He put a hand on his grandfather's knee. Grandad leveled his eyes at young Saul, the cataracts refracting the light in a way that made them green, his gaze locked on the distance. His gnarled hands rested on his thighs, Saul waiting and waiting for an answer, jumping when his Grandmama touched his shoulder and directed him and Orville to bed.

Saul looked at the gravestone now. So there was no body. He might have known; if the girl in Grandad's stories was never found, it reasoned that she was unburied, the soil underfoot holding nothing of her. Saul shivered despite the sunshine edging the cemetery's boundaries. A body without a proper burial grew restless. Troubled.

"Why is she marked here?" the redheaded young lady asked, waiting for an answer. A breeze wove around them. He wanted to say he didn't know, rude as she would find him, but his jaw stuck, his tongue thickened and useless.

She tossed her head back in amusement, and Saul jumped, the hand broom clattering against the gravestone. The delicate flesh of her throat greeted the sun as she bent backward, her chest puffing air. She swayed on her feet, her hands like claws. "Where is she?" the girl cackled. "No one knows. There's not but a soul who knows."

The redheaded girl kissed the cold granite headstone for Mr. Dickey's second wife—her name etched into the stone was Ada Augustine Jackson Dickey. Saul looked away with a feeling of having opened a door better left closed. The girl glided off, passing through the gate without latching it, without turning to acknowledge him at all.

The gate swung wide on its hinges. Leave the door open and the dead might run out. As he left, he took care to fasten it tightly. He trembled to think that the spirits had lulled him into safety, convinced him they held no quarrel, then sent this girl into his path—living or dead, what did it matter, perhaps she was only a creature in the shape of a girl—to remind him who lay beneath his feet. The dead girl's story told him by Grandad Jack was a warning that anyone could be brushed aside to keep Bellerton's prestige intact.

When he returned a month later for his usual routine, the sycamores' debris of leaves and twigs had been collected into a neat pile at the gate. It infuriated him, staring at that loose bundle. The accusation of it. He knew who was responsible. That girl had been back, had left him a message: clean up after my people or you shall pay. He knew her people were unforgiving.

He raised his shears to trim back the grass, and he saw the freshly cut lilies nestled against the second Mrs. Dickey's headstone, another gift, another warning: their petals like bloody mouths open, the shiny insides like white tongues lashing.

Winter
1951

Remember: you must constantly strive
for perfection in your words and actions.
There are girls who look up to you, and others
who will take their cues from your behavior.
Men will expect to be dazzled by your warmth
and politeness. There are eyes always upon you.

—BELLERTON STUDENT HANDBOOK, 1951–1952

Chapter 15

DEENA

DECEMBER arrived cold and windy, but the frigid weather did not deter the Belles from sneaking out and accumulating mottled bruises on their knees and thighs, arms and hips. The varietal colors were like constellations on skin that fomented into the color of their ribbons, deepening to match the campus road.

They began to realize what their bodies could withstand—the miracle of flesh and muscle and bone. Their bruises connected them, garlands adorning their bodies. They gnashed their teeth unapologetically at night, only to become demure and smiling and small again by breakfast, drinking copious amounts of coffee to shake off the prior evening's antics. They found it difficult to focus on lectures for all the delightful, throbbing pain, and took to running their fingertips over spots where bruises hid beneath their clothes until the telltale marks melted away and the body refreshed—mended and cleansed—a cycle akin to the seasons. They felt their strength grow like clouds amassed on the horizon.

Then, their things began to disappear. Prissy couldn't find her favorite tube of lipstick. Sheba lost a favorite sweater. A novel Fred had nearly finished was gone.

Deena slept with her ribbon under her pillow, a thing too precious to lose—the gift that proved she belonged. She was unconcerned about her glass bric-a-brac jar filled with rubber bands, thumbtacks, colorful pebbles, and the like. Who would want to steal her worthless knickknacks? But when the jar vanished, she was frantic.

As a child, it had held every silly, precious thing Deena collected, its contents periodically dumped and sorted to make way for the new. The jar was a story: who she once was and who she wanted to be.

The day before arriving at Bellerton, she had emptied it and selected objects that held the most meaning, including a glass bead that glittered in the sunlight, painted with her initials—her real ones—LJS. She had emptied the jar and sorted through it after Grandmother died of stomach cancer. She had done it as a small girl the night she accepted that her mother was never coming back. She worried that whoever took it would somehow discover the bigger truth, her secrets that must never come out.

"Fred, have you seen my jar? I can't find it anywhere." Deena tried not to inflect her voice with urgency.

Fred's nose crinkled. "That old junk? I'm sure it's got to be somewhere. It'll turn up."

In the days that followed, Deena listened at her door for movements in the hallway, trying to anticipate the thief. Muffled voices drifted past, but when she cracked her door, the hall lay empty. She crept upstairs between classes and hunted for traces of disturbance; she searched the other girls' faces for tacit confessions. She counted her few possessions nightly like a totemic spell, her fingers gracing the objects as she whispered: one pair of black shoes, two white blouses, three wool sweaters, one ugly mustard-colored turtleneck, two sweater sets with delicate faux pearls purchased on sale at Woolworth's, two wool skirts—one plaid and one black—and two pleated cotton skirts for summer, a satin dress salvaged from a charity shop, one pair of blue jeans, a long coat for winter, one horsehair brush, one cracked mirror, fourteen bobby pins, a tin of hand cream. Grandmother's Bible with her real name erased from the family tree, one lovingly stitched quilt, a pair of work trousers yet to be worn at Bellerton.

More precious objects vanished: The locket from Sheba's father that she removed only while bathing. Ada May's blue silk fan and one of her family's Bellerton yearbooks. When Ada May discovered it was missing, she blocked the bathroom doorway and addressed them as a group.

"Those yearbooks are very special to me and my family. We've been at Bellerton since the darn beginning."

It was the strongest language Deena had ever heard Ada May use.

"We're the darn reason Bellerton exists! My great-grandmother and great-grandfather founded this place, and whoever took it, I demand you return the yearbook promptly. I promise I won't be cross. You may keep my fan. But the yearbook—" Ada May spun away, too choked with anger to continue.

Yet the disappearances carried on. Ada May's chevron-patterned scarf. An interesting rock lashed with striations that Deena had found near the horse pastures. Sheba's wool stockings, Prissy's leather kid gloves. Fred's porcelain figurine of a brown-and-white dog.

Fred accused Prissy of stealing it.

The others emerged from their rooms to watch the sparring. Deena bit her bottom lip, unsettled by the argument and that Fred, the kindest of all the girls, was accusing another.

Prissy folded her thin arms, a large bruise on her elbow, and sneered. "You're upset."

Fred raised her voice as she never did. "Give it back."

Prissy huffed. "I didn't take your stupid figurine."

Nell stepped between them, playing the peacemaker, hands held up pleadingly. Deena felt the urge to pull her limp brown hair. "Ladies, please."

Fred pointed a finger into Prissy's face. "You're a thief."

Nell begged them to stop. "Maybe you just misplaced it. Like Sheba's soap was misplaced. Remember?"

The supper bell rang. The girls scurried to their rooms, and for the first time since their arrival, they each locked their doors.

The Belles traipsed stiffly together to the dining hall that night, feeling no safer with keys tucked into hand purses. Deena was near the back of the group, her eye catching upon the dark curls and cape that she recognized as Mary's, but when she leaned over the pointed finials, she saw it was Peggy Donovan walking arm in arm with another senior, Lucille Whittier, who was scarlet with rage and crying.

"Deena, you're dawdling. Is anything the matter?" Ada May swept beside her and clenched her elbow, guiding her gently forward.

"Sorry, it's nothing."

Ada May's voice was tinged with impatience. "You don't want to be accused of stealing next. Best to stick with the group."

The dining room clattered with noise, but the Belles ate in tense silence, the knock of their cutlery loud against their plates. Dessert was set before them: chocolate mousse.

Ada May spread her hands on the table. "What if the housemother has been taking our things? She has keys to all our rooms."

Sheba was blunter. "And she's poor."

The spoonful of rich cream and chocolate curdled on Deena's tongue. She knew just how common it was to pin guilt onto poorness. She had been accused of stealing when she was six or seven, and she recalled the way her stomach dropped when the grocer's assistant forced her to turn out her pockets. She was buying a cut of pork, the tiniest portion, but the butcher wanted to measure a slab larger than she could afford with the coins in her pocket. She remembered how his irritation was communicated in the thudding of his knife. The way his calloused hands squeezed the handle with resentment as she repeated, *Smaller, please, smaller*.

After he handed her the poorly wrapped cut, he whispered to the grocer. And though nothing was found in her pockets, the butcher folded his arms with satisfaction at the charade, and the prim mothers judged her coldly. Deena had burned with shame. She was being forced to pay a price for her tattered coat and broken-soled shoes. Standing proud as Grandmother advised her had done nothing to lessen her leaden embarrassment. She had known there were places she did not belong, but that day, she had learned that her lacking made others uncomfortable, even angry.

Across the Bellerton dining table, Prissy's cameo dangled from the ribbon fastened around her neck. She lowered her voice. "It's true we don't know where the housemother came from."

Deena was sweating, the room suddenly boiling, crammed with one hundred and fifty girls whose throats bobbed with every swallow of food. It was impossible not to feel that the Belles were talking about her. That they had seen right through her.

Sheba swirled her spoon through her mousse. "If it's not one of us, then it *must* be her. She's using our things. Or selling them."

"But what would she want with my porcelain dog?" Fred lightly touched the back of Sheba's hand.

Sheba's mouth twitched. Her expression, typically amiable and open, narrowed. "Someone like that could be capable of anything."

They all began speaking at once, disgusted by the thought of the housemother wearing their clothes and lipstick. They cringed at the thought of her body fondling their soap, their silk fans, their stockings, the pages of their book. Deena balled her hands into fists under the table. The others leaned forward, pearl earrings glinting, pink lipstick shimmering. They were dignified ladies, and therefore believed in the certainty of their imputations.

But wasn't she one of them now? Couldn't she also lay blame? Like Ada May had said: She didn't want to be accused next.

Deena's water glass struck the table. "We search her rooms." She lifted her chin as she had seen Prissy do a hundred times before when she refused to budge. "The sooner the better. We surprise her."

"Tonight," Fred said reluctantly. She pushed a hand into her hair. "Just a brief search," she added. "To check for our stuff."

Prissy added, "She'll be slower once she's been tippling."

Nell threw her hands up in exasperation. "That seems a bit much. Maybe the things will come back." She spoke as if the missing objects were lost pets.

Ada May tossed her head, baring her pale throat. Her eyes sparked like flint. "Don't you know what's vanished never returns?"

◆ ◆ ◆

THE BOARDS OUTSIDE THE HOUSEMOTHER'S ROOMS DIPPED. DEENA rapped on the housemother's door. She heard shuffling on the other side. The door bent back, and the housemother, hair laden with curlers, blinked at them, a confused sea creature unaccustomed to land. Deena was swamped by the sharp, acidic smell of liquor.

"Now," Ada May commanded. Deena hesitated, and the girls shoved past her, flooding the room like water. "Lights," Ada May said, and magically a sickly yellow glow startled the room awake.

Deena was shocked by what she saw. The furniture was dusted, every piece squared to face the blaring radio, the news anchor yammering about a failed appeal for the Rosenbergs. The plaster walls were scrubbed free of marks, the windows spotless. Where was the filth they'd anticipated? The indicators of a torpid life? The room was spare but clean, respectable.

The housemother's bloodshot eyes protruded as she shooed them. "Go, get."

A uranium green highball glass wetted the end table. Fred sniffed it and flashed a thumbs-up: gin. The housemother was on her way to sodden; at least one expectation had proven true.

Nell refused to join the search and stood by the door while Deena and the rest of the Belles fanned out to search the rooms: The adjoining kitchen and narrow dining room, the table already laid for breakfast with a chipped plate and spotted silverware. The linen closet, shelves bare. The bedroom: narrow dorm room bed, same as theirs, shoved to the wall. Nightstand, lamp, bottle of aspirin. Her underthings were ragged, the color of used bathwater. The bottom dresser drawer was empty. The closet echoed, with nothing but a pillbox hat and extra sheets. Did she wear the hat on Sundays? Deena couldn't imagine her in such easily mimicked finery.

"Is this all she's got?" Sheba asked. She sounded taken aback.

"I doubt she's paid very much," Fred said.

Deena retreated to the bathroom of pink tile, reddening in shame at Sheba's question. She resolved to augment her own wardrobe with her next allowance.

A water stain looped the inside of the clawfoot tub. Deena bent to feel around beneath the tub, where there was nothing but dust. She washed her hands at the sink, then dried them on the housemother's hand towel, folding it neatly on the rack.

"Don't." Prissy tugged it from the metal bar and dropped it to the floor. "Let her clean it up." She tutted at her reflection. "I'll get pimples after touching her things."

Though they upturned her cooking pots and her two pairs of shoes, wrenched open cupboards and closets and drawers, they did not find their missing items in the housemother's rooms.

Ada May swayed on her feet, pinching her nose like she had a headache. "The potpourri," she said when Deena asked what was wrong.

The housemother had given up, her bulk sitting in the armchair, mouth opening and closing like a fish's. She patted Deena's arm. "It'll be all right, sweetie."

Deena felt cheated by her empty hands, denied the return of her cracked glass jar. She jerked away from the housemother's touch.

"Tell on us, and we tell on you." Ada May shook the bottle of gin.

"Oh, no, misses, your secrets are safe with me. I remember our agreement." The housemother crossed her heart with a shaking finger. "Haven't I kept hush so far? Youse got nothing to worry from me." She coughed, a wet rattle in her chest, a clenched fist pressed between her breasts. She hunched like a beaten dog. Another cough overtook her, spittle dotting the air. A loose curler clattered to the floor.

Deena twisted her ribbon around her palm, her knuckles tender pink. It was a shame the housemother wasn't the thief, that the suspicion had been thrown back onto them. Things would have been much easier if she was to blame.

Chapter 16
DEENA

THE end of the year approached: Christmas on the horizon, a separation imminent. The Belles' beloved things were still missing. Deena feared her glass jar was gone forever. Nothing else had disappeared after they searched the housemother's rooms—evidence enough, they agreed, that she was the likely thief.

The nights stretched long. The gray days were harder for being snowless. Crisp air sliced their lungs; to inhale deeply was like swallowing knives.

Prissy complained that she had never felt such chill in all her life. "In Texas we have no use for cold weather." She lit her cigarette, then tossed the lighter to Fred, who caught it one-handed. "Though we still put up a Christmas tree, of course. We're not Communists."

Their history final exam had just ended. Deena had chosen a seat near left-handed Fred because it made for easier cheating, and she felt confident she'd done well enough.

Deena eyed Prissy's mink stole jealously. She wore beautiful cashmere sweaters that Deena coveted—though she would never steal such a thing, she told herself firmly. The sweaters she'd ordered through the Sears catalog were cheap wool, not cashmere, layered over long-sleeved thermals for extra warmth. Her newly purchased things were helping her fit in better, but they still weren't enough. She was self-conscious of her dun-colored winter coat that was thinner than anything the others owned, but a new one, even from Sears, was far too expensive. When the Belles snuck out at night, the frigid winds knocked her about, numbing her entire body and leaving her to shiver in her sleep, struggling to get warm again.

The Belles were trudging to South Hall when senior Lucille Whittier and her bright red coat flashed up ahead. She chased after the poet-professor, who moved like a badger, his head down but his ears alert.

"What on earth is she doing?" Prissy asked, flicking cigarette ash.

Lucille called the professor's name, and he kicked up his step. His unbuttoned coat flapped in the wind. A dangerous current buzzed in the air. Lucille tripped, arms wheeling for balance. She called the professor's name again and stumbled, her feet skidding out from beneath her as she crashed to the hardened ground.

"Poor thing!" Fred moved to help.

Ada May stuck out her arm to restrain her. She tutted, "We can only help those who help themselves." Fred seemed reluctant to follow the other girls, but Deena stepped forward and guided her inside, leaving Lucille on her own.

The wall sconces inside South Hall flickered as the girls proceeded upstairs. Deena noticed that in their absence, the cleaning staff had polished the brass doorknobs into a dull shine.

Ada May pressed a bruise on Deena's neck from their recent games. "Best wear a turtleneck to cover that up."

Deena agreed, though she hated the feeling of fabric around her neck. "Maybe we all wear them?" she asked cautiously.

Ada May assented. "Yes, we'll all put on turtlenecks for classes tomorrow." She raised her voice just enough for the others to hear.

Sheba groaned. "I'll look like a giraffe."

Ada May gripped Sheba's elbow. "But you'll wear it." It was a command, not a question. "See you at supper, ladies." They scattered behind their doors.

◆ ◆ ◆

THE LAST FEW DAYS OF THE SEMESTER THE SKIES SPILLED WITH freezing rain. Walkways iced over. Power went out for half a day, and Deena was forced to write her final English paper by the afternoon light pulsing through her window. Thick clouds bore down, erasing the world beyond campus; whenever she looked up, it was like staring into a new landscape laid over the old. She reluctantly delivered the paper to the professor's mailbox when she finished, her hand cramped from writing all day. Prissy's final paper was on top, neatly typewritten. Deena jabbed the tip of a paperclip into her palm, furious at Prissy's diligence, the privilege of owning a personal typewriter. She fled the building before she did something wrong, like foolishly ripping the paper to shreds or blotting out Prissy's name and writing in her own.

The rain prevented the girls from sneaking out, and the Belles grew restless without the exhilaration of release, circling one another with curt politeness like strangers at a bus terminal. Deena felt adrift now that she was detached from the semester's routines, ambling mindlessly around the dorm while rubbing the fading bruise on her neck, irritated by how Prissy played her radio heedless of the others. Deena glimpsed Fred leaning on a windowsill with a cigarette in one hand and a book in the other. In the bathroom, Nell was hunkered before a mirror, popping zits before scrubbing her face with a drugstore's worth of cleansers. Deena washed her hands and was turning to go when she saw Nell swivel to Prissy's basket of bath supplies and remove her bottle of facial toner. When she caught Deena staring, she said hurriedly, "Prissy's letting me borrow it."

On the third straight day of rain, Ada May had the idea they gather in the first-floor drawing room for a change, and with Mrs. Tibbert's permission, she instructed the staff to have it aired out and swept and mopped, the dust coverings removed, the furniture polished. That evening following supper, Ada May pushed wide the double doors and welcomed them inside.

The Jackson Drawing Room had been made cozy. Behind the brocade curtains pulled tight over the French doors, cold December rain smattered the porch, but inside a fire burned in the hearth. Decks of playing cards and dominoes and cribbage boards were stacked on a table. Fred and Nell shoved the sofas and chairs into a group, and Prissy brought down her radio, Kay Starr's high soprano filling the room. Deena swept Ada May into a hug, whispered *thank you* in her ear.

Snug in pajamas and feeling especially grown-up, the girls sprawled across the furniture and sipped steaming cocoa poured from a silver urn on the sideboard. The room conjured images of their futures: intimate meals followed by coffee and dessert, husbands massaging their stockinged feet, a small dog lounging on the rug, and the children asleep in their rooms. The American dream of royalty, each a queen of her own household. Deena recalled Prissy's recent issue of *Life* that was filled with photographs of Princess Elizabeth in her shimmering tiara, her children obedient at her side.

Ada May flicked her glossy copper hair behind her shoulders and reached for the decorative box tucked under her armchair. "I have one more treat for us." She lifted the lid and gingerly removed two books. One was a yellowed collection of papers fastened with string, and the other sported an embossed cover. "My grandmother's and my great-grandmother's yearbooks," she explained, caressing them. Then she scowled. "The thief still has my mother's yearbook."

From the sofa, Sheba was glib. "It's just a yearbook. It'll turn up."

What happened next was quick: Sheba sprawled on the rug like a starfish with Ada May looming above, her jaw clenched. Deena would later try to recall the exact moment when Ada May struck Sheba and she fell to the floor, but all that came to mind was how the usually commanding Sheba had shriveled. Still, Deena knew instantly that she was on Ada May's side.

An unease palpitated in the room. Sheba had spoken carelessly. She had placed herself apart, and for those reasons, no one dared interfere. They knew to fall in line. To keep silent where Sheba had not.

Ada May lifted Sheba's chin with a delicate hinge of her foot and pushed her head back until Sheba choked for breath. Her bare toes nestled at Sheba's throat. She tipped Sheba's chin higher until the crown of her blonde head was nearly flush with the floor. Her throat exposed and head angled unnaturally, she gasped for breath as if she was drowning.

"I'm sorry." Sheba choked out the words, her voice strained. "Those yearbooks are important. To your family. To us all." Tears streamed from her eyes.

Ada May stepped back, melting again into a Bellerton girl. The tension in the room evaporated. Sheba sputtered onto her side, gulping for air. Fred hurried over to her with a biting glare at the others, who looked away, pretending as if nothing had happened.

Deena poured herself more hot cocoa from the urn on the sideboard; she brought Ada May a cup, too, and received a warm squeeze on her shoulder. The girls scooted nearer as Ada May tapped the two yearbooks, fascinated by the depths of Bellerton history in her hands. Even Sheba drew shyly onto her knees at the back of the group, her shoulders hunched. Deena brushed her pinky against Sheba's arm to signal that she had been forgiven.

The binding crackled when Ada May opened her grandmother's 1898 yearbook and the sound was like an ice storm, the snap of tree limbs expanding and contracting. The pages of black-and-white photographs began with the faculty, then ran to sports and societies, followed last by formal portraits. Ada May lingered over a spread dedicated to the basketball team, a sporting craze, she explained, that had swept women's colleges at the turn of the century. Twenty varsity players in bloomers and opaque stockings stood with unsmiling ferocity and determination. The team's coach grinned from the back row, a small terrier perched on his shoulder.

Ada May indicated the girl who had a basketball tucked under her arm. "That's Grandmother Hampton." She turned to the next page. "And these silly pictures of girls dressed as animals. What do you think that was about?"

In photo after photo, her grandmother's face—Ada May's face—hovered on the page: A potato sack race on the lawn. The equestrian team. The May Queen with her court.

"Have all the women in your family been crowned May Queen?" Prissy asked, unable to keep the tinge of envy from her question.

"They have, yes," Ada May said, flicking her hand dismissively as if it didn't matter, though behind the gesture Deena saw her pride. She tried to imagine what it was like to know your family's history was entwined with a place like Bellerton—that one would not exist without the other. She found it astonishing that anyone could trace their family's origins back generations, when all she had were a few names written in the back of a Bible, a list of women and girls but very few men. A crooked, misshapen family tree.

"Show us your great-grandmother's yearbook," Deena said, eager to change the subject from May Queens. She rose onto her knees to get a better look.

The hand-stitched binding was fragile. Instead of photographs, inked illustrations were interspersed with faded, handwritten text. Deena marveled at the lists of classes, instructors, and students. Each girl was detailed by her name, her nickname, her favorite class, and a friend she admired, the list captured by an elegant cursive script.

Ada May said, "There wasn't a printing press for three counties following the war. The girls had to do everything by hand, each responsible for copying out her own yearbook from the master copy. A student made this extra yearbook for my great-grandparents." From her chair that seemed more like a throne, Ada May took the girls in one-by-one, her eyes dancing with the firelight. "Bellerton wasn't supposed to be called Bellerton, you know," she said. "And my great-grandfather William Grayson Dickey wasn't always called by that name. He was born in England as William Gray, and he would later change his name. It never bothered my family. Sometimes, a new identity is necessary."

The Belles nodded in agreement: Fred, whose real name was Winifred. Nell, whose mother refused to fully give up her last name when she married. Prissy's family was determined to shed their nouveau riche trappings. And there was Sheba, whose father had reinvented himself from a preacher into a medicinal, cure-hawking prophet. Deena, more than any of them, understood the need to become someone new.

Ada May held the Belles firmly in her thrall. "Shall I tell you the rest of Bellerton's history?"

•   •   •

WILLIAM GRAY, AS HE WAS THEN KNOWN, ARRIVED TO THE shores of the United States when the country was less than a century old. He quickly tired of Washington's swampy climate and muddy streets and crossed into the heart of the Virginia Commonwealth to live for a time in Richmond before he grew restless again and headed west over the Appalachian Mountains. There, he stumbled upon the land that became Bellerton, purchasing its six hundred acres fairly— Ada May slowed to emphasize the word *fairly* in her telling, which implied to Deena that it was anything but fair—from the handful of homesteaders and one or two Native encampments.

His recently purchased land was isolated; through it ran cool, clear creek water. "He was fluent in the needs of the day," Ada May said, her pride spilling over as she spoke. "People needed a place to rest and recuperate from the stresses of life, and why should they have to go abroad to do so? With good amenities, the isolated setting, and the clean water, he decided to create a retreat that offered rest and relaxation away from life's responsibilities. In 1848, Belle Terre Springs was born.

"People came from all over for the water cures at Belle Terre Springs." From the box that held the yearbooks, Ada May withdrew a mimeographed advertising pamphlet and passed it to Deena, who held the fragile artifact by its edges. Inside the dusty trifold was an ink drawing of a three-story brick building buttressed by woods, mountains in the backdrop and a creek in the foreground. Deena read the pamphlet aloud:

"Take the waters at beautiful Belle Terre Springs, located in the mother of states, Old Virginia. We offer cures for all manner of ailments. From cancer to consumption to gout, there is nothing clean mineral water and rest cannot do! Belle Terre Springs is your home away from home, where comfort and curatives meet. Open to both gentlemen and ladies with stays of one week to six months. Pamper yourself into wellness!"

Nell, in her high-collared nightdress and quilted dressing gown, crowded to Deena's side and pointed to the centerfold drawing. "Look, it's our dorm!"

Ada May glowed as if she had been the one identified. "South Hall is one of three original buildings. The president's house and the senior dormitory are the others." She continued with her story.

The retreat was a huge success, but William Gray wanted more. In 1852, on his land adjacent to the springs, he founded an institution of learning dedicated to the brightest young women. Then, nearly a decade on, came Virginia's ordinance of secession. Relaxation could not be found with the nearby specter of war, and soon there were shortages of sugar, flour, and butter, and reports of soldiers setting fire to fields and homes. There was no cure to be found in streams that ran with blood. Retreat guests dwindled to only an old widow in her eternal black, like a specter of death haunting the grounds.

The school for young women flourished. Girls whose families had taken the waters began to arrive in greater numbers than before, seeking shelter from the war. Buildings once meant for guests turned into dormitories and classrooms. Belle Terre Springs closed, but Belle Terre College was born.

"He was an advocate for women. A great man," Ada May declared, then read aloud her great-grandfather's introduction in the yearbook, deepening her voice for effect: "Let there be no qualms about women's education. God would not have endowed women with capacities equal to that of men only to abandon their minds to unequal learning. With a proper curriculum to sharpen young ladies' minds, they will attain the trappings representative of good breeding: reading, writing, arithmetic, elocution, music, drawing, painting, and wax flower making. Belle Terre College is a superior education for a superior lady."

The fire snapped; the Belles clapped, the newest recruits of perfected young women. Prissy's radio played a sweet tune beneath the thrum of rain, while elsewhere in the dormitory radiators banged discordantly. The building creaked and groaned.

"So how did we get the name Bellerton?" Fred asked. She was snuggled with Sheba on the floor near Ada May's feet. Aside from the way Fred's arms were enclosed protectively around Sheba, Deena noticed that it was as if the earlier tiff hadn't happened.

"An errant splash of ink on a bureaucratic form twisted the name from Belle Terre into Bellerton."

"Wasn't your great-grandfather conscripted?" Prissy asked. "I've always been told that's why there are so few men. They all died in the war, and it's taken generations to replenish them."

Ada May tapped the arm of her chair as if considering the question for the first time. "Yes, conscription was a problem. He wore an eye patch over his left eye—an accident with lye—and a limp from an old childhood incident returned, so he had to walk with a cane. He suffered, too, from terrible migraines brought on by the stress. When the war was over, things could return as they were."

"So, he faked injury and illness to get out of fighting," Prissy said bluntly.

Deena was surprised when Ada May laughed. "My great-grandfather was a man who lived and died on his own terms and no one else's."

Prissy leaned back into her pile of floor cushions with a satisfied, appreciative air. "A thorough businessman."

"But how did your great-grandfather keep the college going?" Deena asked. What she really wanted to know was: Where had he gotten the money to purchase all that land in the first place? That kind of wealth didn't come from nothing.

Ada May leaned forward, dropping her voice to a whisper though the Belles were alone in the drawing room. "Running a school was expensive, of course, and the economy had utterly collapsed. For a time during the war, my great-grandfather found it necessary to improvise currency"— Ada May raised her faint eyebrows to show what she really meant—"but there were other means as well."

Deena found Ada May's tone difficult to untangle, but her pleasure in her family's history and resilience was a bejeweled, flashy emotion. She set her empty cup on the side table. "Of course, I'm sure none of this is *exactly* true. Family lore changes over the years, and some in my family have been known for both their exaggeration and their dark sense of humor. But this is what my grandmother told me."

◆ ◆ ◆

IT ALL STARTS WITH A SINGLE TRAVELER CAUGHT IN THE ISOLATED valley, and as night descends, he requires no persuasion to stay at a girls' school, where he assumes that no harm will come to him among the pretty little ladies. Violence abounds throughout the South during Reconstruction, with bands of roving citizens sniffing out traitors—the weak, the abolitionists, the Republican sympathizers—who in their minds undermine a return to the Southern glory that was.

The sojourner, now a welcomed guest, sits in a polished Chippendale chair in the president's brick house on the hill. Girls from the dormitories down below skip into the parlor dressed in bright baby blues and mint julep greens, white Chantilly lace fanned modestly across their chests, furbelowed skirts rustling. The sojourner listens to a recitation of Horace in Greek, a piano player and her warbling mezzo-soprano sister, and a mathematically inclined girl who performs complex problems in her head. These young ladies hidden away in the mountains like sirens are a collection of impressive, bewildering specimens.

He can see that the acquisition of knowledge—thank Jehovah!—is not the only thing they are taught. They entertain him with polite man-

ners and lively conversation, flittering nymphlike while the mistress sips
her coffee in the corner, watching over the rim of her cup. The traveler
yearns to caress these strange, lovely creatures who are pure, unspoiled.
They giggle behind their hands and flick their eyelashes. Their bare wrists
entice; he longs to snap one to his lips, slather it with kisses and nips of
his teeth.

He adjourns with the lively hostesses to the dining room for supper,
sitting opposite the mistress of the house at the long table. The master is
away on business, oh shame. He hears the news and sits taller; the sweet
ladies will not find his manner gauche in the absence of another man.

Two servants bring out covered silver dishes that punctuate the air
with the most delicious smells his senses have known. There is pork roast,
fried tomatoes, Irish and sweet potatoes cut, boiled, and mixed in a dish,
thick white biscuits, stewed apples, morels from the woods, pig's head
hash, and fried ham. He has paid mightily for an innkeeper's room in the
past and not eaten a quarter as well. He stuffs himself, the embarrassment
of his hunger fading away with each dish that appears before him. The
conversation is gay, the young ladies excellent at carrying it forward. They
are fascinating, and he cannot help but graze a finger against the hand of
the girl nearest him, who briskly glides her elbow back.

And there is dessert! Almonds served in small dishes. Sweet raisins.
Potato pies and boiled custard. Jade candies like jewels that melt on the
tongue.

"You all are the kindest folks I've ever had the pleasure to meet," he
says, careful with his words for there was wine, yes, plenty of strong, excellent wine. "Why, ma'am, this candy is nearly indistinguishable from
your ring!" he exclaims, holding the emerald sweet before his eyes like a
gemologist.

From the opposite end of the table, Mrs. Dickey perches like a feline.
"How apropos."

"Yes, how—" The traveler's brain slurs, the word sliding away. What
is it she has said? Was it French, perhaps a way of complimenting him?
He tries again. "Yes, how—" He can't feel his arm. It's as if his limb has

been cut off, yet he can see it splayed before him, hear the splunk of the candy as it falls from his fingers into his wineglass.

The cutlery clatters as his arm crashes to the table. "Yes—" His tongue seems to swell, and he slumps forward, unable to hold up his head. He lifts his other arm, the shoulder joint aflame. "Ma'am—" His finger points, not in accusation but as if he is prepared to argue a philosophical stance. His head lolls. He hears distantly the shattering of a plate. How embarrassing. The young lady whose hand he touched leans forward to wipe his damp mouth, and when she lifts the cloth away, he sees the white froth bubbling there. He jerks violently, falls from his chair.

The girls' boots hover near his nose, the lace and crinoline of their dresses brushing his cheek. He struggles to sit. He does not want to give the impression that he is untoward, trying for a peek at their ankles, or worse, a look up their skirts. Somewhere in his mind he recalls their uncluttered plates: a few potatoes, the biscuits, the hash. They did not eat, and he begins to understand—what does he understand? His eyes roll in his head, and his mouth fills with a bitter tang. His teeth are chomping, he cannot stop them, and above float the hazy faces of the girls. He reaches out, he manages to close his fingers around the toe of a boot. Then, at last, he is still.

The boot kicks his hand away. Kicks it a second time for good measure.

"Dotty!" a voice calls. A moment later the servant appears. The boot nudges the traveler. "Anything on him is yours."

Dotty snaps her fingers, and a second servant appears. Together, they heft him from the floor, disappearing with him into the night. Where they take him or what they do with him is their business. The girls are already back in the parlor, one having fetched the traveler's bag from his room. The clasps fall away, the bag yawns as if exhausted by what follows. They rummage through his things, taking inventory. When they finish, Mrs. Dickey walks along, a shopper in a bazaar. The girls stand with hands folded behind them and wait.

Discovering what each man brings is the best part; learning what each girl is entitled to keep is the next best part. Sometimes, they are disappointed. Trousers, a clean shirt, socks. A newspaper folded to an advertisement for a job in West Virginia or Tennessee or—if he was going the other way—Richmond or Norfolk. Sometimes, they are surprised. The preacher last year, for example, with five hundred dollars sewed into the lining of his jacket, nine dollars of which was split among the girls. Sometimes there is jewelry: pearls, opals, and gold. Several men carry daguerreotypes with small faces where the humanity is difficult to discern. The jewelry is never for the girls; Mrs. Dickey keeps it all. They never see her wear it; perhaps it is sold. The photographs are theirs. She cannot be bothered with other people's families. Paper and coins stay with her as well—that's what made the night of the preacher so exciting because there was enough even for them. If there is whiskey, that, too, stays in the grand house, but any sweets or snacks go down to the dormitories.

And so it is how Belle Terre College not merely establishes and sustains itself, but flourishes and grows. Only a few trusted young ladies are chosen to participate in the ritual—*the Belles*—hand-selected for their cunning and willingness to do as requested. They are kept to the utmost secrecy. They do not speak of what happens in the big house to anyone except themselves and even then cautiously, far from the others, in whispers and veiled language.

If they are troubled by their actions—if they struggle with moral turpitude—they do not linger upon it, for their behavior has not been unseemly. They are not the glutton who eats apace of his hosts, and they have neither cooked nor served the offending meal. They have no greater ambition than to see and be seen; the balance is on the man and the sum always calculates to a dangerous willingness toward his own blindness, his own fault of being bewitched by girls who are—look at their sweet faces!—nothing more than mere girls.

Chapter 17
DEENA

ADA MAY'S story stunned the Belles into silence. Then, Prissy tossed back her head and cackled, a startling and discordant sound.

"That's one hell of a story, Ada May," Prissy sputtered. Deena had never heard this laugh of Prissy's: loud, grating, uncouth. The laugh of uncomfortable things. She wiped at the tears in her eyes with the back of one hand. "Every important family has skeletons in the closet. My father says ours is my uncle. He's an alcoholic. A very insistent one."

Fred chimed in. "We have a few Boston marriages in my family's history."

Sheba raised her head from Fred's lap and said, "I've already told you about how my father went from holding church revivals to selling so-called miracles." She rolled her eyes. "But it pays for Bellerton." She nudged Nell with her foot. "Tell us your family's dirty little secrets, Nelly."

"We already know," Prissy said. "She's Catholic and her parents are divorced."

Nell's face reddened, and she whipped her head in Deena's direction. "What about you? What's your family hiding?"

Deena grew hot and tugged at the collar of her nightgown. The Belles' eyes were on her, waiting for a confession, a lie—or a blend of both. She looked up at the rococo plaster ceiling that rippled in the fireplace's flickering light. "My father wasn't around much, so I don't really know him."

There was a soft coo of sympathy from the others, except Prissy, who muttered, "That's not much of a family secret. Everyone's father worked." Dissatisfied, Prissy pitched a question in Deena's direction. "Are you acquainted with the Vandorns? I just had a letter from them last week. They're my cousins."

Deena went deadly still. She knew of the Vandorns: their stately, sprawling former home of painted white bricks, the drive lined with boulders dredged from the James River and interspersed with elegant yews and azaleas. They were particular in hiring only light-skinned help, but never whites, and they were important people who had purchased and moved into her father's house when the family relocated north after the incident.

"I've never met them," Deena said, and it was the truth. Her body felt heavy with fear, her cheeks stinging with heat.

Prissy held her gaze. Deena, unable to withstand its directness, pushed away from the rug and began gathering the playing cards scattered under the couch. Was Prissy onto her secret? Deena was lightheaded, terrified that she might be forced to confess what she'd done.

Maybe Prissy knew nothing. Perhaps the families were not acquainted beyond the exchange of deeds. The Williamses and the Vandorns might have belonged to separate clubs, dined at different restaurants. Deena had no idea how it worked, and the thought caused the muscles to tighten in her neck. Her father—though he refused to acknowledge himself as such—had returned to Massachusetts with his wife, but what if the Vandorns had kept in touch? What if, over Sunday coffee and croissants, the Vandorns raised their eyebrows and said to one another in reedy, disbelieving voices, "I understand the Williams daughter had a breakdown of sorts, that she . . ."

And here, they trailed off out of respect for what could not be said. It would not do to gossip. Best to dispense with the facts in quick euphemism and leave it alone. They might say, *she was troubled* or *she had always been a little lost.*

And if Prissy had mentioned casually in a letter or a phone call that she went to school with Deena Williams, might the Vandorns have carefully said, *You know what's curious about your college friend . . .*

Her half sister's birth certificate was folded inside her grandmother's Bible, her fingers having traced and retraced the letters of her new name. Would Deena be forced to present it as evidence and pretend she had miraculously recovered? Was it even possible for a damaged brain to be healed?

Or would Prissy find out about the institution where the real Deena Williams spent her days in an unresponsive state except for the occasional flicker of her eyes? Would Prissy bring the evidence directly to them, wheeling her catatonic half sister into the drawing room while the other girls watched with curiosity? Deena chilled, imagining how it would unfold.

Look, look! Here is the real Deena Williams! Prissy would say, tapping the half sister's head as drool trickled from her mouth, then pointing an accusing finger at Deena—who they thought was Deena. *That girl is an impostor!* Prissy's grin would be smug and triumphant. *That girl is a cheat! She's taken us all for fools. She's not truly one of us, and we must drive her out. We must make her go away.*

Make her disappear.

"Oh, well, never mind then," Prissy drawled. "I guess I was mistaken. They probably know a different Williams family."

"It's a common name," Deena agreed, exhaling. Her secret was intact. Her hands shook with relief that Prissy's prying had failed. Deena tucked the playing cards into their tin, her nerves settling, then went around collecting the girls' empty cocoa cups.

The energy of the room shifted into quiet contemplation. The radio clicked twice, and Deena watched as the dial rotated, moved by an unseen hand. Or was it just a trick of the light? Midnight had come and the stations should have gone dark, but the Ames Brothers billowed forth.

Prissy jumped up and swayed to the laconic, watery beat, pulling drowsy Sheba and Fred to their feet. The three girls moved in unison until Prissy stepped back, leaving Fred and Sheba together.

"I've never danced with anyone," Fred admitted.

Sheba slid her arms around Fred's waist and nudged them closer. "You can be the boy and lead."

Fred went redder than one of Nell's pimples.

Deena coaxed Ada May to join her, and they spun and shimmied until the song gave up its last shivering note. Deena's cheeks flushed with heat, and she poured a glass of water from the sideboard, then gulped it down.

"Thank you for the dance, Miss Wyatt." Fred bowed deeply.

Sheba responded with an exaggerated curtsy. Fred bowed again. Prissy, who had been watching, curtsied to them both, and Nell bowed. Deena joined them, her giddiness rising. Ada May stood off to the side, her hair the brightest thing in the room's dim firelight.

The radiator suddenly clanged in its corner, and they screamed, their fright launching them into further silliness. Soon, they were jumping and shouting, spinning around the room, knees and shins banging into furniture. The mirrors quaked; the porcelain cups jittered on the sideboard.

The Belles shoved the furniture back to clear a space, then formed a daisy chain, dancing and skipping in a circle beneath the room's chandelier that wept tear-shaped crystals. Their heels kicked up, knees raised, their bare feet smashing against the oriental rug. They were being bad, yes, so very bad, behaving nothing like the ladies they were raised to be.

Deena tripped and flung her arms out to catch herself, nearly cracking her head against the brick hearth. Fred dropped down to check that Deena was all right, and her foot tangled in Prissy's nightgown, knocking her off-balance and sending her crashing to the floor. The other girls sunk to their knees, dropped onto their backs, tossed their limbs wide. Deena's chest heaved to catch her breath, and her sweat-damp nightgown stuck to her skin.

"I'll require another bath," Nell exclaimed. She wiped her sweaty face on her sleeve.

"Let's go to bed filthy," Fred said.

The hour had grown late, and the fire had burned to embers. The rain hushed to a drizzle. Prissy's radio fell silent. Ada May was flopped like a lily on her sofa, an arm thrown over her eyes, and she hummed an unhurried tune—Deena recognized but couldn't place it. She had settled on the floor nearby and was trying to conceal her yawns.

Ada May's fingers curled around the edges of her great-grandmother's yearbook wistfully. She turned to the final page, and Deena's eye caught the elaborate hand-drawn crest adorned with the words:

In Memoriam Our Sister
Mary Burden, 1848–1865
Requiescat in pace

Deena's hand shot forward. Beneath her fingers, Ada May's pulse throbbed, but her skin was cool, and her ice-blue eyes flashed when Deena tightened her grip to keep Ada May from stowing the yearbook away. She read the inscription again, then for a third time. The room rocked; her thoughts grew hazy. She had spoken and dined with Mary. She had chased Mary across the lawn—only to have her vanish around the corner of a building.

Deena lurched to her feet, goose bumps on her arms. She jostled Ada May, and the yearbook tumbled to the floor.

"Watch out!" Sheba cried, startled into alertness by Deena's sudden movement.

"For heaven's sake, Deena," Fred admonished.

Deena stepped on something cold and sharp, and lifted her foot. Her key had sunk into the rug. Her hand flew to her neck, as she remembered move-in day months ago when the same thing had happened. *Mary.* Deena's vision blurred, gray splotches floating like dust motes that, when she looked up, were five pairs of brows drawn with concern. Behind the Belles stood Mary, lit by the lamp's sallow glow. Her hood was shoved back, finger to her lips. *Don't tell.*

Deena stumbled to the sofa and dropped onto the cushions. "I'm sorry. I thought—"

Don't tell.

Fred wrapped Deena in her grandmother's quilt; earlier, the others had fawned over it, admiring the stitching and colors, and she had blushed at the pleasant fuss over something she owned. Now Fred crouched next to Deena and rubbed her arms. "What's gotten into you?"

Deena made an act of yawning and rubbing her eyes. "I'm tired, that's all."

Ada May tucked her yearbooks away, then nestled beside Deena while the other girls withdrew to paint one another's nails and cinch pin curls with Prissy's endless supply of hairpins.

"Let me braid your hair." Ada May's voice was delicate satin, and Deena closed her eyes, soothed by the gentle tug of Ada May's fingers and the scratch of nails across her scalp.

Deena wanted to ask Ada May if she knew how Mary had died all those years ago, but she was afraid that if she broke the spell, her sense of security might break, too. She settled for Ada May's hands in her hair, weaving a braid that Deena would go to sleep wearing.

Don't tell. And she wouldn't. Mary had chosen to reveal herself only to Deena. Besides, if she kept Mary to herself, Deena would have a piece of Bellerton all her own, something no one else had, not even Ada May. She rolled the name Mary Burden in her mouth, stashing it like a secret candy under the tongue.

All her life she had wanted what the others had: the safety of family and wealth. That special clutch of belonging. Like her half sister, these girls had been given everything, yet somehow didn't know it. You can have anything you want, long as you're smart about it, Grandmother had often advised. You just got to be able to take what's yours.

She had fought for and earned her place with the Belles. She would do whatever it took to remain one. She wouldn't let go of what was now hers.

Chapter 18

DEENA

THE semester finished; the freshmen waited at the gated entrance to be claimed by families or whisked away in taxis. Even the housemother had left campus to spend Christmas with one of her sons, calling him a good-for-nothing as she hobbled to his puttering car, her ugly olive-colored carrying case thumping against her legs. Fred had played spy and reported back, much to their delight, that the son was bald and had a frog-faced wife. With the housemother gone, Mrs. Tibbert had minded them for the night, her shrewd presence curtailing their plans to sneak out one final time before the new year.

Only Sheba and Deena stayed behind. Mr. Wyatt, Sheba's father, was passing near Bellerton for business, and on Christmas Eve sent a driver to pick up his daughter for dinner and an overnight stay in town. Deena stood for the second time that week at the entrance gate, struggling not to feel abandoned: the girl with nowhere to go.

Sheba wore leather gloves cuffed in mink. A light snowfall descended in the solemn afternoon. "My mother said snow was the frozen tears of angels. She was rather dramatic. At least, she is in my memory." Deena understood Sheba's mother-longing, that smudge of recollection for a woman barely known. They had both been motherless from young ages. The difference was that Sheba had a father she could rely on. A man who at least claimed his daughter.

Sheba pressed her hands together, gloves creaking. "Do you remember your mother?"

The question startled Deena. She had forgotten she had shared this partial truth: She was an orphan raised by her grandmother. "I rarely think about her," Deena said honestly, spinning the toe of her boot against the frozen ground. But she had thought of her mother constantly for months after her death. Deena was six years old at the time, and her half-formed blurry memories were soon supplanted by her domineering grandmother, eventually leaving her with only a distant impression of who her mother had been.

Headlights suddenly slid down the road, slowed, then hurried onward, the driver obscured by the windshield's cold reflection and the slice of the wiper blades flicking away the snow.

"I hope that wasn't him," Sheba said. "Say, you haven't got the time, have you?" Deena shook her head. "It's all right. If I'm late meeting my father for dinner, it's the driver's fault anyhow." She reached for Deena's hand. For the first time since the mix-up with the rooms, Deena felt that Sheba actually liked her. "I'm sorry you'll be alone tonight and tomorrow morning. I expect to return no later than two o'clock. Then, we'll have a celebration with just the two of us. I promise."

"That would be nice. I'd like that."

"Do you find it strange that you don't think about your mother?"

Deena hesitated before answering. "Not really, no."

"Sometimes, I wonder if I'm broken. I half believe I've imagined all my recollections of her. I was ten when she died. That isn't so young. Certainly, my memories are real. Oh!" Sheba waved, signaling. "It's the same car returning. I'm certain it's the driver my father sent." The black Chrysler turned into the drive and rolled to a stop before them.

The driver came around and opened the back door. "Miss Wyatt?" he said, bowing. He was withered, his hands and face cut with deep wrinkles.

Sheba bent down to kiss Deena's cheek. "Take care, dear. I'll see you tomorrow." The driver shut her inside the vehicle, then moved her suitcase to the trunk. Sheba rolled down the window. She seemed so grown-up and glamorous inside the black town car with her blonde hair pinned into an updo. "Don't do anything foolish all by yourself." Deena must have looked startled because Sheba laughed. "I'm only tickling you." Sheba pinched Deena's cheek. The car disappeared at a bend on the narrow road.

A man stepped forward and locked the Bellerton gates. His name—Saul—was stitched above the breast pocket on his navy work shirt, and Deena immediately recognized him as the porter from her very first day. A sense of confinement gripped her. She had not left the grounds since arriving; the outside world had nothing to offer her yet. Not until graduation when she'd emerge as a young lady ready to become a wife. If she was clever, she would marry well and never have to lift a finger for all her days—the very thing she and Grandmother had plotted. The very hope embodied in becoming Deena Evangeline Williams.

Saul retreated. She wrapped her hands around the gate's cold iron bars and traced the disquieting whisper of the trees, their shorn heads charcoal against the slate-gray sky. She was untethered from the familiar comfort of Bellerton's routines. How was she going to fill the time without the others? She had no magazines, no radio, not even a set of dominoes or a deck of playing cards. The sleepy-faced library was locked for the break. In her melancholic mood, Bellerton seemed somber, and she resented the solitary day she would have to pass until Sheba's return.

Deena decided to go on a walk, bundling into long underwear and her warmest clothes before heading out, her breath fogging the air. The chapel bells rang twice for the hour. The snowfall had ceased but the temperature had dropped, and the ground grew slippery. Her mind cloudy, she headed in the direction of the stables, cutting across the empty pasture and its frozen clumps of dirt. The wind tugged her hair from beneath her wool hat. Where the pasture ended, Deena crawled between the fence slats.

She saw the path immediately, though she had never noticed it before. No wider than her own two feet, it carved narrow purchase along the unnamed woods. A line braced between the known and the unknown.

Her lungs ached from the cold. The woods leered, the trees hungering for a lost girl. If she went missing, how soon would anyone know? Not for a full day at least, when Sheba returned and found her room empty. Fear spiked in Deena's limbs, but her feet marched independent of her mind. She seemed locked into her forward motion, her curiosity the stronger emotion, as if she was a boat and a current tugged her from shore. Rustling echoed on the path ahead, and she drew in a sharp breath. "Mary?"

Deena heard faint giggling and chased it, uncertain if she was running away from or toward Bellerton. If the black ribbon road ended where it began, she might somehow return to South Hall.

The path did not arc toward the dormitory but opened onto a rutted dirt road. Winded, Deena bent over, hands on knees as she counted twenty-two tin-roofed houses crammed together, hemmed in by hills. Though Bellerton felt far away, she could still see snatches of the brick wall enclosing the grounds. Seeing the bleak houses, an image immediately came to her: home.

Her gut twisted. She had done everything in her power to forget her humble past: houses built from unvarnished boards, newspapers shoved in the chinks for insulation; the banging of acorns on the low tin roof.

Deena's father—her grandmother's employer—was a man who had come down from the North and believed himself better than his Southern neighbors. He spoke often of his family's progressiveness, his word for goodness. He hired white maids to prove he did not debase others for the color of their skin. Yet his contempt for his workers was plain.

"You're his daughter, too." Grandmother pinched Deena's chin between her fingers. "He wanted your mother and none of the consequences." Grandmother spit. "You'll take what is rightfully yours."

And that was when it happened, really happened, for the first time: A crack appeared in her life and she pressed her eye to it, looking out upon all she could own and possess. If she could get to Bellerton, she would survive. She would become a lady with a maid, rather than that woman's maid. Her home might have a doorbell and a television and glass windows and water running clear from a tap. She would have things no other women in her family had ever imagined could be theirs. The alternative, without her grandmother, was unthinkable. At Bellerton, her body would never know hunger or pain. Bellerton offered the guarantee of acceptance into a realm otherwise forbidden to her.

She was tired of the world she came from. She hated the dirt clinging to the hem of her dress. She hated the battered wash flapping ignorantly on lines strung between the houses. She hated her drab and ugly home filled with discards found and fixed or remade—the wooden apple box that, turned bottom up and covered with last week's newspaper, became a stool. The empty tin of tobacco that became a milk saucer for stray cats. Everything made new by becoming something else: If the wooden box and the tobacco tin could, then why not her?

She had strived and plotted, scrabbled and lied, and become someone else, all for the purpose of leaving behind a hard life she did not want. A life that denied her everything, including a father and a mother.

"Mary," she whispered. Her fingers numbed with cold. "Why did you bring me here?"

Mary gave no reply, and Deena, alone and afraid, shut her eyes to the past.

A door to a house creaked, and Deena watched a woman emerge wearing a wool cloche snapped tight over her head and pinned with a small brooch like an eye. Deena recognized her as Alice, one of the cleaning women she had seen all those months ago on her first day at Bellerton, and she realized with satisfaction how much more confident she felt since then.

A woven cloth basket bumped against Alice's leg as she locked the door. She dropped the key into her handbag, snapped it shut, and adjusted her hat. She had begun to walk up the dirt road when she caught sight of Deena. A breeze whistled. A sheath of cold scaled Deena's spine.

"You lost, miss?" Alice called.

Her directness was startling. Deena fumbled. "I'm studying at Bellerton—"

"I know you're one of those girls. I'm asking what you're doing here."

The words slapped, and Deena's stomach clenched. A hot, piercing spike of shame spread through her chest. "I've got no family, and all the other girls are away—"

"And you decided to walk here."

Deena didn't understand her flush of guilt. She had only gone where the path had taken her, led by Mary's invisible hand. Why should her walking the grounds cause this woman any upset?

"I don't appreciate your words." Deena was firm, her tone uncompromising. She would correct this impertinent cleaning woman. "I'm merely out for a walk—"

Alice interrupted her. "I'm sorry you got no family to be with, but that don't give you the right to bother me and my kin. We don't come uninvited to where you are and gape at what we see." Alice's voice was taut. "We don't come around unless we're told to. We got to be invited. And yet, here you are on my doorstep when you have no invitation." Her glare cut Deena up and down. "I know what you are."

Deena's skin prickled. The brooch's eye regarded her with a stabbing gleam. The woman's mouth twisted in disgust. Deena had let herself be seen.

Her resolve hardened.

"You don't know anything about me. You have no idea what I'm capable of."

Alice laughed—a jarring, braying sound. Deena felt the crawl of many scrutinizing eyes, although the hunched houses were still. A shaggy mutt trotted past, nose to air.

"You." Alice jabbed at Deena, her words mocking. "Exactly the same as the others. No matter where you came from. You girls all the same. Every last one. You'd kick a sick dog if you thought it'd help you. You'd nurse that same dog to health if you thought it'd help you, too. Because the first and last thing you got on your mind is yourself. You don't think I see you? I spent my life watching you. I got no choice. I see you better than you see yourself."

She snapped her fingers, and the mutt leapt to her side obediently. "Maybe you come from nothing. But you still got the single most important thing that lets you into that school. You'll get more than I'll ever have, even if you came from dirt." She scratched the dog's ear. "You fit right in with those pearl girls. All that shiny perfection. But inside is rotten." Her face puckered with malice. "You worse for getting your little piece. Well, like I said. I know what you are."

She gave a sneer. Then, like a shade rolling over a window, Deena watched her features melt into blankness. She adjusted her hat, patted the knot of her scarf.

Deena felt like she had been set on fire. How dare she be spoken to this way. She bent and patted the dirt, closed her hand around a rock. She straightened, drew back her arm, and threw it.

The rock thudded at the woman's feet, but she showed no reaction. Deena burned with dismissal. How dare this woman say she came from dirt. As if she was no one, as if she didn't matter. Her fingers clenched. Her rage burst. She scooped up another rock. She took aim and hit the woman between the shoulder blades.

Alice wheeled and flicked a hissing breath. "Miss," the honorific rumbled with warning. "You best take care now." She tugged her skirt and whistled for the dog. Together, they walked rapidly up the road.

"Come back here!" Deena screamed. She heaved another rock. "Don't you dare leave! You're awful! Mean!" But nothing forced Alice to turn back. The rush of nightfall quickly enveloped her.

Deena breathed heavily, hands shaking with anger at Alice's insults, yet something else stayed with her. Alice had said she was just like the other girls. Exactly like she and Grandmother had planned.

◆ ◆ ◆

LATER THAT EVENING IN SOUTH HALL, DEENA DREAMED OF MARY. Her limbs ached; the rocks she had thrown were heavier than she'd realized. Had Mary been watching her? Had she led Deena to the ramshackle homes because she knew what Deena had done to earn her place at Bellerton?

In the dream, the ground shone white, and stars dotted the sky. Mary stood in the middle of the lawn wearing her long black cloak, Deena shivering beside her in her nightgown. She was not afraid, only curious. She felt singled out by Mary, special for being chosen, and sensed that Mary wanted something from her. Deena didn't yet know what.

Mary reached for Deena's hand and a trilling sensation danced up her skin. Mary whispered at Deena's ear, but her meaning was impenetrable, the words distant. *I don't understand*, Deena said, Mary's cold hands squeezing hers. *Please, I don't know what you're trying to say.* Mary dissolved, fading into effervescence.

Deena awoke to the poet-professor shaking her. She twisted away from his grasp and realized she was outside surrounded by fresh snow. She lifted her palms, wet and red and stinging with cold. Deena grasped for Mary's words—Mary, who had led her from South Hall to the campus's edge, who walked through her dreams—and she didn't understand why.

The poet-professor draped his coat across her trembling shoulders. "More snow soon, I expect," he said. "Let's get you inside. I doubt Mrs. Tibbert finds sleepwalking agreeable."

He helped her into her dorm and stood inside the foyer, the black-and-white checkered floor a welcomed sight. The snow melted on his thick hair. "At least you didn't lock yourself out." Up close, he was less gangly and more confident. He sat on the bottom stair, blocking her path to the second-floor rooms, and propped his chin in his hand. "Are you the only one here?"

Deena tugged the coat tighter, mortified at the thought of her nightgown's thin fabric. "No," she lied.

He studied her with one arm felled to his side, his fingers drumming the carpet. Deena shifted on her numbed feet. "This is one of the freshmen halls?" She nodded. "Bellerton has a reputation," he said. The ceiling creaked. "A reputation for ghosts. And for pretty, compliant girls."

What was compliance? Her mind flitted to apple-cheeked Lucille Whittier chasing him down. Deena had the sensation of nearing something important, but her mind was sluggish from the bone-deep chill. The poet-professor reached out to tease the lace frills of her nightgown.

A door slammed above, and footsteps pounded. He sprung like an arrow to his feet. Deena felt a presence with them in the hall and realized he did, too.

He touched the brim of his hat. She stood at arm's length and handed over his coat.

"Merry Christmas," he said. He pulled the door tight.

Deena waited for Mary to reveal herself, but the air had gone stale. Her skin puckered into goose bumps. She bolted the front door and turned on every light, then drew a warm bath and slid into the water up to her neck, lying submerged until her teeth ceased clacking. She drained the tub and refilled it with hot water until gradually her skin pinked, her chill evaporated. A double bath: another luxury granted to Bellerton girls. She dipped her chin into the water. She sucked in a breath, puffing her cheeks. She slid under.

◆　◆　◆

DEENA SAID NOTHING ABOUT ALICE OR THE PROFESSOR WHEN Sheba returned from the overnight trip with her father. When asked how she spent her Christmas, Deena complimented Sheba's stylish new hat.

Sheba was flattered, petting it like a puppy. "A gift from my father. He always finds the exact right shopgirl to help him pick things out. They have impeccable taste. And"—she leaned in as if to divulge a secret—"the cost doesn't matter."

The other girls soon returned, but their interactions were stiff. Deena resented how their individual sojourns to the outside world disrupted the group's ties, straining their former sense of ease. Had the others been changed by temporarily leaving Bellerton? Had Bellerton changed them in a way they struggled to reconcile with who they were in the outside world? She disliked not knowing.

The housemother commented on the change when she came in to sweep the fireplace ashes. "You're a deathly quiet lot," she said, unfolding a newspaper to kneel at the hearth. She scooped the blackened cinders into a bucket, then scrubbed the bricks clean with a bristled brush. "I expected more chitter-chatter. I hope youse had a nice Christmas. My son had Christmas Eve snow, but it didn't last." She rolled onto her heels and stood slowly, one hand on her knee, the other steadying her against the wall. "The new year is upon us now. With luck, we'll all be richer by the end of it." She dusted her hands on her skirt. "Good night, misses."

Her uneven steps trundled downstairs. She left the ash bucket at the back door to carry out in the morning for disposal, then dragged herself up three flights to her rooms.

The Belles waited until they heard her lock shudder into place, then screeched and danced around the common room.

"With luck, we'll be rich," Prissy mocked the housemother's speech.

"Filthy rich!" Sheba toddled her body in mimicry of the house-mother's bosom-heavy figure, using two beaten throw pillows to heighten the effect.

Deena joined the teasing because Alice had been right: She was exactly like the others. Their awkwardness melted, and they were Bellerton sisters once more. As a child, Deena had frequently taken buckets to the ashpit at the end of her street, but at Bellerton she had no idea where the ashpit was. She wasn't the girl heaving the ash bucket anymore.

"While you all were away, I found a hidden path in the woods," Deena said. "We could go there." Her grandmother had taught her to want more, but it was the Belles who had shown her how to take it.

One by one, the Belles turned their pale faces to the window. How gentle the moon-sparked grass seemed, how inviting the unlit pockets between the trees. They grasped hands, a tacit agreement forming. They would push the boundaries of Bellerton, go further than they had ever been—into the woods. The words passed breathlessly from mouth to mouth like a kiss. *The woods.*

Deena tingled at the thrill of it.

Nine days apart had been too long.

Chapter 19
PRISSY

JUNE 2002

PRISSY had always known Deena wasn't who she pretended to be. From the moment she introduced herself and told them where she was from, Prissy began to count her lies.

It was a matter of chance that she had met the real Deena Williams—just once, at a holiday party her cousin Esther's family hosted. Their mothers were sisters, and her family was staying with the Vandorns that year. The two girls had to share a room, which Prissy hated because Esther was particular about her things, slept in, was lazy with her studies, and was a huge snob. She remembered the real Deena clearly because she was just like Esther. From the moment she arrived at the party, the two were inseparable, and Prissy had been left alone to sip Shirley Temples.

Prissy hadn't thought of Deena or Bellerton in years, until she received an invitation for the school's one hundred and fiftieth celebration. Prissy cursed, unsettled by the sudden rush of memories. She had only applied to Bellerton because her father was a trustee, and Esther had said it would be fun to attend together. Except Esther was a year ahead of her in age, and by the time Prissy's turn came, Esther had dropped out of college, recently wed and with a baby on the way. But Prissy went anyway, completing her four years, then quickly putting the school behind her. Now the invitation was dredging up the long-buried past.

Prissy stood from her desk and stretched, then wandered downstairs. In the kitchen, she sniffed the leftover turkey sandwich she had planned to eat for lunch and threw it into the trash. She hadn't been that hungry anyway.

Prissy relished secrets: having her own, keeping them for others. She had never begrudged Deena for hiding things. She figured there might be a good reason for it. Prissy had kept a whole writing career secret from her husband, who wasn't all that observant to begin with. A romance novelist, she published under the pen name Daphne St. James and deposited her earnings into a separate bank account. A woman needed to have something of her own. Just in case. Besides, she was very good at writing romances and proud of the income she earned. Her husband didn't deserve to spend any of it.

He'd said once that she must really like this Daphne author because her books were scattered everywhere throughout the house, and Prissy had rolled her eyes. She played it like a game, leaving clues everywhere, but her husband, bless his heart, was a man whose attention was only for things that interested him. So yes, she understood Deena's desire to hide parts of herself. Even to lie about who she was.

She meandered into the backyard, where the light shone divinely, the day perfect. She lowered herself onto an Adirondack chair and closed her eyes, ignoring the creeping feeling that the day was about to crack wide open.

It hadn't been her place to act on Deena's lies. Besides, Deena's secrets had given her something fun to poke at, and she took pleasure watching the other girl squirm under her questions. Deena had been an odd duck trying to swim among the swans, and Prissy had pitied her. The truth was often more complicated than it seemed.

The sun grew too bright, the heat too biting. The phone in the hallway began to ring, and Prissy hauled herself from the chair, annoyed. She checked the caller ID, sucking in a sharp breath: Ada May.

She cursed again, her pleasant day having gone south. She would never be free of that damn place.

Winter
1952

No man, not even a father, may go to a student's room
except with the knowledge of the housemother.
We cannot be blamed for what might happen
should you choose to ignore this rule.

—BELLERTON STUDENT HANDBOOK, 1951–1952

Chapter 20
DEENA

THE year turned, January 1952. It was at last Bellerton's centennial, an auspicious anniversary. The power of a hundred years stacked like bricks, the solidity of tradition and accumulated time. Deena felt it like a heartbeat on campus, and the pressure to be an ideal Bellerton girl was stifling. But night remained a place of refuge, of freedom.

Deena's breath cracked the frigid, dry air. She had bought a new coat finally with her saved allowance, poring over the ones in the Sears catalog, but it was still too thin for the moonlit cold. She didn't want the others to know her mistake—she had only been trying to copy what they owned—and bit her tongue to keep from trembling.

The Belles formed a chain and snaked toward their newfound destination: the woods. Deena's palms tingled knowing she had been the one to suggest it. She rubbed the smooth belly of her ribbon in her coat pocket, unwilling to leave such a precious gift behind.

The night quivered with unease.

Although the handbook was clear that the woods were prohibited, the Belles were already regularly breaking curfew. The woods were the next rule to break. A place where not even they could keep each other safe.

The Belles halted at the edge. Creatures darted from the brush. The rattle of cicadas echoed—an impossibility in winter. Deena pressed her thumb into the hollow at her throat, her pulse throbbing wildly. Purple fruit glistened on the berry bushes dotting the woods' edge. Nell stretched to pluck one, but Prissy slapped her hand.

Ada May said, "On the count of three."

A breath, a chance to collect themselves. On three, they crashed into the trees, scrambling over roots and pushing through brambles. Deena was disoriented by their ricocheting echoes. How far was it to the brick wall enclosing the grounds? Would they see it rising before them or would they crack their bones against it? She hastened to catch up, falling in line with the rest. Sheba's blonde head was a bobbing beacon, her loud call echoing through the trees. "Olly olly oxen free!"

The ground dipped and slanted, luring them toward the trickling creek that was hedged with rhododendrons. The opposite bank was unreachable, the creek wide. The water looked black in the night.

A shivering fit gripped Deena, and she doubled over with the sharp, clean scent of the creek in her nostrils. Her convulsions were acute. Water seemed to wash around her. She gritted her teeth. The girls circled, and Fred scrambled to her side, rubbed her back soothingly.

"I'm fine." Deena straightened, winded. "Just some dizziness."

The Belles regarded her with concern, and she resented how her sudden fit made her pitiful. She was finished with the pity of others, and how it quickly could shift into revulsion. She yearned now for admiration.

"It's a damn shame, really." Prissy was uncharacteristically earnest. "A place this lovely shouldn't be off-limits."

The branches overhead were a black cathedral. Tree limbs shook, vibrating with a murder of crows rising in perturbed silence. Deena gasped. "I thought they were leaves."

Ada May asked them to hold hands. Her nearness was intoxicating, her hair shimmering with a metallic gleam. Deena rested her head on Ada May's shoulder. Who might she be if Ada May had not accepted her into their group, if Deena had not given herself over completely to the Belles? When she tried to picture it, she saw only emptiness.

"This is our place. Our secret," Ada May said, an echo of their earlier oath. She dragged her fingers through the creek, then flicked the water at each Belle. An anointing.

The Belles agreed, yes, yes, yes, yes, yes. The trees clattered as if in approval.

Deena sensed Mary hovering at the edge of her perception and turned to search for her, but only the empty dark stared back.

Ada May smiled pearls. "No matter what happens here, this place is our secret, and Belles never tell."

Chapter 21
DEENA

THE following week on an overcast February afternoon, Deena accompanied Ada May and Sheba to the barns, eager for a brisk walk after a long day spent inside studying.

Ada May had put in a call ahead of time, and the groom had the horses saddled and waiting when they arrived. Deena watched the two girls fasten their helmets with admiration before they mounted and rode off—the horses sleek and strong and the girls as straight-backed as warriors.

Gray clouds amassed in the sky, foretelling a winter storm. Deena thought of a magician she had seen at a carnival once, a man who conjured words on blank paper with a flick of his wrist, who vanished objects, only to make them reappear. The ease of his tricks had impressed her, how quickly the solidity of reality could change. Bellerton was like that: here and not here. Sometimes Deena felt she also existed in this in-between state.

She watched the horses canter into the far fields and was about to return to the dorm when a cloaked, hooded figure caught her eye, creeping between the pasture and woods, trailing behind the riders at an impossible pace. The wind kicked the hood back, and Mary's dark curls tumbled out.

"Mary!" Deena stood on her tiptoes and waved. The wind spit her cries back into her face, and Mary slipped into the woods at the same spot where the Belles had entered just a few nights ago. Deena called after her, but the ghost girl did not show herself again.

When she looked down, an object sparked in the grass. Deena crouched and stretched an arm through the wooden fence slats, her hand closing around it: Ada May's gold ring with its striking green stone. She slid it onto her finger, admiring its beauty, startled when seconds later Fred sprinted up behind her, face buckled with worry. Deena quickly shoved the ring into her coat pocket for safekeeping, squeezing until the jewel dug into her palm.

"Something's wrong!" Fred jostled past her to climb onto the fence and began frantically waving her arms. Deena turned toward the sound of hooves. Sheba was galloping Beauregard at full speed in their direction, aiming as if to trample them. The horse skittered to a halt just feet from where they stood.

Sheba gasped for breath, her usual blitheness gone. The reins tremored in her hands. "Brutus bucked."

Deena didn't understand, but Fred snapped into action. "You," she commanded the groom, who had emerged from the stables at the commotion. "Get two horses ready. Any horses. Hurry." She instructed Deena to call for a doctor. When Deena didn't move, frozen in her fear that Mary had done some awful trick, Fred shoved her. "Deena, *go*."

Deena clutched Ada May's ring in her hand and flew.

◆　◆　◆

ADA MAY WAS RUSHED BY AMBULANCE TO THE NEAREST HOSPITAL, in Sharpsburg. She was there a full day for X-rays and probing before being released, and was immediately sequestered to her room in South Hall.

The Belles didn't know the extent of her injuries, whether she might have broken bones or ruptured discs or a concussion. Fred and Sheba superstitiously refused to describe the accident. Sheba said only that Ada May had looked like a crumpled handkerchief when she fell from Brutus. Supper became a subdued affair, and not just at South Hall's table; it seemed to Deena that every Bellerton girl ate solemnly over her plate, and the predominant sound was the gentle scrape of the silverware against porcelain.

Deena split from the Belles after supper. "I have a paper to research in the library," she said, sensing their judgment. She brushed off their disapproving looks, and as soon as they were out of sight, she careened toward the pasture, led by an idea forming in her mind. At the bend in the trail where she had seen Mary enter the woods, a flap of burlap stuck out from the dirt, flickering like a tongue.

She worked for the better part of an hour as the wind pawed insistently at her thin coat. Her nails cracked on the frozen ground, and several sticks she was using to dig snapped in two, but eventually she was able to wrestle the thing from the earth: a box, the rotted wood giving way easily. She unfurled the burlap and found a diary. Her hunch had been right. Mary had tried to lead her to this spot for a reason.

She unwound the ribbon tied around the diary. Her intuition was again proven correct. Inside was a name: Mary Burden.

◆　◆　◆

DEENA RETURNED TO SOUTH HALL AND LEARNED THAT MRS. TIBbert had summoned the Belles to Ada May's room. She stashed the diary at the back of her closet and hurried to join the others.

Ada May lay half-prostrate in her ruffled bed. Her head was wrapped in a white cotton bandage that partially concealed her face, and only one swollen eye was visible. The cotton contrasted sharply with her pink complexion, her cheeks rosy with unexpected color. Her red hair was braided and damp along the edges. She reflexively reached to scratch at her bandages, though something stopped her—a remembered admonishment, perhaps, or a belated recognition at the unladylike action. Instead, her fingers froze clawlike at her cheeks, then knotted into a fist that she lowered to her side. Deena's own hands were filthy from digging, and she hid them behind her back.

Mrs. Tibbert emerged from the dark corner. "How did this happen?" she demanded from the Belles.

Ada May's good eye rolled in its socket, the uncanny movement like a doll or wooden ventriloquist's dummy. The eye locked onto Deena and blinked.

Sheba took a half step forward. "Brutus bucked, ma'am."

"Yes, but why?" Mrs. Tibbert snapped.

She dipped her head. "Something must have startled him."

Ada May's fingers twitched atop the white duvet. Her eye was a roaming glacial blue marble. When she spoke, her voice was ragged. "Brutus doesn't spook." She might as well have declared Sheba was outright lying.

Sheba's confidence evaporated. She fiddled with the tips of her hair. "I'm sorry," she whispered. "It happened so fast. There was a shadow—"

Mrs. Tibbert sneered incredulously. "The horse was frightened by a *shadow*?" She tugged Ada May's blanket down an inch and adjusted her pillow.

Ada May's finger lifted, then dropped. Lifted, then dropped. Her single eye hunted them for information, a tell that would give up the truth. The radiator hissed and Deena could sense the beginnings of a nascent mistrust, a suspicion of apostasy among them, because it seemed most likely that Brutus had not acted without provocation. Deena wondered if Mary had somehow been involved in Ada May's accident. Maybe in trying to show Deena where to find her diary, she had unintentionally startled Brutus.

"She is fortunate she's not worse off," Mrs. Tibbert said. "That does not change my disappointment in you ladies. You must look out for one another. You must especially look out for Ada May."

A chorus of *Yes, ma'ams* answered her.

Ada May shifted beneath the blanket. Her good eye closed.

They had been dismissed, the matter unresolved. Mrs. Tibbert shooed the Belles out the door.

◆ ◆ ◆

LATER, DEENA SNUCK INTO ADA MAY'S ROOM. SHE HAD EXPECTED Ada May to be asleep, but a glint let her know she was being observed.

"Deena." Ada May patted the bedcovers. "Come."

She was hideous with her bandaged head, more frightening without the buffer of the other girls clumped around her, and Deena had to force herself to approach. The incongruity of her frilly lace nightgown and the white ruffled blankets against her damaged face made Ada May even more monstrous. A bruise that stretched from her cheek to her hairline, invisible earlier, seemed to darken as they sat together.

Deena held out her hand, revealing the gold ring with its emerald stone. Ada May plucked the ring from Deena's outstretched palm, surprisingly dexterous with just one eye. "Where did you get this?"

"I found it on the ground, just before your accident," Deena said.

"How strange." An accusation girded her words. "Were you there when my accident happened?"

"I was at the stables." Deena hesitated. "Fred showed up. I ran to the switchboard, and when the doctor arrived, he and Fred rode to where you were."

"You didn't want to ride to my rescue?"

Deena blushed. "I can't ride. I don't know how."

Ada May examined the ring, her single eye crawling along the gold band. Deena wondered whether the other eye hurt. Whether it could see despite being swollen shut and buried in gauze.

"Yes, that's right. The girl who has never been on a horse." Ada May wrapped her fingers around the ring and cocked her head. "You had my ring with you this entire time?"

"I wanted to return it sooner but you were at the hospital." Deena flushed with the sense of having wronged her friend, though she was certain she hadn't done anything. She felt a slackening, then tightening between them, like a string held taut.

"We never did find the thief," Ada May said, clacking her tongue.

Deena had the urge to defend herself but knew that her denial might read as guilt. Still, she let slip a small defense. "It wasn't me."

Ada May tossed the ring into the air, catching it in a swift gesture. Her eye blinked. "This might surprise you, but I hold this ring as a sort of talisman. It contains the strength of every Delacourt woman who has worn it. I never take it off for riding, yet you found it just before my accident."

"It's very odd," Deena agreed. The words tasted metallic.

"Strange that you were the one to find it." Ada May clenched her palm tightly around the ring. "I'm very tired. Sleep tight, Deena Evangeline Williams."

Chapter 22
DEENA & MARY

WITH Ada May bedridden and the Belles taking turns nursing her nightly, there was no sneaking out. Deena didn't mind; she had Mary Burden's diary to read.

Bound in leather, the pages were fragile. Black ink spotted both sides of the paper and blurred the words, sometimes incomprehensibly. What legibly remained were wild, unspooling stories about Bellerton, things forgotten and lost to time. It was the writing of a girl straddling two selves: one who belonged at Bellerton, and another who languished as an outsider. Deena understood Mary's fracturing and the ways in which she could never be whole. Like Mary, two people breathed within her: the person she had once been and the girl—her half sister—she pretended to be. It was impossible to put on another identity and not have it tangle with what remained of your own.

The basic facts Deena learned about Mary were these: She grew up in Manassas the youngest of two girls. She was her father's favorite and often assisted in his mercantile. Then came the war, and the glorious rose of Mary's life wilted.

• • •

November 24, 1862

Father has been conscripted and Mama tells me I am to be sent away to the mountains for my safety. She does not send Eliza, who is making herself useful at the field hospital in Centerville. Mama says she will call for my return soon, but when I think of the five-day journey here by cramped coach, my stomach turns.

A horrible journey it was. We were three women and one man, and the other passengers were siblings. On the second day we rode past a string of gaunt and hollow-eyed gray-clad soldiers caked in dirt, and I felt chilled by their stares. I will never forget their slick lips as they worked their jaws. For miles after, a rotten and fetid smell clung to the carriage, rendering each of us passengers ill, until the whole party was forced to stop at a dirty little tavern where the owner grinned like a devil at us, never moving from his post. I swear he would have shot us in the backs and buried us in the ditch for the opportunity to raid our possessions if the driver hadn't paid him a tidy sum in Federalist greenbacks.

I arrived at Belle Terre where there are other girls whose families also seek a safe haven. Though it's the cusp of winter Belle Terre is beautiful indeed, untouched by the wolves of war. The grounds are idyllic, with a creek running through, bordered by mountains and shielded by forest. We are told to stay clear of the latter. I suppose there is fear we will get lost in the woods, though I have a good head for direction and might go strolling there anyhow.

I am homesick but determined to make the best of my situation. Amongst the eldest girls here, I have made myself useful by letting the younger girls cry in my lap while I run my hands tenderly over their hair and sing them lullabies.

The man who runs this place, a Mr. Gray, once received a grand favor from Papa (though what that exact favor was, Mama refused to disclose, the reticence unlike her), and he repays his debt by allowing me to stay without remittance. Unlike the other girls, whose fathers pay significant sums to keep them here, I am a shopkeeper's daughter, a mere pigeon among the ostriches. But we all have been abandoned here, even if the abandoning, we are told, is for our benefit.

January 14, 1863

What an industrious group of girls are we! We are doing our part to make our temporary home cheery by organizing quilting circles and French lessons, Bible study, natural philosophy walks, piano lessons, canning tutorials, and basic arithmetic and reading lessons from primers two sisters packed in their trunks. Girls scribble algebra equations from morning to night. One girl recently arrived with an orrery, and we study the planets and stars.

My friend Clara, a lively and good-humored girl, leads informal classes in geology and botany that everyone lines up to attend, and we go marching through high grasses and down to the sphagnum bog that buttresses the forest. Jane, my other friend, is a serious girl with a sober demeanor, and leads needlepoint lessons. I taught the younger girls the quadrille, and they have taken to plaiting my hair and shining the pearl buttons on my boots.

At supper tonight, Jane said how strange it is to live in isolation from men as if we were women from myth, for the only man here is Mr. Gray, who supposedly has a wife, though none has ever seen her. Clara said she was happy for the company of more intelligent creatures. Then, she told us a story of ladies gone to fight.

"Not in petticoats and lace," I asked her.

"In disguise," Clara replied, her dark eyes gleaming. I do love Clara's way of having fun. "In uniforms with brass buttons and mud-splattered breeches and boots pounded flat from the endless marching."

Jane was scandalized! "And they shoot?" she exclaimed.

"Aye, they shoot! Dead shots, right between the eyes!" Clara laughed.

She insists these stories are true, says the ladies shear their hair and tie down their bosoms, and when they are injured—if they are injured—it is in this way they are discovered and discharged.

I caressed my hair and mused what I might look like shorn, and Jane very nearly passed out at the mere mention. I later told Clara she was driving Jane's innocent heart to an early grave, but she only broke into a wide smile.

April 3, 1863

Strangeness is underfoot. Though the trees dress in tiny buds and the grass thickens and greens, with spring's heralding something dangerous has reached us.

It began with the arrival of four new girls: the nearly identical siblings Sarah and Sophie Gannon, who are referred to as the Gannon sisters, as if they are two bodies but one mind; Lydia Booth, sly-faced and manipulative; and Ada Jackson, a copper-haired beauty who takes assessment of each girl and situation as a surveyor might, compiling the information for her own gain. Circumstances threw the four together—though Clara says circumstance in this instance is another name for the devil—and over the course of their journey here, they became committed friends.

Their first act was to command a desirable corner room on the second floor by forcing out the girls already living there! I was astounded by their audacity. Their second act was to claim seats at the head of the table as if they were the masters of us all. They questioned us on our families and our fathers' offices and seemed to weigh our worth accordingly. All week went on like this, an endless demonstration of proving that we are worthy. When I said my father ran a mercantile, their lips curled and Lydia jeered, "Shopkeeper's daughter," as if the words were dirty, and I felt my face redden. It was the first time I have ever felt embarrassed of my father, but I was held as if by a spell and could not move my tongue in my defense.

We are tucked away here and sometimes it is easy to forget the world outside, but these four girls have brought wickedness to Belle Terre. They are planning harm. I am certain of it, but I cannot speak to anyone of this—not Jane, not Clara. Who would believe me? Still, a shiver climbs my spine when I hear Lydia Booth's hissing accusation again in my mind. Belle Terre, once beautiful and peaceful, is becoming a different place.

July 12, 1863

A clutch of younger girls went out for a walk along the creek yesterday and came back screaming to where the rest of us were sitting on the porch, taking turns fanning one another against the rising humidity. Clara, fast thinker that she is, deciphered their babbling, and took off instantly at a run, the whole of Belle Terre following.

Little Betty Kindrake had drowned.

The creek is less than a foot deep in the spot where she was found, the bank level and the water calm. Her friends reported that she appeared to have been pushed into the water, then thrashed as if fighting off an invisible foe, who forced her head under.

Clara did not believe them. "Nonsense," she muttered. "They are hysterical. They don't know what they saw or did not see." I shushed Clara—what did it matter now that their friend was drowned?

The night Betty Kindrake died, two queer things occurred. The first was one of Mr. Gray's men was seen stalking the grounds with a rifle. He had only three fingers on each hand, and he moved light and quick with an obvious intent to kill. Mr. Gray informed us girls that we were not to fear him. We were to ignore the man, that he was there to protect the grounds from trespassers, looters, and marauders.

The second queer thing happened when Jane led the girls in prayer that evening for poor little Betty Kindrake. The drawing room was filled with wailing and reminders that misfortune could befall us even in the heart of our sanctuary. Every eye spilled with tears—except the four newest girls. They held hands and bowed their heads, but their expressions were free of anguish or sorrow. When I looked at them, a terrifying idea held me. What if these newcomers are somehow responsible for what happened to little Betty?

January 13, 1864

The new year has brought news and tribulations from the world outside.

Mama is gone and buried. I am bereft but numb. Eliza insists I stay at Belle Terre for a time longer, saying there is nothing to be gained by making the long journey home. I cannot silence the voice that says my sister does not want me back. She did not write of Father, last seen with his regiment near Petersburg, and I quietly draw my own conclusions. Lincoln might have declared emancipation a year agone, yet the war marches on interminably.

March 20, 1864

Another girl is dead: Savannah Mason. And here I thought our sorrows were almost ending.

Lydia Booth delivered the news at breakfast, instructed by Mr. Gray. When we asked what happened, Lydia said, "She grew confused strolling in the mist, strayed too far, and fell clear off the mountain." Lydia painted on a respectable somber face, but several of us girls knew that Savannah was a thorn in Lydia's side. Her insouciance for proper etiquette irritated Lydia and her wicked friends, and she cheerfully refused to kneel to their whims as the rest of us have learned to do. She did not readily conform to their ideal of true womanhood.

I cannot liberate myself from the certainty that there was something false in Lydia's story. Monsters, I thought uncharitably when Lydia left the room, closely followed by Ada and the Gannon sisters. Clara squeezed my hand as if she had read my mind, but later when I approached her to discuss my philosophy that Belle Terre disposes of those it deems unworthy, she put her hand on my shoulder, said she needed to think, then closed the door. And perhaps Clara is right to shut me out; my theory, even to my ears, sounds like madness.

December 1, 1864

I am unraveling. Even Clara is on edge these days. I once believed we were shielded from the country's ugliness here in our little hideaway, but now I see that ugliness is everywhere, and, worse, I have been part of it all along.

This evening as I prepared to walk to chapel, whispers caught my ear. I drew back into the shadow of the porch, and who did I see exchanging caresses with our benefactor? None other than Ada Jackson! She trailed her fingers along the wool of Mr. Gray's coat.

"Sir." She nodded, her voice soft. She did not look back; she did not need to. I saw how she was a flame burning through him, red like the color of her hair. She spoke but a single word, but I saw how *he* flushed. I saw how she broke him.

Then Lydia Booth bumped into me from behind. "Best be cautious," she said, a cackle in her voice. "We are watching you."

January 10, 1865

The news is official. Mr. Gray has taken a new wife: Ada Augustine Jackson. What happened to his first wife? There were rumors that she was a recluse who never left the big house on the hill, terrified for her own safety, but none of us girls know what has actually become of her. Regardless, the path has been cleared for Ada Jackson. One can detect in the shimmering glow of Ada's cheeks and the way she carries herself that she is already with child.

Snow swirled outside the windows all morning and, this afternoon, she stood in a stately manner on the porches to oversee the servants move her things into a cart and lug them to the big house. A double-gold band with a green stone weighted her finger, and her hair glowed like embers. How beautiful she looked; how proud. The grand couple have new names to mark their union: Mr. and Mrs. Dickey.

February 24, 1865

The war drags on. Fees have been raised for all girls. If one cannot pay, you are put to work or turned out, a policy Lydia and her compatriots, the Gannon sisters, enforce with relish. They have put me on the laundries where the labor has turned my hands red and chapped.

They have always bullied others, but now that their friend is Mrs. Dickey, the president's wife, they are empowered to punish girls who fail to fit in or follow the rules. Lydia and the Gannon sisters move amongst us girls with newly scornful airs, traipsing weekly up the hill to dine with their old friend and returning to the dormitory flying, as if they are sodden with spirits. None can fathom what occurs up there, and they hold their secrets tight, but I wager it is nothing Christian. I have carried clean linens to the great house; I have seen the metalwork above the parlor doorway, two writhing, entwined serpents. Who would hang such a symbol in their home?

April 1, 1865

I cannot slough the feeling that they are coming for me. What was once a formless, creeping dread has become a shape that crawls upon me at all hours, squeezing my lungs and choking my breath. I am no madwoman, no deranged soul.

I am in danger.

◆   ◆   ◆

THAT WAS MARY'S FINAL ENTRY. DEENA RAISED HER HEAD FROM her feverish reading, startled by the lateness of the hour. South Hall lay in slumber. She ground her palms into her eyes, exhausted but unable to sleep, Mary's words drumming through her head.

Was Mary one of the girls in Bellerton's ghost stories? She had been deeply troubled, her homesick spirit broken by the uncertainty of a long war and the loss of both parents. Perhaps Bellerton had nothing to do with her death. Maybe illness had gotten to her, or she had grown increasingly paranoid and harmed herself. Deena had seen it happen in her old life, a personality that turned suddenly. Maybe that was why her restless spirit was unable to cross over.

Snug beneath her grandmother's quilt, Deena ruffled the diary pages with her thumbs. *What happened to you, Mary?* she wondered. She was no closer to knowing Mary's actual cause of death than before she'd found the diary. She was also intrigued about Ada May's ancestor, the president's second wife. Deena understood what it took to reinvent oneself. To make alliances in order to rise above the station in life you were born into.

Deena and Ada May were more alike than she had known.

Chapter 23
DEENA

THE new semester's classes were harder than the last. Headaches began to gnaw behind Deena's eyes. The days, which held too few hours, had taken on a predictable shape. Deena had once craved such stability. Before Bellerton, life bent toward staving off inevitable catastrophe, where a single season of drought could become a disaster that unmoored a person or a family, stabbed the thinness of their survival. She had seen it often in her other life. One day a family trying to hold on; the next, gone. Bellerton girls lived innocently, their lives cocoons of invulnerability.

Deena wanted both. The assurance of certainty, but not at the cost of the expectations that wrapped around her like a fist. She began rushing onto the porch at the edge of curfew, risking being locked out of the dorm. Risking demerits, suspension. Hands gripping the porch railing as she swallowed night air, fantasizing about aching limbs and bruises and blood.

The stress of her schoolwork left Deena bleary and exhausted, and she tripped over Prissy one afternoon as she left the library, catching herself before she fell but banging her elbow against the door. She clutched it and cursed. Prissy stood coolly at the entrance, door propped with her foot and a cigarette pinched in her right hand, snug in her mink coat. She didn't bother to apologize. Earlier in the year, Deena had been annoyed that Prissy owned multiple furs. She wanted now to rip a chunk of silky hair from the sleeve.

"You said your parents are deceased?"

She was fog-headed, the pain shooting up her arm. "That's right."

Prissy regarded her smugly. "I never much liked my cousin Esther."

"Who?" Deena checked that she hadn't dropped any homework papers.

"Esther Vandorn." Prissy drew out the syllables. "You're *certain* you don't know her?"

Despite her striving and cleverness, she was not that far removed from who she had been less than a year ago. And it terrified her. Everything could be undone.

Before she could answer, Prissy lifted a stray hair from her collar and let it drift to the floor. "Well, Esther's awful. One can't trust half the things she says." She squinted at Deena. "I suppose I can tell you this, as you've made it clear you've never, not once, met her. That you're an *orphan*." Her eyebrow twitched. She snubbed her cigarette against the radiator and flicked the butt into the trash. The door shuddered closed between them, leaving Deena paralyzed on the library steps, winter surging around her.

• • •

WITHOUT ADA MAY AROUND, THE BELLES WERE LOST. DEENA FELT unmoored and she saw the others had the same aimlessness. They gathered in Prissy's room each night, trickling in after supper and homework, but they had lost their collective sense of purpose.

One evening, Prissy offered to do pin curls for Deena, and Nell joined them, passing around a paper bag of taffy her mother had sent from home. On the bed, Sheba laid her head in Fred's lap and Fred traced her fingertips over Sheba's face and neck.

When Fred left to use the bathroom, Nell confronted Sheba.

"Aren't you worried?" She half-whispered it, but Deena still looked up from where Prissy was rolling her hair. Nell rubbed her teddy bear's ear. "Aren't you afraid?"

"Afraid of what?" Sheba stretched her legs and wriggled her red-polished toes.

Nell lowered her voice. "What people will think about you and Fred." She tugged the bear's ear viciously. "You're terribly close."

"What people?" Sheba sat up. She locked eyes with Nell, ice and fire at once.

"Don't you think people notice?" Nell turned to them.

Prissy coughed and spritzed hair spray in a sweeping arc around Deena's head. Deena opened her mouth to say it didn't matter but Prissy gave a hard tug of her hair, then bent forward under the guise of adjusting a hairpin and whispered, "Stay out of it."

"What people?" Sheba demanded, louder and more stridently now. "Who on earth are you talking about?"

Nell tucked her chin into the bear's soft head. "Others," she whispered. "Everyone."

Sheba stood up, her jaw tight. She snapped her fingers in front of Prissy and Deena. "Does she mean the two of you? Are you talking about me behind my back?"

Nell said softly, "You're making such a scene."

Fred returned at that moment, her face drawn. "I'm turning in," she said. Her glance lingered not on Sheba, but on Nell, and Deena wondered how much she might have overheard. Prissy pinned a final curl on Deena's head, her touch rougher now than it had been, the hairpins digging into Deena's scalp.

Ada May would have known how to smooth things over; instead, Deena worried the Belles were beginning to fall apart.

◆ ◆ ◆

Two weeks after her accident, Ada May—improved by bedrest and constant ministrations—was released from confinement. She rolled up and down the corridor in her wheelchair, the bandage wrapped around her head dangling like a loose hem, her impaired gaze steady as she observed the other Belles.

When the last class ended for the week, Ada May declared she did not wish to eat alone in her room. Could they please have supper in South Hall? Deena and Sheba went to the housemother, who was skeptical.

"Old Mother Hubbard isn't going to like that," she mumbled, tying her shawl and tromping off to the switchboard to put in a call to the grand brick house on the hill.

To everyone's surprise Mrs. Tibbert acquiesced. Last-minute arrangements were made for the girls to dine in the common room. Tables were carried upstairs and draped with white linens, set with white cloth napkins and polished silverware. Deena quickly scanned the servants' faces for Alice, and to her relief she wasn't there. Deena had been avoiding the staff as much as it was possible since throwing the rocks. She couldn't bear their judgments and tried to convince herself that what had happened didn't matter, but each time she saw any of them, shame flooded her.

The girls were expected to maintain formal dress for their special supper in South Hall, and the second floor filled with excited chatter at the evening's departure from the usual. Ada May required assistance getting ready, blinking steadily through her bandage while Deena and Nell slid her navy gown easily over her head.

Nell bit her bottom lip, tugging at the fabric. "It doesn't fit."

"It fits," Ada May insisted.

Deena called into the hall, and a moment later Sheba came in to examine the dress that was now loose at the waist and gaping at the shoulders and breasts. She squeezed her palms together. "Keep up this illness, Ada May, and you'll soon disappear. Prissy will be furious."

Sheba set to work pinching fabric, securing it with tight, nimble stitches—she had learned a thing or two in boarding school—then found two pairs of socks in Ada May's bureau. Ada May regarded the socks with open disdain as Sheba explained, "Press them into the cups of your bra. We've got to fill you out somehow."

Ada May's mouth pinched with displeasure. "I'm not a harlot."

"You're also not a little girl."

Convalescence had made Ada May compliant, and she turned around for privacy to do as Sheba said. When she spun to face them, hands on her thin waist and elbows jutting, they gasped at her natural beauty perfected. Even with the bandage still covering one eye, Ada May was stunning.

"You're the envy of us all," Sheba exclaimed.

Nell dashed to her room and returned with a sharp-edged holly twig, red berries shining, and presented it to Ada May.

"My hair," Ada May said, and Deena pinned the offering in place.

Deena wheeled her to the common room on the girls' floor where Fred and Prissy were already squeezed in at the table. Ada May preened like a peacock as she settled at the table's head, the floorboards creaking under the gleaming metal and polished wood of the wheelchair. It was impossible not to be enamored by her beauty.

At the table's opposite end, Prissy was openly envious of Ada May's thinner shape. "Illness hasn't been entirely terrible for you."

"It's a terrible thing for anyone," Ada May said, taking up her fork. "What injures one, injures all."

The waiters set the first course of lamb croquette with dill cream sauce. The girls ate in silence, the evening a thin gauze that might tear with too much exertion. Prissy picked at her food. The fire crackled, the room overly warm. At the start of dessert—banana pudding topped with vanilla wafers and meringue—Fred cracked the window and frigid air rushed in. The waiters brought coffee on a silver cart.

"Deena, will you fetch my hairbrush?" Ada May asked. "My room is unlocked."

The hairbrush lay beside Ada May's hand mirror and comb. The brush's ivory handle was smooth and heavy in Deena's palm, its stark whiteness like a bone peeking through skin. The bristles were thick but soft, the shield-shaped head painted with two garlands. A chill wound up Deena's arms, but when she turned around the room was empty.

"I saw someone step from the woods into Brutus's path," Sheba was saying when Deena returned to the common room. "As if they were waiting."

The hairbrush clattered to the floor. The girls turned in Deena's direction, and she fumbled to retrieve it, her thoughts spinning. She had seen Mary moments before Brutus bucked, but that didn't necessarily mean she was responsible. Still, the coincidence felt like too much.

"This confinement has been awful," Prissy said. "We haven't snuck out since your accident. It doesn't feel right."

Ada May took the brush from Deena with a courteous thank-you. She said, "You are permitted to break curfew without me."

The girls protested this remark. How could they leave one of their own behind? They were bound; they had sworn allegiance and fidelity with their oath. They were expected to live within degrees of weakness, obedient to the extreme. But together they had discovered ways to hold power, to exist briefly outside of the expectations pressed upon them, so that they might experience meaning beyond the lives they were being trained to inhabit.

"We could never," Sheba said. And that was that.

The girls, pleasantly full from the meal and the coffee, drifted into comfortable chatter. Ada May counted brushstrokes. A gap in her bandage exposed the throbbing, monstrous bruise around her swollen eye: sickly puce edges underneath, the hardened crust of a laceration. Deena reached for Ada May's hand, but Ada May tutted and pulled away. The fire's embers polished her single blue eye into shining coldness. Pity for Ada May clotted Deena's throat. With her injury, she was a girl apart. Sterner and less patient with them. Guarded and watchful. Yet she was more beautiful for it, too.

◆　◆　◆

THE EVENING ENDED. THE GIRLS WASHED THEIR FACES, THEN RE-treated to bed. Bolts slid into locks. Deena listened, and when she was certain the others lay ensconced in their rooms, she tiptoed to the first floor, searching for Mary, desperate to know what had happened the day of Ada May's accident—whether Mary was the figure who had stepped in front of Brutus.

She crept into the Jackson Drawing Room, its glass doorknobs smooth beneath her palms. The last time she was in this room, it had glowed with warmth, and Ada May had showed the girls her old Bellerton yearbooks. Now, emptied of the girls' presence, it was leeched of vibrancy and color. The settees hulked beneath their dust coverings, and the air was stale. The radiator flues were shut, and cold crept up Deena's back. She searched the elaborate plaster crown molding for eyes she felt certain were watching.

Finding nothing, she faced one of the identical twin mirrors.

"Mary, are you here?" No reply. "I want to say hello." She waited for several minutes, but nothing stirred.

Deena's hand stretched until her palm flattened against the glass. A mark that would have to be wiped clean, but not by her. Grandmother said the past lives inside of the present, a constant heartbeat. Deena's reflection was a smear, barely visible.

"Are you dead, Deena Williams?" she asked herself in the mirror. "Are you dead, or are you living?"

A shadow moved behind her, but when she spun to look, nothing was there. She crept into the reception room, where the girls were supposed to host their male visitors, and to the study room. Both rooms were vacant and chilly with disuse. Mary wasn't here either. Deena tried the other doors on the first floor and found them locked. The only sound she heard was her own throbbing heartbeat.

Unable to find Mary anywhere, Deena crossed the checkered floor to the back door and spied a mysterious light floating near the woods. She thought she saw a fox or coyote slink across the back lawn. Or maybe it was a stray cat. But no sign of the ghost girl.

Mary, Mary, quite contrary.

She walked to the opposite end of the foyer to check the front quad, her face pressed to the glass, and saw nothing but the stalwart trees with their bare winter limbs. Moonlight illuminated the black-and-white floor pattern, and although she had never played chess, Fred and Sheba often set up a board and had taught her the names of the pieces: rooks and pawns, bishops and knights. She knew the queen was more powerful than the king, but it was the king you had to dethrone to win because the king mattered most of all.

A rush of dizziness overwhelmed her, and to steady herself she spread her fingers along the striped wallpaper of pale green and canary. Her gaze fell onto the back porch. A face looked in from the other side of the glass.

Deena ran down the hallway and flung open the door. "I've been looking for you."

Mary frowned. Dampness moved past her into the hall, and the crackle of winter was in her hair.

"Mary, did you frighten Brutus?" The other girl gave a small nod. "On purpose?" She nodded again. Deena felt betrayed by Mary's cruelty, and the secret of her turned sour. Could she be trusted now? "Mary, you hurt my friend. I would have found your diary, without there needing to be any accident."

Mary's black curls writhed. "There are no accidents at Bellerton."

Deena shivered at the ghost girl's revelation. She recalled the final entry of Mary's diary. So, she *had* been in danger. "Mary, tell me what happened to you."

The toes of Mary's black boots nudged the threshold. "Go," Mary whispered. Urgency sprung into her voice. "Leave this place."

Deena put a hand to her throat to strangle the sudden laughter bubbling there, giddy at the presence of this strange girl. Giddy at the suggestion that she give up everything twice. Mary smelled of wet clay and muck. When Deena dropped her hand, the back of it grazed Mary's cloak.

"But I can't," Deena said. "Don't you see? I'm a Belle now. I'm one of them. My place is here at Bellerton."

Mary snatched Deena's wrist and tugged.

"No," they both said, a single voice. Mary, because she did not wish Deena to stay, and Deena because she did not want to go.

"Deena?"

She startled at hearing the name. Ada May wavered on the stairs, the white of her nightgown shimmering. She inched forward on bare feet. "What are you doing? I thought you were in bed."

"I couldn't sleep," Deena said.

"Why is the door open? You weren't about to go outside alone, were you?"

The doorway was empty. Mary had vanished. Deena closed and locked the door, hands trembling. She put them behind her back and leaned against the wall.

"There was just a strange animal I wanted a better look at," she said. When Ada May didn't respond, Deena added with a shrug, "Only a squirrel in the end." Deena noticed that the hem of Ada May's night-gown was damp, a stray thread of grass stuck to it. Had Ada May gone for a walk? There was a side entrance the girls rarely used. But that made no sense. She had been in a wheelchair all week, including two hours ago at supper.

"Squirrels are strange animals." Ada May picked up a yellowed oak leaf near the door and rubbed the stem. "They have little fingers and toes, and those beady black eyes on the sides of their heads." Ada May looked thoughtful. "What a pretty leaf this is, a reminder of fall." Her bandage glowed in the dark. "Oh, but I like winter best."

She fixated on Deena. The smell of damp clay had been overtaken by Ada May's lavender scent. Deena saw a streak of dirt near Ada May's elbow. So, Ada May was not only faking the extent of her injuries, but she was keeping a secret from them, too. Something with dirt and per-haps rot. Deena had to admire it. She knew the pleasure of withholding a thing for yourself.

"Aren't you going to ask me why I like winter?"

Deena considered telling her no, emboldened by the late hour, by the things she was learning about Bellerton—and Ada May's family.

The ceiling creaked and they both froze, waiting for the sound to resolve into footsteps. Deena stared at the white of Ada May's hands, her dove-colored fingers pinching the leaf.

"Why do you like winter, Ada May? Tell me," Deena said, the giddiness of earlier returning. More than ribbons or bruises, Ada May was confiding in her, letting her in on her game of pretend. She was special after all.

"Because winter is the time when pretense is stripped away, and everything is laid bare. Literature tells us winter is a time of death, a fallow period of absence, of stillness. I disagree. Winter is when things typically outside our perception become visible. The truth emerges. We are cleansed."

The tiles were cold beneath Deena's feet. She held her breath, waiting for Ada May to say more, but the other girl turned, a pirouette that sent her nightgown rippling. Her arm looped through Deena's. The truth, Deena thought. The truth.

"What a lovely chat we've had, Deena Evangeline Williams. We should return to our rooms." At the top of the stairs, she kissed Deena's cheek, her lips warm with reassurance. The leaf fluttered to the carpet, and Deena shut her door.

Chapter 24

MRS. TIBBERT

MARCH, the cusp of spring. Days when the weather swerved from brisk, bundled mornings to a sleepy golden warmth in late afternoon. The time of year in her attic perch when she threw open the windows to the breeze.

It was from her attic watchtower that Mrs. Tibbert observed the door to the humanities building open. She raised her binoculars to study the stream of girls flowing to a sunny part of the quad, where they settled down, their knobby knees kissing blankets stretched over the grass, their class textbooks spread upon their laps.

The poet-professor joined them, and Mrs. Tibbert scoffed at his haphazardly knotted tie and scuffed shoes, then marked her notebook. If she could laden demerits upon the men, this impudent professor would have dozens from last month alone. She dabbed at her brow with a handkerchief. Insolence always did make her perspire.

She had not wanted him hired, but her campaign to convince Reginald had failed. The men were enamored with his vitality, his New Englandness. Reginald thought it was a remarkable sign of Bellerton's growing prestige that such a man was interested in a professorship among them.

"His family is rather prominent," Dr. Tibbert had said over breakfast the morning after his interview. He stirred ketchup into his eggs. "A boon for us, certainly. It could bring a new caliber of faculty and new attention to the college." Her husband's knife sliced cleanly through his blood sausage.

She did not like it one bit and stabbed at her plate, crimson dots flickering obscenely in her vision. She distrusted poetry. It was fanciful. It was opaque and infused with secret meanings. What use would such a thing be to the girls? Reading Milton and Shakespeare was fine, but beyond that, why give them such expansive modes of self-expression? Would they stir supper with one hand and pen verses with the other? Doubtful.

She lifted her binoculars again, traced the groupings of girls, then slid her lenses back over to the professor. His hands glided with small movements while he lectured, and the girls clung to his every word, their faces open and innocent. His gaze frequented one in particular: Lucille Whittier. A girl who was possessed of narcissism and too much bosom for her own good. Her older sister had been a rotten apple, and now Mrs. Tibbert wondered whether there might be an infection of the whole tree.

She recalled discovering the sister just outside her attic door, enmeshed with another girl, their mouths suckling like fish. She had them expelled immediately. At the end of the year, she found their faces in the school yearbooks and meticulously used correction ink to remove them. When she finished, it was as if neither had ever existed. She could not abide a permanent stain. Remove them bodily from campus, then excise them from the record.

When the lecture ended, Mrs. Tibbert waited until the girls dispersed before she marched from the library to the English department, eager to nail the professor to the floorboards.

Four quick knocks, then she pushed into his office. His feet were kicked onto his desk, and he clattered upright when she entered, slamming his knee, then scrambling to locate his jacket and reengage his tie, all the while mumbling and blushing. She took her time sitting; she crossed her ankles and straightened her back. Newspapers were stacked scattershot on a chair and his movements knocked the pile over. *The New York Times*, she noted with annoyance. Did he believe the *Times-Dispatch* was a farce not worth his attention? This man was like being in a semi-private train compartment with a stranger who could not stop elbowing you at every jostle along the tracks.

"Agnes," he muttered finally, standing to shake her hand.

"That's Mrs. Tibbert," she snapped.

"Ma'am." It wasn't quite a correction. "What a pleasant surprise." He gestured vaguely about his desk, as if his brilliancy could be found in the disarray.

Looking at him, her mind imagined all manner of silly creatures: Giraffe. Fawn. A stick-like insect that was easily crushed.

Though she held no jurisdiction over him—that was Reginald's job—the girls were within her purview, and since he was responsible for their academic education, she felt justified in meeting. She had learned over the years how a girl's missteps might ripple and grow. Wasn't that the very lesson her old Wesleyan friend Ginger had taught her? Men might indulge, but girls paid the price. The answer was to protect the girls, to keep them in line. But that didn't mean she was ignorant of what was really going on.

That was the other lesson she had learned from Ginger on that long-ago day: the importance of keeping one's eyes open to possible troubles a girl might step into.

Mrs. Tibbert, then only Agnes, had gone to Ginger's room for their usual afternoon card game, and instead she had found Ginger bleeding out after a botched procedure too close to the quickening.

When she demanded to know who was responsible, Ginger only said, "It's not what I wanted."

"The child or the carving it out?" She clamped Ginger's hand, confused by her boiling anger. She recalled her mother's barbed admonishments during the war. "You are lucky to be born a girl, Agnes. You are safe here, while the men have no choice but to fight."

But the so-called luck of womanhood was a war, too, she thought.

Ginger's head rolled on the pillow, her spark fading, and Agnes was left with an unshakable conviction that crystallized then into her life's purpose. Certain mistakes were permanent. Going forward, she would interfere long before a girl capsized, before scandal—or worse—erupted.

"We have disobedient bodies," Ginger whispered.

"Not me," Agnes replied. "Not me."

Ginger's throat pulsed with the effort of swallowing. Agnes was swift. She pulled sheets from the closet. Pillows and a down coat. She shoved them between Ginger's legs to staunch the blood, but nothing could stop what was coming. The room shrank. She held Ginger's hand until it was cold, then walked to the campus exchange to phone the doctor that there had been an accident. She remembered how the sky that day was colorless and flat. How a flock of starlings slipped over its face.

◆ ◆ ◆

THOUGH DECADES HAD PASSED, SHE COULD STILL REMEMBER HOW powerless she'd felt when she lost her dearest friend. Sitting in the professor's dusty office, a window set high in the wall behind him emitting a rectangle of horizontal light, Mrs. Tibbert lingered over her memories that still ached like a bruise. She had spent years reflecting on Ginger's words about disobedient bodies, the remark just as sharp as it ever was. How unfair that the man sitting before her would never be called into account for *his* body.

"I am here about the girls," she said.

His office was grimy and disordered. Books toppled across every surface. Coffee cups stood abandoned, liquid surfaces floating with scum. She recoiled, her disgust as thick as clotted cream in her throat.

"The girls?" He sounded as if he didn't know of whom she spoke. Then, he bounced in his chair, and leaned forward eagerly. "The girls! How they have delighted and surprised me! Their observations are astute, and they possess such active minds and voracious desires. Now that I know them better . . ."

He trailed off, shifting his hands uneasily from the desk blotter to the tops of his thighs. His left collar stood at salute, and she resisted tamping it down. Still just a boy, she thought. A child inhabiting the figure of a man.

She interjected before he could speak. "Was it your class I saw on the quad?"

He looked surprised. "Yes, I believe it was."

"In opposition to the edict that classes remain indoors?"

"I'm afraid I didn't understand it was mandatory. I find the classrooms a bit stuffy, though I suppose I'm not used to the weather here, it's not at all like Massachusetts. The quad offers a change of scenery for the ladies. To get them thinking in expansive ways." He was red now and sweating. "To open their minds." He tugged at his tie.

She regretted that she had not spoken directly to him until now. Who knew what trouble he had already managed to stir up. Mrs. Tibbert clamped her nails into the skin on her wrist to control herself. She had half-believed he was light in the loafers—Reginald claimed that most poets were—but now she realized he had pulled the wool over her eyes.

"To what, exactly, are you opening their minds?"

His gaze fumbled upward, as if the words he sought drifted midair. A heavy tread approached, and the door opened, the literature professor leaning around it. "My pal, you wouldn't believe—" He stopped, his words halted by Mrs. Tibbert's glare. "Excuse me, ma'am. I didn't realize you were—" The door closed with too much heft, the air stirring for several seconds before settling. She waited until she heard the literature professor retreat to the end of the hall before speaking. Her words were hot and barbed.

"Our girls do not need independent thinking. They do not require self-expression. You might be training their minds, but I am preparing them for the roles they will inhabit once they leave. And of that, you know nothing." She enjoyed how he squirmed. Let him be afraid. "I would advise, going forth, that you stick to the curriculum for which you were hired, and you teach them in the lovely buildings in which we have given you space. Furthermore, I would advise that you maintain your distance from the girls outside of the classrooms. Am I making myself clear?"

He was as still as a mouse hiding from a hawk. They sat in silence, the room darkening as the sun dropped behind the mountains. She was startled when he pulled the chain on his desk lamp and the flush of green-tinged light spilled forth. His face took on a strange pallor as he stood, hand extended. "Yes, ma'am."

His politeness might sound benign to others' ears, but she saw that he meant to undermine her. She wouldn't allow it, not from him. There would be no further shenanigans with the girls. If Lucille was too far gone, she would make an example of her for the others. If Lucille and her sister were both rotten apples, then she would chop down the entire wretched tree. Order must prevail. No matter the costs.

Chapter 25
DEENA

AT long last, Deena was the one to catch the thief. She awoke with a start from a nap, clammy and short of breath. The fraying quality of the light signified late afternoon. She kicked off the quilt and threw the window open to let the cool air wake her, leaning her forehead on the glass.

A faint metallic scraping was perceptible, a scritch-scritch that arrowed across the room. Her door groaned as a weight shoved it from the other side, but it stuck fast. A shadow flickered underneath.

Her first thought was of Mary, then of the housemother. The grating noise reverberated from the end of the hall. Deena flattened her face to the crack under the door, surprised to see Nell jiggle Prissy's lock with a thin tool, biting her lip in concentration. The door popped open. Nell checked over her shoulder, then wormed inside.

Deena bolted to her feet. Nell's deception undermined everything it meant to be a Belle and their trust in one another. She tiptoed across the hall to where Ada May was propped on pillows in bed, a book on her lap and the smell of lemon cleaner in the air. Her bandage had been removed recently, and her newly uncovered left eye blinked myopically, the skin around it buttery and puckered.

"Come quick. I discovered who's been taking our things." Announcing it, Deena felt only sadness and none of the elated zeal she had expected. A rough pebble of betrayal lodged in her throat.

Ada May followed her into the hall, the rug swallowing their footfalls. She pushed Prissy's door wide just as Prissy ascended the stairs. Behind her, Sheba was pulling Fred by the hand.

"Get away from my room," Prissy screeched. "In it together! You rotten—"

"There's your thief," Deena said, pointing.

Prissy's mink hung from Nell's shoulders. She gawped in surprise at the girls standing in the doorway. Prissy roared. She grabbed the awl Nell had used to pick the lock and threw it to the floor, then snapped the mink away and dragged Nell roughly to the bed.

The girls charged into the room, demanding answers.

Nell crossed her arms defiantly. The medallion on her necklace seemed to wink.

Ada May's composure fled and fury reddened her face. "How dare you. I should snap your neck. That yearbook you took is priceless, a family heirloom."

"Oh, please." Nell started to get up, but Ada May shoved her down with a violence Deena felt coursing through all of them. The room pulsed with their collective anger. Sheba swatted the side of Nell's head.

Nell pouted. "I was going to give your things back."

"Where are you hiding it all?" Ada May was formidable, terrifying. When Nell refused to say, Ada May twisted the skin on her arm until Nell grumbled that everything was under her bed.

Ada May's finger flicked in Deena's direction. "You go. And you—" She indicated Fred. "Go with her."

Deena put her hands up in refusal. She wanted nothing to do with the thievery. Ada May glared, her words blunt: "We trust you, Deena."

•   •   •

DEENA AND FRED WERE GREETED WITH CHEERS WHEN THEY marched into Prissy's room with the vanished treasures in an old apple crate. Fred immediately dug out her porcelain dog from the box, but as she clutched the figurine to her chest, her face bunched. "It's broken."

A piece had chipped off. Deena was grateful she had nothing at Bellerton so valuable it might break. She set the box down and began to root for her cracked glass jar, but Ada May shoved her aside. When she found her missing yearbook, she sat back on her heels. "I can't forgive you for taking this. My family's history is in these pages."

Prissy tossed items onto the bed until she had found her favorite lipstick. One by one, they reclaimed the things they had lost: Fred's book, Sheba's locket. Nell groaned, swinging her feet like a child, unable to stay still. Deena couldn't believe her insolence.

"Where's my jar?"

Nell tossed her hands up. "I didn't take everything, jeez." She seemed flustered. She wriggled her hand into her shoe, drawing out the small stone Deena had found, its onyx body crisscrossed with tawny striations.

Deena reached for it, but Fred exclaimed, "Oh!" and swept the rock from Nell's hand.

"That's mine!" Deena cried.

Fred tightened her fist around it. "No, it's mine."

"I found it on the path near the stables."

"And I found it behind the library."

The others didn't seem to notice Deena's hands were empty. To the last, every girl had been given back what was taken except for her. Her body stung at the unfairness of it. Her jar was still gone, and the stone that might have assuaged her hurt feelings—negligible, but special, an object of her own—wasn't hers, according to Fred. Deena stomped her feet. "It isn't fair!" she yelled.

Her outburst silenced the room. The criticism was swift.

"Gosh, Deena, it's just a rock." Disgust marred Prissy's pretty face.

Sheba patted her arm. "There are plenty of rocks. We'll get you another."

Deena didn't know how to make them understand. She repeated under her breath what Prissy had said. It was just a rock. She pinched her arm to make it true.

Dusk flooded the room, casting ghoulish shadows over Eisenhower's face on the campaign poster Prissy had tacked to her wall. She dragged her nails down her arms, ashamed she had behaved out of turn. She had forgotten who she was supposed to be.

"All right, we have our things back," Ada May said. She stared pointedly at Deena, who was gripped by a gnawing sense that she was being chided.

Prissy switched on the lamps, and in the window's reflection, Deena saw Mary standing behind her. She spun around but Mary wasn't there.

The supper bell rang, and the girls hurried off to dress. On her way out, Ada May attempted to soothe Deena. "Don't worry, we'll find your things, too."

She wanted to believe Ada May. In the window's black panes, Deena's reflection frowned, the image a ghostly wavering—as if it didn't believe Ada May either.

◆ ◆ ◆

The girls retired early that evening, armed with a plan. They weren't going to let Nell get off so easily. If the Bellerton handbook detailed consequences for an infraction as minor as wearing the wrong type of shoes to dinner, then the Belles would lay down their own punishments for the egregious act of stealing.

Deena hunched cross-legged on her bed, unable to focus on her schoolwork, tense with anticipation. The chapel bells guided her: nine o'clock, then ten. At eleven, Deena flicked off her light. The hallway was a river of darkness, its waters pulsing with impatience.

Light shone from under Nell's door, and inside, she hummed cheerily. Deena bristled at her infuriating lack of remorse. A ripple passed from girl to girl—a convergence. Ada May snapped her fingers, and Nell's door screamed open, a dam breaking. The room went dark.

Deena stumbled into the bedpost, spit a cussword. She shoved Nell's face into her pillow, and its cotton batting silenced her yells. Sheba squatted like a gargoyle on her kicking legs. Fred and Prissy each pinned one of Nell's arms to the mattress. Deena snapped the necklace chain Nell always wore and dropped it to the floor.

Ada May surged from the inky black, spread her hands along Nell's skull. She wrapped several strands of hair around her finger, crooked it, and pulled. Nell screamed into the pillow. Deena pressed her down with greater force. Nell didn't deserve kindness, not when she had violated their trust.

Ada May yanked her hair again, then cleared space for Prissy. Nell pleaded, the words muffled by the pillow and her tears. Please, *please* stop. They were hurting her, *really* hurting her, didn't they see she wasn't enjoying this. It wasn't like their usual hair pulling game. Though they hadn't played that game in months.

The Belles sneered, leaning in. They took turns punishing her, tugging strands from a patch at the back of her head, denuding it. A hot intimacy shot through the room, and when Fred's fingers brushed Deena's arm, the touch was two elements melding.

When it was finally her turn, Deena thought of everything she had done to enter Bellerton's gates. How Nell was different, too, but not like Deena was. Nell's ambivalence enraged Deena, who could never afford to take anything for granted. She dug her nails into Nell's scalp, hooked her fingers. She heard Grandmother's cajoling voice warning her about choosing her Bellerton friends wisely. Deena needed to show what she was capable of doing. She needed to show that she could fight.

Mary appeared suddenly, her presence rippling the air. The others seemed not to notice, except for Ada May, who turned and searched the gloom. Mary's brow was troubled. Her fingers plucked at her velvet ribbon—knotted not around her hair, as usual, but around her neck. Deena rubbed absently at her own aching muscles there.

"I have to," Deena whispered to Mary.

She closed her fist around a clump of Nell's hair and pulled hard.

◆ ◆ ◆

TO NOT LOOK AT NELL THE NEXT MORNING: THAT WAS THE HARD-est part. The Belles' bodies ached, mottled with fresh bruising from Nell's initial resistance.

Deena was scrubbing her face at the bathroom sink when Nell crept in, hair arranged to conceal the throbbing bald patch. Her face was red with a fresh acne outbreak. The Belles all had bruises, though none so deeply colored as Nell's.

The South Hall girls called sunny *Good mornings*! and whirled through their routines, wrapping themselves snugly in their coats for the chilly walk to breakfast. Outside, the sky was white and cloudless, the air stinging like nettles in Deena's lungs.

Behind, a voice called, "Wait for me."

Deena stopped, as did the others. Nell hobbled to catch up, her coat unbuttoned, her sweater rumpled. A scratch marred her lip. When she shakily raised her chin, Deena noted the goose egg throbbing under her jaw.

"Why? So you can lie to us some more?" Prissy said, the corner of her mouth rising into a snarl.

Sheba said, "I bet there's other things she's keeping from us."

Nell was in tears. "Please," she begged. "I accepted my punishment."

"Why did you do it, Nell?" Fred asked pityingly. She sounded ex-hausted, her short hair more disarrayed than usual. Dark half circles had formed under Fred's eyes.

"I just wanted nice things. It's been harder for us since my mom left my dad," Nell muttered. "And some stuff, like Ada May's yearbook, I was only borrowing. I was going to return it, I swear." She started to cry.

"Then you can return my jar," Deena said, unmoved by Nell's tears. She had coveted the same nice things the others owned, yet she wasn't a thief.

Nell wiped her nose on her coatsleeve. "I told you, I didn't take it."

Deena decided she no longer wanted to protect Nell's secret, the one she had learned months ago the night the girls had slept in the barns, because Nell had done more than steal from them—she wasn't living up to the name of the Belles.

"Her sister is an invalid with polio."

Nell's face reddened. She balled her hands into fists. "How dare you."

"Then say it isn't true."

Nell hesitated for just a moment before rushing at Deena with her arms extended, as if she meant to shove her over the porch railings. The Belles stepped forward and folded protectively around her, and Nell reared up short, one fist raised threateningly.

Ada May detached from the group and stepped swiftly toward Nell, teeth bared. Nell shrunk back, frightened. "I was only having fun."

Deena started to speak, but Ada May silenced her. She drew close to Nell, reaching up to adjust her coat collar and sweeping Nell's hair behind her shoulders. When Ada May finally spoke, her honeyed voice was laced with poison. "We were only having fun, too."

Chapter 26
DEENA

DEENA was amazed by how the Belles' confidence and influence had grown in the months since they had begun their games. Whispered awe trailed in their wake. The other freshmen could not look away,
and the upperclassmen gave them wide berths. The Belles wore their
ribbons prominently, ends dangling like temptations. Deena thrilled at
their amassing power on campus and the reputation they had made for
themselves. They had grown feral; they were in total control. Bellerton
belonged to them.

For the first time ever, they let their games become visible: Swollen lips and dark contusions. Goose eggs and welts. Scratches and cuts.
Nell might have been the one to receive punishment, but she wasn't the
only Belle who had been bruised. Ada May, recovered finally from her
horse-riding injury, had a throbbing scar through her eyebrow and a grin
lighting her blue eyes.

Midway through breakfast the same week as Nell's punishment, Mrs.
Tibbert's heels could be heard crossing the floor before she burst into the
dining room like a torpedo. Talk ceased immediately. Cups slid onto sau-
cers and cutlery clanked into position on plates. Students sat at attention.

An unplanned visit from the president's wife was unwelcomed. It meant something had happened.

"Good morning, ladies."

"Good morning, Mrs. Tibbert," the students responded in apprehensive unison. Three hundred and fifty-two Bellerton girls twisted their hands nervously in their laps.

"Today, I remind you of our community's rules." Whispers sprung up, then quickly died down. Mrs. Tibbert's sharp eyes picked at the girls like they were crumbs. "Rules that are for your safety and well-being. It has come to my attention that these rules are being violated."

The Belles' attention snapped to Nell, who dragged the back of her hand across her nose. Deena twisted her cloth napkin in her lap and glanced at the others, whose faces all showed the same fear: that Nell had tattled. Nell's face was a crimson color so deep it looked as if she had been boiled, and that was proof enough to Deena. Her stomach knotted when she thought of how she might be forced to leave Bellerton with nowhere to go.

Mrs. Tibbert continued. "I would like for our seniors to recite Bellerton's expectations. Miss Donovan, from the top of the handbook. You may please begin."

The seniors were grim. Peggy Donovan smoothed her skirt. "The first rule is what to wear and when to wear it. Ladies must always be conscious of how they look. The consequences for straying from approved clothing styles and lipstick colors is a failing mark for that day."

Ann Goodchild went next. "The second rule is that quiet hours must be observed from nine p.m. until seven a.m., with no exceptions."

Desperation clawed at Deena. At every table eggs went cold. Toast hardened, and coffee curdled. The recitation felt excruciating, but when Deena turned her face away, she found herself staring at William Grayson Dickey's portrait, his patrician features beset with sternness. What would he have done, Deena wondered, if he knew he was about to lose everything?

When the seniors finished, Mrs. Tibbert commanded all students to stand and repeat the community agreements. She thumped her foot against the floor. "Louder, ladies. I cannot hear you. We have pride in our community and its rules."

Deena gripped the table's edge, lightheadedness swamping her. The knot in her stomach hardened. She grew short of breath. She could not allow herself to be removed from Bellerton and planned to beg for Mrs. Tibbert's mercy. She would do whatever it took to stay.

"Very good, ladies. I expect that you will—"

A high-pitched shriek lanced her words. Mrs. Tibbert's eyes flashed. She started again. "I expect that you will keep to these values, and you will not—"

Yelling echoed from the walkway outside, sharpening from noise into declaration. "I won't go!"

Mrs. Tibbert pitched her voice above the disruption. "Keep to the guidelines, and you will flourish into your brightest, most diligent selves. Refuse these guidelines, and you will dishonor Bellerton—"

Lucille Whittier burst into the room. Several girls gasped and jolted to their feet.

"Sit down," Mrs. Tibbert barked.

Deena gaped at Lucille's dishevelment: her tangled hair and wrinkled, untucked blouse. Her bare legs prickled with goose bumps and blue, unseemly veins. She wore no makeup and her cheeks blazed scarlet. She looked younger than her twenty years, childlike in her wildness. An untamed girl. Deena was immediately soothed by the realization that Mrs. Tibbert's morning visit didn't involve the Belles at all.

Lucille begged on her knees. "Ma'am, please have some understanding!"

Mrs. Tibbert's lip curled. She took two steps back from the indecorous creature at her feet. "Ladies, you will—"

Lucille snatched the hem of Mrs. Tibbert's skirt. "He loves me," she crowed. "We're going to be married. It's all okay."

Mrs. Tibbert kicked her, and Lucille toppled onto her back. Her stomach swelled and the situation became obvious to even the most prudish in the room: Lucille was in the family way. Anxious chatter burbled up. The room of polite, well-trained Bellerton students did not know what to do or where to cast their eyes.

Deena thought of the day she had stood with the others outside South Hall, watching Lucille chase the poet-professor. Then, she recalled the night in December when he had found her sleepwalking and led her into South Hall. A dawning came upon her as she watched Lucille sprawled on the dining room floor.

"Pull yourself together, child," Mrs. Tibbert snapped. "He's denied you."

Lucille wobbled to her feet, unsteady inside her changing body. "You're lying."

"Is that so? How are we to know it wasn't a boy from town? A distant cousin? There is no evidence beyond your own body."

Lucille bellowed. Mrs. Tibbert signaled for the staff. "She's hysterical. Remove her to the infirmary until her father gets here."

One of the waitstaff grabbed for her, but Lucille darted away. "Don't touch me!" She spat at the man, and a globule of white phlegm struck his face then dripped onto his collar. She backed into Peggy Donovan, who put a hand on Lucille's cheek.

"Hush. It's done now." Peggy wrapped her arms above the lift in Lucille's belly.

Lucille slammed her elbow into Peggy's ribs. "I won't go!"

Mrs. Tibbert called for attention. "Ladies, you are dismissed." Not a single girl moved. She grabbed a water glass from a table and smashed it to the floor. The glass burst with tyrannizing force. "To your classes! Now!"

Chairs scraped. Plates clattered. Girls threw their jackets on in haste.

An animal-like fear flashed in Lucille's face. She crashed into a chair. "Don't let her send me off!" she screamed. She slid to the floor, fighting off the waitstaff who attempted to haul her to her feet. "I'll never go! I'd rather die here! It isn't fair that he's permitted to stay!"

The Belles bunched at the threshold, shoved along by the crowd hurrying to leave, but Ada May hurled herself toward Lucille. Deena followed close behind, grabbing unsuccessfully for Ada May to pull her back in line.

Ada May towered over Lucille, who shrunk back. "Betraying Beller-ton like this. How dare you." Though the words scalded, Deena was the only bystander near enough to feel their heat.

"How dare *I*?" Lucille screeched. "You're insane!"

Lucille attempted to push herself up, but Ada May's foot jabbed her side, and she slid back down. The scar above Ada May's eyebrow pulsed, her rage at Lucille's behavior flushing her face and neck. Deena snatched Ada May by the elbow.

"Come on," Deena whispered, thinking of the horses in the barn, animals whose unpredictable natures had been tamed into compliance, but who still had enough power to hurt. "She isn't worth it." At her feet, Lucille was sweaty and seething.

They joined the Belles on the porch. Before the dining room doors slammed shut behind them, Deena caught sight of Mrs. Tibbert slapping Lucille.

Beside her, Ada May cleared her throat. "Ladies, we'll be late for class."

Like a doll torn apart and stitched back together, she put on her regal bearing once more, as quickly as she had thrown it off.

◆　◆　◆

THEY RECEIVED FOUR TARDINESS DEMERITS FROM THE HISTORY professor, who refused to reschedule that day's test, mumbling, "Girls and their drama, girls and their gossip." He flaunted the test papers. "No more chitchat. Get to work."

Deena's stomach rumbled as she picked up her pencil, her thoughts scattering like pebbles with all she had witnessed that morning. Around her, the other Belles bent diligently over their desks as if nothing had happened; beside her, Ada May was pristine and pink-cheeked.

Ten minutes into the test, the professor grunted like a feral hog, asleep at his desk. Fred snapped twice, then sent her test paper sliding over the floor. Sheba snatched it up and mouthed *thank you*. Deena laid her head on her desk, hungry and exhausted. This was a test she seemed likely to fail.

Prissy sidled toward the pencil sharpener at the back of the room, which grated, then stalled. She gave a breathless "Lucille!"

The girls clambered from their seats, as the professor at his desk continued to snore. Fred raised a window sash, and they all stuck their heads out to gawk at the commotion below.

Lucille was running back and forth across the quad. A crowd had gathered before South Hall: the entirety of the senior class, Mrs. Tibbert, Saul the caretaker, and a man in a heavy wool coat who must have been Lucille's father, who pleaded with her each time she zipped past, snarling at anyone who approached.

"She's mad!" Sheba exclaimed.

"She's beautiful," Fred whispered.

"What will happen when they catch her?" Deena asked.

Lucille stumbled, slamming onto the ground. Mrs. Tibbert's sharp rebuke echoed across the quad, and more Bellerton students gathered to watch the spectacle, girls grouping on the porches and the lawn, pointing from the sidewalks. Commanded by her father, Saul rushed at Lucille, but she shoved him back, and he crashed into Mrs. Tibbert.

"She definitely won't be May Queen," Prissy said, twisting the nub of her cigarette on the windowsill.

Lucille kicked her feet in the air. Her skirt slid down her thighs, revealing the garter snaps dangling from the bottom of her girdle. She twisted recklessly onto her stomach, sweeping her arms across the dried grass, bleating with madness. Her father turned away in disgust. Peggy Donovan attempted to usher students into the dorms. Mrs. Tibbert jerked Lucille to her feet like a rag doll. She barked an order at Peggy, who flew to her side.

Deena leaned back, spied Ada May a few paces down from the other girls. She gripped the window ledge with barely concealed delight as Mrs. Tibbert and Peggy dragged the twisting, howling Lucille away.

Chapter 27

FRED

JUNE 2002

FRED was sitting on her porch when a glint of metal flashed through the trees: a car weaving up the mountain. A glass of iced tea sweated in her lap, drops of condensation running between her naked thighs. The summer mornings in the Appalachians were chilly, but by midday the sun blazed and a cold beverage was called for. Though she had given up drinking along with smoking years back, times arose when the itching returned and she dreamed of the whiskey burn in her throat, heard the chink of ice in a glass.

A sleek, four-door sedan the color of a robin's egg rolled to a stop on the gravel. Its engine purred from exertion on the incline. The driver's door opened.

"I'm surprised that thing made it up here," Fred called, deciding to play it light. "I don't make myself easy to reach."

A woman emerged, her face blotted by large, reflective sunglasses. She was dressed smartly, in a loose cotton blouse and white sandals beneath calf-hugging chinos. Fred spread her knees wider in her chair, matchstick legs poking from the bottoms of her ratted jean shorts. She loved the air on her bare skin, the freedom of exposure. Her hemline had grown younger as she had grown older.

The woman took her time tottering elegantly to the porch on her wide wicker heels. She swept off her sunglasses and folded them into the front pocket of her purse. Her blue eyes, still sharp after all these years, unsettled Fred. There was no trace of her long-ago riding injury except a thin scar jutting through her eyebrow.

Fred made no move to stand and instead sunk deeper into her rocker. In the intervening decades, Fred's brunette hair had grown to drape her shoulders and was threaded with gray. The sides were swept back with two sparkling butterfly clips. Fred saw Ada May staring and touched one.

"Delia's granddaughter. A gift." Fred gestured. "Welcome. Have a seat."

Ada May lowered into the rocker, her purse held primly in her lap. She cleared her throat. "Delia's your friend?"

"My wife." Fred's jaw hardened. "As a matter of speaking." She wished for a cigarette right then, to go with that phantom whiskey. "Official isn't possible for us."

Ada May gave a trilling *hm* in the back of her throat. She smoothed her pants, the center crease razor crisp. Pink pearls sat upon her earlobes. Her hair was glossy red and sheared into a bob. How clever, Fred thought, to match it to the color of her youth. But she had always been vain about her hair.

"We haven't spoken in so long, Winifred."

"You haven't been getting my Christmas cards?" Ada May looked stricken, and Fred started laughing. Almost felt bad for pulling her leg. "It's been over half a lifetime since we last saw each other." How had Ada May found her? With her family's ties to Bellerton, no doubt she could weasel her way into alumnae files. But Fred had carved a life here in the Allegheny Mountains of Pennsylvania that had allowed her to disappear.

Ada May touched her throat with delicate, manicured hands. "It's rather warm today. I underestimated the weather up here."

Fred gestured toward the house. "Pitcher of iced tea is in the fridge. Water's in the tap. Help yourself." She paused. "Where are you these days, anyhow?"

"Richmond." Ada May added, "Virginia," as if it needed clarification. "Well, just outside the city. Wyndham. My husband's a senator for the commonwealth." She abruptly stood, and the screen door clattered.

Ada May's sandals clacked on the kitchen floor. In the yard, a lonely cicada sawed mournfully from the limb of a sycamore. Time had grown malleable. Even though she was no longer seventeen, and Bellerton was fifty years behind her and far away, time was not the calcified thing it had been that morning,

"To seeing old friends," Fred said, when Ada May returned. Their glasses clinked.

Ada May sipped her iced tea. "Why did you choose this place?"

"It chose me." Fred crooked her knee, picking at a bit of chipped red toenail polish. "No matter where I try to go, I keep coming back to the mountains and the woods."

"You moved around quite a bit." It was not a question but a statement of fact.

Fred tensed. Ada May had known about her wandering, of course, probably tracking her in all the ways a person could be tracked. She'd gone from Bellerton back to Baltimore, then down to DC and up to Philly. She'd tried being on a sort of commune in West Virginia. She'd lived for a time with a ceramic artist on the Eastern Shore. Shaming her family all the while. And then, fourteen years ago, came Delia and this place.

She dug a fingernail beneath a lip of loose polish, peeled off a thin strip. "Delia found this land. Fifteen acres, miles from nowhere. I built the house myself. And the porch, the shop out back. These rockers." Fred rapped her knuckles on the rocker's arm. "It's a quiet, simple life. Don't tell me you came here to ruin that."

Ada May twisted the bracelet around her wrist. "I'd like to meet her. Your wife."

"She'll be back later."

Ada May uncrossed her ankles. Fred sensed a shift in the day. They had been circling Ada May's true purpose for being there and they both knew it. Ada May said, "I don't know whether things reach you given how . . . removed you are."

Fred watched a woodpecker circle a tree trunk, the rat-tat-tat-tat of its work echoing in the forest. "What is it you want? Money for Bellerton? To build a new dormitory, endow some scholarship?"

Ada May's jaw tightened. "You know exactly why I'm here."

And she did. Fred had known from the moment she realized it was Ada May driving the sedan the color of an untroubled sky.

Fred surged to her feet. She resented Ada May's intrusion into her life. "Dammit. I knew this would come back to haunt us."

Ada May fingered the ends of her bob. "Bellerton will want only to close the matter quickly, lay things to rest. If they can identify who it is, that's what we must prepare for."

Fred saw that Ada May had surrounded herself with the means of protection, walling herself behind a powerful husband and her own connections. Behind her Bellerton legacy. Ada May wasn't dirtying her hands.

"Would it have been me if it hadn't been her? Because I'm . . ." Fred couldn't say it, not to Ada May, and she hated herself for it, just as she still hated herself for cutting things off abruptly with Sheba back then. But she hadn't wanted to give the other Belles any reason to target either of them next. So she had ended it after freshman year and hadn't spoken to Sheba since.

"You knew I loved Sheba." Fred was surprised at the emotion clogging her throat. She hardened her voice. "You were always so damn good at convincing others to follow your lead."

The high-pitched whine of a motor broke the day. Fred recognized the familiar sound of Delia's dirt bike engine. Now that she was finally settled and happy, she had everything to lose.

"Just say nothing." Ada May's urgency grew as the dirt bike became louder. "Do that, and the past will be past. We can all move on."

"Ada May, how—" Fred hesitated, though she was desperate to have it out while there was still time.

"Peggy Donovan and Ann Goodchild went for a walk along the creek at the all-class reunion last weekend. They found—" Ada May gave a strangled laugh. "Peggy thought it was a rock, at first."

The dirt bike crested the last rise and shot across the gravel, skimming past Ada May's car and roaring to a stop around the side of the house.

Delia appeared, boots crunching the gravel, hands tugging at her helmet. Her hair fell in long, blonde waves that sported a painted purple streak she tucked behind her ear. She was in her mid-forties, twenty-five years younger than Fred, fit where Fred was gaunt and thin, her face cut with angles and a single mole. She bounded up the steps and gave Fred a kiss before turning to their guest.

"I didn't know we were expecting anyone this week. Are you here for the cabinet?"

"This is Ada May. She's an old friend come to say hello."

"Goodness!" Delia stuck out a calloused hand, thumb crooked from a long-ago motorcycle accident. "Freddy never talks about any of you, even when I prod." She tickled Fred's side. Fred slapped her hand away. "I hope you stay for dinner, Ada May." Delia unzipped her leather riding jacket and shrugged it off, tossing it over the porch railing.

"We could grill up the hocks from that hog John slaughtered last week." She bent to unlace her boots, tugged them off without using her hands. "The hogs are free range, organic, all that. My friend John has a pig farm out that way." Her mouth quirked. "You seem like the type of woman who needs to know where her hog's been."

Fred put a hand on Delia's elbow. "Ada May was just telling me she must get back to her hotel. She has a . . . a thing tomorrow."

"A fundraiser," Ada May put in, her lie smooth. "I'm sorry I can't stay. It sounds like a wonderful treat. Another time."

"Suit yourself." Delia shrugged. "It's a long drive back down that mountain. Darling, I'll get her some snacks for the road." The screen door slapped behind her.

Ada May lowered her voice, her fingers pinching Fred's arm. "I refuse to let her destroy everything my family created."

Fred wanted to force Ada May to say out loud what they did. Make it real. But she knew that Ada May kept everything vague on purpose, so she could scrunch her nose as if detecting a bad smell, and someone else would rush to take care of the problem. It was how people like Ada May handled life's unsavory things—by appointing someone else to clean up. It was all about protecting her legacy and had nothing to do with Fred or the others.

"We could have been kinder to her."

Delia returned just then, a brown paper bag in her hands. "There's bottled water, some trail mix, jerky. Did Freddy show you her woodshop? She's a superb carpenter, the best on the mountain, but she gets so gun-shy about sharing with others—"

"Delia," Fred cut her off. "Ada May needs to go."

Delia stuck out her hand. "Nice meeting you."

At her car, Fred asked Ada May to wait. "I have something to give you." She ran barefoot to her carpentry workshop, where she dug through the top drawer of her tool chest for the palm-sized wooden disk she had made years ago: a six-pointed white star bisected by shades of navy, its points piercing a thin red border. It was the first one she'd made, and she had saved it, without any idea at the time of who would be its recipient.

Fred passed it through the sedan's open window. Ada May pinched it between her thumb and forefinger.

"It's called a hex."

"Is that so?"

"It's a barn decoration used by Dutch and German immigrants. Old folk art of sorts. I use a bandsaw to cut these, then paint them to sell to tourists. Twenty bucks a pop." She thwacked her palm.

Ada May twisted it between her fingers. She still wore her double-band ring with its green stone. "Six points to the star. Six Belles." She tapped each point with a finger.

"That isn't why I'm giving it to you." All these decades later, and they were bound by what they could never reveal. Time unspooled, stories bent and twisted, and with each retelling so went the curve of memory. What else had she missed or forgotten? What other events had she wiped away?

Fred said helplessly, "I just thought you might like it."

"Winifred, thank you. It's lovely," Ada May said. "No spells required, I hope."

"Only tongue of dog, eye of newt."

Ada May nestled the hex into her purse.

Fred gripped the window, an urge overtaking her. "You can rely on me," she said, drawing an X over her chest with her pointer finger. "Belles never tell." The old girlhood patterns of leader and follower locked again into place. With a pang, Fred remembered that it was Sheba who had painted the X marks across their palms.

Ada May squeezed Fred's arm, rolled up her window, and wheeled the car around. She raised her hand in a quick wave through the back window. Then, the blue sedan was gone, and Fred was left awash in Bellerton memories she'd tried, and failed, to erase.

Spring
1952

Bellerton girls are responsible to themselves
and to one another. If you find a girl is not
meeting the expectations of a Bellerton lady,
it is your duty to correct her.

—BELLERTON STUDENT HANDBOOK, 1951–1952

Chapter 28
DEENA

FOLLOWING Lucille's removal from Bellerton, never to be seen again, Nell shrunk further into herself. She stopped wearing her ribbon. She went mute at meals and in classes. She declined to study with the other Belles, and she avoided them in the hallway and bathroom.

It was only a few days after Lucille left that Deena heard unusual sounds coming from Nell's room next door: dresser drawers opening, clasps unbuckling, the weight of a trunk being dragged across the floor. The others must have heard the noises, too, because when she peeked into the hall, the girls had circled Nell's room. Ada May knocked with forceful authority and the scrabbling inside abruptly ceased. She knocked again, and Nell opened the door a crack, flinching when she saw the group amassed at her threshold.

"I'm leaving," she said flatly, then moved to shut the door.

"Nellie jelly, no!" Sheba cried, sticking her foot into the crack.

"We like you," Prissy said in a tone of mild conviction, examining her nails.

Fred reasoned with Nell. "What will you do if you go home now?

Bellerton won't have you back, and you won't have any degree. All this for nothing!"

Ada May added, "It's over now. What's done is done."

Nell opened the door wider. Over her shoulder, Deena saw piles of clothes and bedding. Nell's dresser had been cleared of her framed family photographs, her curtains pulled from the rod. Through the window, the barest green fuzz could be seen on the trees.

Deena pushed her way inside and forced Nell into a hug. "Please stay," she whispered into her hair, pity welling in her throat.

The other Belles threw their arms around Nell, too, until she was squeezed ferociously between them. The message was clear: her punishment levied, Nell had been brought into line, and there she would stay so long as she didn't betray them again.

"You're now and forever a Belle," Sheba said, making clear what forgiveness meant. She combed her fingers through Nell's hair and formed a loose braid. Deena saw Nell flinch, though whether from pain or fear, she didn't know.

"Okay, I'll stay," Nell said finally, her tone resigned.

To mark the occasion, and to renew their closeness, Ada May suggested they sneak out—their first time since her injuries had healed.

They gathered in the foyer that night after curfew, listening to the reverberation of the midnight chapel bell. Ada May kissed the key and released the lock mechanism with a firm, smooth thud.

The night was overcast and cold. Deena's breath hung in the air, yet she was renewed by the ritual, and the release from the staid, corseted self she inhabited by day. She was comforted, too, by the sense of belonging it gave her. They were Belles, and their bonds would never break.

Ada May demanded they go to the barns, her longing for Brutus too large to ignore, and the others capitulated. Their flashlights bounced eerily in the stable's rafters. Mice flinched from the bright beam and the horses released humanlike sputters. The girls squeezed into Brutus's stall, his musk stifling, while Deena hung back, still frightened by his power and size. She flattened herself as far from Brutus as possible.

His black lips blubbered around an apple in Ada May's hands, his teeth gnashing. "I forgive you," she said, running her hand up his muzzle and scratching at the spot where his mane tumbled out, her affection akin to love with all its attendant blindness. "We'll go riding again soon," she whispered.

Deena's flashlight caught the gleam in Brutus's gaze. His black eyes rolled from Ada May to her. She felt a strange compulsion to touch that eye, squish the soft meat of it in her hand. The others began to wander, too restless to stay long in one place, but Deena stuck close to Ada May, who ran her hands over Brutus's flank and buried her nose in his neck. Her voice was muffled when she asked, "Did your jar ever return?"

The question prickled Deena, who was still bitter about it, though she reminded herself that she had forgiven Nell. Before she could answer, Ada May lifted her head, her blue eyes piercing even in the half-light. "What makes that broken jar so special, anyway?"

The truth rolled like a psalm down Deena's tongue. The jar and its junk were the only evidence of her former self—but she swallowed her explanation at the last moment and said, "Ada May, the others are waiting."

The Belles were clustered along the path that edged the pastures. Together, the six began to walk, and they had almost reached the woods when Sheba cried out, "My ribbon!" She had left it hooked around a barn post and dashed off at a sprint to retrieve it, her body ungraceful but strong. Deena grew impatient when Sheba didn't return right away. The longer the Belles waited, the more Deena grew certain that something was wrong.

Fred must have thought the same. "I'm going to check on her." Before the others could react, she cut swiftly to the barn and disappeared inside.

The Belles followed as quickly as they could. The fizz of excitement from breaking curfew had worn off, and Deena's limbs were stiff with cold. As soon as she stepped inside the barn, she realized that they weren't alone. Unlike earlier, the horses swayed uneasily. A crunch of footsteps echoed. Deena's heart thudded in her chest. Too late to hide or scramble away. She tightened her grip on her flashlight and steadied herself for whatever reckoning was about to come.

A figure materialized, clinging to the nearby stall. The apparition limped closer, resolving into Sheba, who was hunched-over and smaller than Deena had ever seen her.

Sheba couldn't meet their eyes, and she had a flat vacancy in her expression. A sense of something gone horribly wrong spread through Deena's chest and rippled across the other Belles.

Fred rushed forward and wrapped Sheba in her arms, though it was clear to Deena that Sheba was numb, her body inaccessible to her.

"It's nothing." Sheba spoke with chilling stoicism. "It's my fault anyway."

"What happened?" Fred asked carefully, her voice trembling.

A nearby clatter echoed; it sounded as if someone was trying to leave undetected. Prissy trained her flashlight beam on the interloper, who recoiled like a captured rat, his face ghoulish in the light: the poet-professor.

"Greetings, ladies."

They turned their flashlights on him in a collective spotlight that pinned him in place. He grimaced, then drew a pack of cigarettes from his shirt pocket, lit one, and shook the pack in their direction. When none of the girls moved, he shrugged and stood smoking in short, quick puffs while his other hand tugged his hair.

The Belles formed a blockade around Sheba, and Deena felt the protectorate of the girls rising as they pieced together what must have happened. A whiff of something rotten drifted into the stables.

"He's filthy." Nell spat the word as if she had cussed.

"He's a poet." Ada May was blunt.

He was wrapped in the stink of booze and hay. His white shirt was wrinkled and stained, one-half of the collar pointing up and the top several buttons undone, exposing a chest the color of raw chicken breast. His slicked-back hair was unwashed, the strands greasy in the dim light.

He's slippery, Deena thought, with a wicked kind of charm that lets him get away with anything. She couldn't believe she had once found him suave. She thought of her mother, of the hurt a man had inflicted upon her. Bitter resentment filled her mouth.

"Say, none of you has my Housman by chance?" He squinted at their faces. "You aren't my seniors." He sighed and crushed the cigarette with his shoe, looking down at its remains.

Deena was enraged by his casualness after whatever perversion he had inflicted on Sheba. All the protections stacked around them were still not enough, not even here at Bellerton. But her feelings of powerlessness were gone. Bellerton had changed her. She wasn't vulnerable like her mother was, because she was a Belle. Deena raised both hands, the beam of her flashlight arcing wildly, and shoved him.

The poet-professor stumbled into the slatted boards of a stall. "What's wrong with you?" he admonished. He straightened, reaching as if to adjust a necktie. He wagged his finger, not taking them seriously. In a faux accent, he said, "Lassies, for this you'll get the lash."

The night curdled. The Belles tightened their positions and Deena snatched the poet-professor's wrist. He teetered, caught in their snare, and flashed a full smile, the hideous grin of a scarecrow.

"Don't hurt me, ladies." His tone was mocking and sarcastic. His fingers pried at Deena's grip. She squeezed tighter and a bone loosened with a sickening snap. Deena bent his arm behind his back until his knees buckled. He was half-crouched and half-standing, his eyes rolling as he realized his mistake.

"Please," he whimpered pathetically.

Who had shown her mother mercy? She was not backing down, not ever again.

"Are we going too far?" Fred whispered.

The poet-professor's face hardened, his tongue curling. "Out after curfew. I wonder what will happen now." He squirmed in Deena's grasp, knowing he was right—no one scrutinized the professors. He could ruin everything for them. He was a threat.

The Belles traded wordless glances over the top of his head.

Deena let go. Freed, he crumpled to the ground like a coat. She raised her flashlight and cracked it on his head. The beam went off. The darkness surged around them. Here, at last, their nighttime fury could be released. In a unified motion, the Belles descended upon him.

Chapter 29

DEENA

THE STORY went like this: The poet-professor tripped, lost his balance, and fell down the hill behind the barns, where the stable groom discovered him the next morning unconscious and covered in bruises. He was taken to the campus infirmary for recovery, the better to keep the matter private, especially as he was discovered to have been drinking in flagrant violation of campus rules against alcohol.

A doctor arrived from Sharpsburg to sew the laceration above his left cheek and diagnosed a concussion. The nurse tended to his bruises and his sprained wrist. All morning Bellerton girls flitted about with concern, and a banner-decorating committee formed to brighten his front door with buntings and cut-out hearts and an enormous bubble-letter sign: WE HOPE YOU HEAL SOON. The Belles drew a cluster of crimson hearts in one corner of his banner before hurriedly moving on.

They had needed to make him understand his behavior was unacceptable. They all agreed they had done what was necessary to protect themselves, and their actions had been a warning of the punishment they would mete out if he—or anyone else—tried anything like it again.

When they saw what they had done, how their rage had been turned into something else, the Belles grew wild with adrenaline. With the poet-professor laid up in the campus infirmary, they crept to his house after curfew, unearthing his key from under a flowerpot, then seeping like floodwater into his ugly little home.

The Belles spread out to dig through his closets and cupboards and bookshelves. Ada May stuck to the kitchen, perching at the Formica table shoved against the wall that was dotted with the grit of a hundred meals. Deena joined her, careful to avoid the broken metal trim whose exposed edge was as sharp as glass, and observed details of the poet-professor's small, boxy home. Cluttered and dirty, the walls bland. Dust gathered on surfaces. The air was speckled with grimy motes.

"It's gross in here," Deena said. "I thought it would be nicer."

"If he spent less time going after us girls, maybe he'd have more time for cleaning," Ada May said with disgust.

Deena had thought a professor's house would be more like the home in which her half sister had grown up: airy and open and grand.

She remembered the morning when Grandmother took her inside the Williams home and ground up the stolen medications into orange juice mixed with liquor, promising the plan was foolproof. Even then, she hadn't fully understood what was about to happen. Or so she told herself.

Later, she wished she'd gone with Grandmother to see her half sister just once, to look at the girl who shared her blood but who was the only one their father claimed. Deena was the mongrel, the cast-off, and she regretted never having the chance to grab her half sister by the arm to say, *This life should never have belonged to you alone.*

It didn't take long for all the pieces to come together. Grandmother had rendered Deena's half sister unconscious by drugging her with the deadly concoction that was intended to kill her. Her strength had caught Grandmother off guard, her body thrashing against death. Even coddled dilettantes could be strong. The aftermath was swift: the medics whisking the unresponsive, catatonic teenager's body away. Mrs. Williams wailing uncontrollably, removed to a hotel where she would remain until the house was sold.

Grandmother's story was at the ready. She came to the house to clean, as usual, and because it was quiet, she thought the whole family was gone, but when she went upstairs, she found the girl in a poorly state.

The doctor labeled it a failed suicide attempt, and that was shame enough for the family. A scandal to contain. But then there was the other matter: that the girl remained alive, though with only her basest functions. To spend her days staring emptily at the world. Deena wondered if that was a fate worse than death—to be alive but not to live.

Grandmother had held no compunction about what she had done. She spoke only of the future.

"It's all yours now, Nee-nee." By then, the cancer was not far from taking her. "He kept you secret from Mrs. Williams all these years, acted like you ain't exist. Well, what's worse than a bastard? A daughter who tried to kill herself. Stains they can't bear. So, I made a deal with him: You become the Williams daughter. You take your half sister's name and her admission to that fancy school. Her monthly allowance, plus a little more. You save the family from scandal. And he saves his own hide. Mrs. Williams thinks you're a charity case, has no idea you're his own." Coughing shook her. Blood flaked her handkerchief when she pulled it from her mouth.

"An eye for an eye, Nee-nee. Folks like them got a debt run up over centuries. And yet they in the hole *and* on top." Grandmother snorted. "Can those who hurt others so bad feel pain? *Real* pain? Pain like yours, like mine. Like your mama's?"

Deena remembered the way her hands moved uncertainly over her half sister's things, dumped from a flour sack onto their kitchen table.

"They're gonna say it's just mean rumors that Deena Williams tried to kill herself. And you is proof that she's alive because from today on, you *are* her. You live her life. Stay clear of the family, and he'll write you a check every month. Got the bank account all ready. Now's your chance. You hear me, girl?" Grandmother tugged hard on Deena's ear. "Make it all yours."

And she had. How readily she had slipped on the exquisite coat of her new life.

The other Belles joined Ada May and Deena in the kitchen, the adventure wearing off. But Deena wasn't quite ready to go. They had punished him, but she wanted more.

She said, "Let's each take something." A further push. A deviation.

Ada May regarded her with surprise. "From his house?"

"He'll never find out unless we want him to."

Ada May's lips parted as if to issue a refusal, but the Belles didn't wait for her words. Quick as mice, they skittered off to make their claims.

Ada May's mask slipped. Beneath her unimpeachable perfection Deena saw fury erupt across her features at how quickly the others had forgotten their obedience to her. How readily they were willing to follow someone other than Ada May. More than ribbons or bruises, Deena was truly on the inside now. She smiled wolfishly.

Ada May grabbed Deena's wrist, dragging her palm down the kitchen table's jagged metal trim. Deena cried out in pain. "Don't be foolish, Deena. Don't behave rashly."

Blood pearled along the cut. Deena's eyes watered, but Ada May was already at the door, calling out, "Ladies!"

The others charged back into the kitchen, showing off their prizes: Fred a forbidden bottle of vodka, Prissy a tie clip. Sheba had tucked rolls of Necco wafers into her pockets. Nell had selected a fragile glass unicorn.

Ada May grabbed a slim leather-bound volume of poetry and commanded, "Let's go."

Deena had wrapped a dishtowel around her palm to staunch the bleeding from her cut and already the blood was soaking through it.

"Deena, are you okay? What happened?" Fred asked.

Ada May's look of reproval was swift, and Fred said nothing more, falling into lockstep as the Belles followed Ada May out the door, clutching the small objects they had filched from another person's life. Stolen curios they would never give back.

◆ ◆ ◆

DEENA'S HAND REQUIRED STITCHES. THE SHARPSBURG DOCTOR had returned the following morning to check on the poet-professor, and he agreed to see Deena as well.

Fred accompanied her to the infirmary first thing, her large, dark eyes widening at the sight of the medical needle and suture. She covered Deena's face with her palms. "Don't watch," she said.

When the doctor was finished, he handed Deena a bottle of medication to numb the pain and the campus nurse wrote an appointment slip for a follow-up in five weeks' time. Deena examined the grotesque black stitches across her left palm as Fred walked her back to South Hall, remembering the X Sheba had painted there the night of their oath all those months ago. Did this mean her ties of belonging had been severed? When they neared the dorm, she shoved her hands behind her back, self-conscious of how the stitches were ugly, as if she was a doll that needed mending.

The Belles took turns hugging her when she got back to their dorm. Sheba petted Deena's hair and Nell clung to her the longest. Ada May was last.

"Get well soon," she said. The sentiment was edged: the words correct, but the delivery was wrong. A chill climbed Deena's spine.

Chapter 30
DEENA

BY THE TIME Deena's hand began to show signs of heal-
ing, it was mid-April. Sunrises lit the clouds pastel, brightness cracking over the mountains. She regularly paused at the window above the
second-floor landing, her breath catching at the mauve sky and the
sanded peaks of the mountains buttressing campus. How had she not
noticed the beauty before? She was exactly where she needed to be; she
had made her grandmother's dream for her a reality. Girls bustled in and
out of the bathroom behind her, but Deena lingered.

"I never want to leave this place." The truest thing she had said since
her arrival at Bellerton, spoken aloud only for herself.

Her thoughts were interrupted by the curious sight of Peggy Don-
ovan striding purposefully across the quad, trailed by two juniors.
South Hall's front door whined open, and they ascended the stairs.
Deena moved to let the group go by, then followed on their heels.
Peggy produced a tiny bell from her pocket, its high treble reminding
Deena of the county bus's shrill breaks while she waited with Grand-
mother on cold mornings. The Belles emerged into the hallway at the
sound.

"We're waiting for one more," Peggy said.

At that moment, Mrs. Tibbert emerged at the top of the stairs, formidable in her somber navy dress. Her attention cut across them, and her mouth puckered. The Belles shifted uncomfortably. Caught half-dressed, their teeth were unbrushed and slippers were still on their feet. Prissy's hair was in curlers, and Nell had a scum of soap streaking her jaw. Only Ada May was put together, dressed in an apple-green blouse with pearl buttons, lips dashed with muted pink lipstick, her cheeks rosy.

Mrs. Tibbert cleared her throat. "Ladies, the time has come for May Queen nominations."

The Belles exploded with excited chatter, and Deena gasped at the thought of Bellerton's most beloved tradition come alive at last.

Mrs. Tibbert curtailed their babble with a silencing gesture. "Names will be tallied and the top three nominees will be voted upon at supper this evening. The most votes determine the winner." The brooch on her shawl caught the light. "I do not need to emphasize how imperative it is that the May Queen reflects Bellerton's values, especially in this all-important centennial year. She will be crowned at a ceremony attended by parents and alumnae. Her name and photo will be added for all posterity into Bellerton's official records. I trust that my Belles will nominate *only* a girl who embraces Bellerton as it is today, yet who carries within her the spirit of Bellerton's past."

Peggy Donovan passed out slips of paper and the girls dashed giddily to their rooms for pencils. Deena rummaged through her desk drawer, her bandaged hand itching. The stitches were nearly ready to come out. Beneath them, Deena could see the puckered scar forming, a reminder of what could happen for stepping out of line.

Fred called from the hallway, urging her to hurry up. Deena smoothed the edges of the blank nomination slip and wrote on it Ada May's name, flashing it openly at the other Belles—Ada May nodded appreciatively—before dropping it into the varnished mahogany box.

It was a shallow show of loyalty. Prissy had already complained that the May Queen was always a senior, but the meaningless nomination was a peace offering after the tension at the poet-professor's house. Deena hoped Ada May would take it as such.

Peggy shook the box with enthusiastic gusto. "See you ladies at supper!" she called, waving as she pounded down the stairs. Mrs. Tibbert followed at a curt pace, but not before her black eyes lingered on Deena's stitched hand and her lips twitched with displeasure.

Deena curtsied and retreated to the sanctuary of her room.

◆ ◆ ◆

THE DINING ROOM THAT EVENING BUZZED WITH GOSSIP AND SPEC-ulation. Bellerton girls arrived in freshly pressed formal gowns, their hair pinned into sweeping updos. The usual mealtime clatter was amplified, food largely untouched. Even Deena, hungry since childhood, could barely eat in their shared excitement. Finally, the dessert course was removed and the waiters departed, making a show of their exit. Mrs. Tibbert, whom Deena hadn't noticed until now, watched from the service doorway at the back of the room, her head swiveling on her neck like a vulture's.

Sheba said, "Now it's only us students." Two juniors locked the doors. A collective breath was drawn, every Bellerton girl taut with anticipation.

A wall light blinked out, dowsing a table of girls in shadows. Satin-clad hands flitted nervously with pearl and ruby and diamond jewelry. Evening in Paris perfume choked the air. Deena nervously played with the seam of her modest dress.

Peggy Donovan glided to the front of the room, elegant in a floor-length black satin gown, bias drapery rippling down her backside. She looked as stunning as Elizabeth Taylor in any photograph, and her radiance was infused with the pleasure of serving as mistress of ceremonies. An entitlement of the senior class president.

Deena took in her own dress, the color of unripe hay, which she had thought looked chic when she bought it in the department store in preparation for Bellerton, its wrongness now apparent. Under her matching evening gloves that concealed her stitches, her hands itched. She wanted to tear them off, try again. Buy a dress like Peggy wore.

Peggy held the moment a beat longer before she flung both hands into the air and declared, "Tonight, the election of the 1952 Bellerton College May Queen officially begins!"

A roar erupted. Girls spilled to their feet, hollering with the intoxication of tradition. Fred pinched her bottom lip and let rip an ear-piercing whistle. Mrs. Tibbert leered from the edges, and although she did nothing to interfere with the ebullient girls, the room seemed to tilt in her direction. Deena dropped dizzily into her chair just as two juniors scuttled forward carrying wax-sealed envelopes. Half the girls sat, and the other half remained standing, and the room was like a teetering, roiling wave.

Peggy tore into the top envelope, smug at the name written on the white card. "Our first nominee is none other than my best friend, Ann Goodchild!"

Ann squealed to her feet. Girls threw their arms around her, smudging their lipstick against her cheek. She glowed beside Peggy, and to Deena it was obvious Ann was the future May Queen.

Peggy slid her gloved finger under the wax seal of the next envelope and lifted the flap. "Our second nominee is Brenda Carter!" Also a senior, Brenda's frizzy hair haloed her small face and made her head appear a smidge too large for her body. She jumped from foot to foot beside Ann, her capering ridiculous in heels and an evening gown. Prissy, always on top of the campus gossip, whispered loud enough for the Belles to hear: "It's a pity nomination after her fiancé dumped her. I hope she has other qualities to recommend her."

Peggy broke the final envelope's seal. "Our third May Queen nominee is—" Her voice faltered. She tossed the envelope aside dismissively, her tone flattened with disapproval. "Ada May Delacourt."

A girl at an adjacent table loudly whispered, "Who?" Deena twisted to look at the other Belles, but they were as startled as she was, heads bobbing with confusion. Ada May rose to her feet, and the room gasped.

"A freshman can't be a nominee!" a senior cried out.

Another declared, "It simply isn't done."

Girls exclaimed about tradition and called Ada May's nomination a ridiculous farce. Despite the girls' commotion, Mrs. Tibbert's expression was smug. She didn't look the least bit surprised, as if she had expected it—or had a hand in making it happen. The thought coated Deena's tongue with a sour taste. If that was true, then Ada May had even more control over Bellerton than she'd realized.

As Ada May wove between the tables to the front of the room, she brushed past Deena, hissing in her ear, "Thank you for your nomination, *Lettie*."

Deena gripped the edges of her chair, lightheaded and clammy, her body going cold. That name, *her* name. How did Ada May find it out?

The seniors banged their fists on their tables. Bellerton's accepted order had been turned upside down, and Deena's world was spinning. Ada May had discovered her secret, and there was no telling what she would do with the truth.

Peggy's mask of polite civility was cracking, and she pointed to Brenda Carter without preamble. "Give your nomination speech."

Deena could hardly pay attention, though Brenda was obviously doomed in the contest; if Deena could tell as much, the girl knew it, too. Sweat streaked the talcum powder she'd dotted across her chest. Her reedy voice rambled unintelligibly, and Peggy didn't bother to intervene when other students began to talk over her.

Ann was next and easily gushed at her own credentials, which included her wedding in two months, her participation in several college clubs, her charity work, her friendship with Peggy and, added as an afterthought, her good grades.

"Not stellar grades though!" a senior quipped. Ann blushed.

Then, it was Ada May's turn. Deena flattened a palm against her chest and forced herself to take deep breaths. Maybe she had misheard, or maybe Ada May had been speaking to another girl who coincidentally shared her name.

Every perfumed breath in the room converged, every gaze was drawn to the freshman nominee. Ada May's copper hair burned against her midnight-blue gown. Large teardrop pearls anchored her ears and drew the eye down to her swelling bosom. Her presence was like a flame, and her speech was simple: She was Bellerton's own creation.

She gestured to William Grayson Dickey's portrait. "The man in this painting is my great-grandfather. So you see, I was forged within our beloved college's heart. I *am* Bellerton."

Necks craned for a better look. Deena didn't need to see it; she had stared at the portrait her first day with the whole year yawning in anticipation before her, worried that she would never fit in. She had long envied Ada May's ability to trace her lineage backward to an auspicious origin, to be able to tap her finger on a starting point a hundred years past and say: *Here is where I begin.* Deena's beginning was Bellerton, but now that Ada May knew she was a fraud, would it also be her ending?

"I am the perfect choice for May Queen." Ada May shimmered gloriously with the gaze of every Bellerton girl upon her. "I promise to uplift our founder's ideals. To do everything in my power to maintain the special sanctity of this place we love. I will ensure every girl here truly belongs at Bellerton."

Deena sensed the mood begin to shift. Ada May was winning over the room. The air grew thick and sweet with awe. Her softness and beauty pulled others in, and Deena saw how girls were desperate for the beacon of her attention. She recognized this desire, understood the longing. She had first felt it on the day Ada May emerged from South Hall into the throbbing heat and shook Deena's hand.

Ada May turned her gaze to the Belles and held them in her icy blue eyes for a long moment before locking onto only Deena. "The world is changing, but that doesn't mean that Bellerton must change with it. You should vote for me because I know what Bellerton is and what Bellerton needs. If a girl who shouldn't be here breeches our threshold, I'll know what to do. I know how to protect our beloved college. How to keep it ours."

Ada May bowed and the room of girls erupted into applause.

Deena sat stunned, unable to move. Had Ada May just threatened her? It didn't matter if the other Belles wanted to protect her. If she was exposed, there was nothing left and nowhere for her to go. Her life would be over.

But Deena had made it this far, and she would show Ada May that she wouldn't cower like a dog. Ada May might hold all the power, but Deena had sharp teeth.

Peggy said, "Time to vote." A smattering of hands went up for Brenda, who flopped despondently into a seat, weeping softly, and Peggy didn't bother hiding her satisfaction. Then she indicated Ada May. "Raise your hand if you'd like to vote for our freshman nominee." Her voice dripped with too much sweetness over the word *freshman*.

The Belles' fingertips speared the air, but Deena balled her fists atop her thighs, refusing to comply. She kept her expression flat. Nell urged her in a low voice not to be foolish, that she was embarrassing them by making a spectacle of herself. Sheba kicked her under the table, and Fred dug an elbow into Deena's side. Prissy gave her a look of caution, one that seemed to say, *Remember what happens when you ask for milk?*

What had Ada May ever done to specifically earn Deena's vote? Loyalty was one thing, but Deena had stumbled upon something more powerful: her refusal to submit.

She folded her hands in her lap. She held her chin higher, determined in her dissent.

Peggy indicated Ann Goodchild. "Now, raise your hand to vote for my best friend as May Queen."

Deena raised her hand. Her palm sweated beneath her glove, and the wait was excruciating. One of the counters was flustered and restarted twice. The longer Deena held her arm in the air, the more exposed she felt. She could not bring herself to look at anyone, Ada May least of all, but she felt the pierce of those frigid blue eyes upon her, witnessing her betrayal.

"Deena, you can still fix this." Prissy pinched her. "For heaven's sake, put your hand down. Tell them you made a mistake."

The room grew stuffy. The oak paneling hardened beneath the lamps' glaring light. Deena's arm began to ache, but she refused to withdraw it. Ada May wielded her authority as if it was a given, not something to be earned. It wouldn't hurt her to be denied something for once in her life.

"Come on, Deena. Stop it," Fred whispered.

The other Belles joined the entreaties. Deena ignored the increasingly desperate and distressed cadence of their voices. She closed her eyes to strengthen her resolve.

Peggy Donovan clapped inelegantly for attention. Her cheeks were flushed, and she fumbled her words. "It seems—" Ann frowned, clearly exasperated, but Ada May was deferential, patient. Deena twisted her dress in her hands, her stomach knotting. The floodwaters in her chest threatened to consume her.

Peggy flicked the top of Ada May's head, a rough yet affectionate gesture, then snatched Ada May's hand and threw it into the air. "I present Miss Ada May Delacourt, your 1952 centennial year May Queen!"

No one moved for a long moment. Then the Belles, without Deena, leapt screaming to their feet and rushed upon Ada May. Ann's supporters gaped with astonishment, Deena among them. It wasn't possible; it couldn't be true. Ann furiously shoved Mrs. Tibbert aside and banged at the dining room doors until one of the juniors hurried to unlock them. Mrs. Tibbert watched her flee, then threw her head back with a cackling laugh at the turn of events.

Deena stumbled to her feet, numbed by Ada May's unexpected victory. If she didn't make amends immediately, there was no telling what would happen to her. How could she have been so stupid as to think she held any power? Ada May's and Bellerton's stories were indivisible, and any threat to her was a direct threat to Bellerton.

Girls grasped for Ada May, desperate for her touch, their fingers grazing her dress. They shoved each other aside to reach her, tripping over the hems of their gowns, feverish with emotion. The new Bellerton hierarchy was about to descend on them all.

Deena withdrew from her clutch the velvet ribbon Ada May had given her—the object that bound them. She tossed her hideous gloves aside and coiled the ribbon around her palm, her stitches prickling and her knuckles raw. She pushed through the undulating, frantic bodies and made her way toward Ada May, the glowing, dewy mirage at the center of the frenzied horde of girls. The four other Belles protectively shielded her from anyone who came too close.

Ada May dismissed them with a flick of her hand. They refused to acknowledge Deena as they withdrew, having already cast her out. But she would claw her way back into their good graces. She had no choice.

Deena had once believed that the highest wall to climb was that of entering Bellerton itself, but it was Bellerton that had showed her how foolish she had been. The wall was never scaled; the summit was never reached. There was no end of having to prove herself. Ada May had every opportunity available to her and still, she felt the need to exclude others. The only thing left for Deena now was to apologize.

She sunk to her knees before the May Queen.

Ada May, the others: They had forgiven Prissy her failure when she had asked for more milk. They had forgiven Sheba's quip about the missing yearbook, and even moved past Nell's thieving. Despite their disgraces, each girl was brought back into the fold, and Deena believed they would do the same for her. Surely, she would be forgiven. She was forever a Belle.

Ada May stroked Deena's hair.

"Ada May, I—"

Deena could not say she was sorry for voting against her because she wasn't—she had only miscalculated Ada May's ability to win. In her hesitation, a pall dangled over them. She touched Ada May's cheek and whispered, "I love you." Her throat tightened, choked by the familiar smell of Ada May's lavender perfume. "I love you, Ada May."

It was truthful, though it was a complicated love.

Ada May bent down as if for a kiss; she pinched Deena's chin and squeezed.

Deena's eyes watered. Ada May's fingertips clamped her jaw, and Deena told herself she didn't mean to be so rough. Ada May didn't mean to hurt her. She bent forward until they were level, her lips at Deena's ear, sharp with a warning.

"How dare you," Ada May snarled. "You of all people. I know all about you." Ada May's grip on Deena's chin tightened. "I know who you really are."

Deena could barely get her words out. "You have no idea what it's like. Please, I'm sorry."

Ada May flung Deena's chin from her grasp and was swept away into the crowd before Deena could grab hold of her. She stumbled back, cast out from the circle of adoring girls. A chasm had opened between them.

Sheba climbed onto a chair, towering above the girls who clamored for Ada May's attention. "We love you, Ada May." Fred jumped beside her and whistled.

Nell pulled herself onto the table, shouting, "Ada May, forever! Three cheers for Ada May!"

The declaration spread like the sparks of a wildfire and soon the room was aflame with cries of adulation. Girls kicked off their heels and clambered onto the tables, shucking the linen tablecloths aside to pound the tops with their stocking feet. Ada May opened her arms to receive the feverish exaltations.

Deena loved Ada May, she did, she did! She hollered the words, but her voice was lost in the crush of a hundred other voices, the mob of girls sing-shouting their adoration. A flash of movement caught Deena's eye and she turned her head just as Mrs. Tibbert slipped from the crowd.

Not a single Bellerton girl noticed. The chanting cohered into a melody that made the room quiver.

"Oh, Ada May, we love you.
Ada May, oh yes we do.

Oh, Ada May, our love is true (so true!)
Ada May, how we love you."

An ache crept along Deena's jaw where Ada May's fingers had latched. She had fought to make it this far, and she would fight to stay.

Deena bowed before the May Queen.

Chapter 31

DEENA

THE next day, Deena was delirious with illness: vomiting and sweats accompanied by a fever that left her quaking. Fred checked on her after she failed to appear at breakfast, but it was Ada May who took over the ministrations, tucking Deena beneath Grandmother's quilt and laying a damp cloth across Deena's forehead in the gauzy haze of her room, where the curtains were drawn against the April light.

On the second day of her illness, Ada May stayed with her between classes. Deena tracked her comings and goings loosely, awakened by the clatter of voices in the hallway each time she entered or left. She woke once to see the Belles crowded around the foot of her bed, faces crumpled with concern; she was woken later by scratching that she took to be varmint. She opened her eyes to find Ada May shuffling through her papers and going through her desk.

"What are you doing?" Her voice was weak but Ada May froze, her back stiffening. She pivoted to Deena's side, her expression careful, her soft hands upon Deena's forehead testing for fever. The floral scent of her hand cream was overpowering and Deena coughed. Ada May left the room and reappeared several minutes later, carrying a tray with a bowl of broth that she spoon-fed to Deena.

"Were you going through my things?" Deena asked when the bowl was nearly emptied, and the broth had cooled to room temperature. Ada May brought another spoonful to her mouth, but Deena turned her face away in refusal.

"You need to eat. It will get your strength back up."

When Deena still refused, Ada May left with the tray and bowl. Deena dropped her head against her pillow, her body weak and her mind fogged.

She woke next to the clang of the chapel bells signaling ten o'clock and by the stirring light determined she had slept past the afternoon, evening, and into the next morning. Her mouth was cottony, and a headache throbbed at her temples. Her stitches itched. She sat up, startled to find Ada May in her desk chair, bent over a pile of embroidery in her lap. She hummed a tune Deena didn't recognize, and her hand moved in swift, assured strokes across the pillowcase she was stitching with a floral motif. Her emerald ring flashed. Without looking up, Ada May said, "The Junior League is collecting items for the destitute."

"Can I have water?" Deena dangled her legs over the side of the bed, relishing the cool air hitting her skin. A stab of headache pierced her skull, and Deena jabbed her thumbs to her temples, hoping to stave off the worst of it. "Ada May, please. Water."

"No one's blaming you." Ada May put aside her embroidery. She swung Deena's legs back onto the bed and tucked her beneath the quilt like a child, then brushed a stray hair from Deena's face. The unadorned walls stared ferociously. "I took pity on you. But charity only goes so far." She pressed a small object into Deena's palm. It was a glass bead painted with her true initials. The one in her lost, cracked jar.

Panic seized her. She had gambled, and she had lost. The shape of things was irrefutable. The tiny glass bead proved it. If Ada May knew Deena's name, what else might she know about her past?

Ada May laid a cool, damp cloth on Deena's forehead. "You're still running a slight fever." Deena tried to sit up again, but Ada May pushed her back down. "Let me tell you another Bellerton story to take your mind off things."

Her dry, itching throat was painful now.

A wavering silhouette shimmered on the other side of the bed, resolving faintly into Mary, who reached for Deena's hand and held it in her own. Her touch was warm.

A hacking cough overtook her, squeezed her eyes shut with tears. When the cough subsided and Deena looked around, her room had changed.

Gone were the dresser and bulletin board that hung above it, replaced by a large cabinet with two doors. Her bed was draped in a gray wool blanket she'd never seen before, and she was alone, with no sign of either Mary or Ada May.

Deena crossed the room and opened the cabinet, the glass bead with her initials tucked in her palm. Various garments—petticoats and the like—were folded and tucked on evenly spaced shelves. Heavy wool and crinoline dresses hung from pegboard to the right of the cabinet. She turned back to the bed, where a wooden trunk with metal clasps sat at the foot. A small, round table stood under the window where her desk was supposed to be. A hand mirror and a thick-bristled hairbrush lay atop the table; beside them was Mary's diary.

The diary's leather binding shone richly in the light pulsing through the window. The pages were crisp, the ink fresh. She reached for it but stopped at the sounds of footsteps in the hallway. The room's door flew wide, and Mary entered along with two other girls, the three of them laughing. None of them noticed her. It was as if she was invisible—or a ghost.

Mary sat while the others flittered around her, brushing and pinning her hair. Deena was struck by her beauty. She smiled often, concealing it shyly behind her hand. She had never seen Mary smile before.

"Clara, tomorrow we'll go for that hike," Mary was saying. "The fresh air will do us good." She tugged playfully on the other girl's skirt. "Jane, you're coming, too."

Clarity shot through Deena—her room and Mary's room were one and the same. She backed away from the trio, knocking into the small table. The diary thudded to the floor. The girls' chatter abruptly ceased, and they stared at the fallen book in silence. Still, none of them noticed her.

The diary lay open on the floor. On the left-hand page, Deena saw the haunting entry Mary had written ending with *I am in danger*.

Mary snatched the diary from the floor and snapped it shut. "I must have set it too close to the table's edge," she said, stashing it under her pillow, just as Deena had once done with her glass jar. She gestured for her friends to continue pinning her hair.

"I can't fathom why I've been invited to the president's house for supper. As Lydia has reminded me more than once, I'm a mere shopkeeper's daughter, after all."

"You must tell us everything," Clara said giddily.

"You'll bring up the burden of the new fees?" Jane asked.

Mary squeezed Jane's hand. "Of course. Perhaps motherhood will have softened Ada, and she can be persuaded towards generosity."

Clara said, "At the very least, the meal will be a welcome change from the food we have been served of late."

Mary sighed, moving toward her wardrobe. "What do you think of this dress for the evening?" Clara and Jane nodded appreciatively.

Deena remembered the night in the drawing room when Ada May had told the story of the poisoned travelers. Mary's sudden invitation to join supper at the president's house, the incriminating final entry of her diary—it all made sense. Mary hadn't been sick in the head, and she hadn't harmed herself. Her paranoia had been real.

Mary had been poisoned.

Deena wanted to warn her somehow, but it was too late. She was suddenly outside and, up ahead, Mary was walking quickly toward the president's house. The mountain laurel hadn't been planted yet, and the hill was a barren, grassy field. Behind her, the trees on the quad were smaller; the buildings fewer. It was nearing sunset, and the mountains Deena loved looked taller, their peaks blocking the horizon like sentinels.

Deena called out for Mary to stop. There was a brief hitch in Mary's step as if she had heard, but she raised her hand to the door and knocked anyway. Above it was a metal decoration of two serpents, the same one Deena had seen during the campus tour. The door opened, and Mary was admitted inside.

Deena was desperate to intervene and raced indoors, still wearing the same nightgown she'd put on when she had fallen feverish and ill. A table had been lavishly set with dishes. The Gannon sisters were on one side. Opposite was Lydia Booth with Mary sitting beside her. At the head of the table, unmistakable with her copper hair and piercing blue eyes, was Ada May's great-grandmother, the woman who had become synonymous with Bellerton.

To her horror, Deena saw that the meal had already been served, and Mary had eaten most of the food on her plate. Mary reached for a half-full glass of red wine that Lydia topped off with a bottle set apart from the others, its neck tied with a ribbon. Deena lurched forward to knock it out of her hands, but there was nothing she could do.

Mary's mouth began to foam. Her hands shook, and she tumbled sideways from her seat, collapsing into a heap on the floor. Ada May's great-grandmother didn't break her conversation, continuing to talk to the Gannon sisters as if nothing had happened. Eventually, Lydia knelt beside Mary's unmoving form and felt along her neck for a pulse. "It's finished," she declared. She stood and brushed her hands off on her dress. The quartet each grabbed one of Mary's limbs and dragged her outside, where a man with a horse and cart was already waiting.

Money was exchanged. The women went back inside.

Deena still didn't understand *why*. What had Mary ever done?

"It isn't what she did, it's who she was," a voice behind her said.

Deena turned to find Ada Augustine Jackson standing in the doorway looking directly at her.

"Or, rather, who she was *not*," Ada clarified. "We have certain values, and not every girl is worthy. We must protect our ideals, and that means being selective on who should be allowed to attend. The natural order of things must be enforced." She reached out and brushed Deena's hair behind her ear, her eyes hard like flint. "I see so many similarities between you and her."

Deena pushed Ada's hand away and shook her head, disbelieving. She had thought the stories Ada May had told about her ancestors were only exaggerations, even playful macabre. Now that she had witnessed the stories, she understood that Bellerton was wicked. She saw how those origins breathed inside the grounds one hundred years on. History had wrapped around her like a shroud, and she felt as if she was being buried alive.

The old nursery rhyme crept onto Deena's tongue.

"Mary, Mary, quite contrary, how does your garden grow?"

And then the brick house was gone, and Deena was back in her Bellerton dorm room beneath her own quilt with Ada May at her bedside, a hand pressed to Deena's mouth, silencing her. "We'll have none of that now."

"I'm so thirsty," Deena said when Ada May removed her hand. Her body ached all over, as if she had fallen from a great height.

"Come," Ada May coaxed, dipping a cotton swab into a cup and rubbing it against Deena's clenched lips. "You'll feel better. It must be so exhausting to live the life of two people."

Deena was terrified to drink or eat Ada May's offerings. For months, Mary had been trying to warn her about the Bellerton girls who had disappeared, but Deena hadn't understood. And now that Ada May knew she didn't truly belong at Bellerton, what would happen to her?

Ada May forced apart Deena's lips with her pinky and raised the cup, liquid spilling onto Deena's nightgown and Grandmother's quilt, flooding her parched throat. It felt like relief.

Deena's eyelids immediately went heavy. As she sank into snarling blackness, she had a vision of Ada May as May Queen, a crown of green boughs laced with white ribbon upon her head.

She gripped her glass bead tighter, unsure if she would ever awake.

Chapter 32
DEENA

IT took several more days, but Deena at last recovered from her curious illness. Although she had been nursed back to health, she was convinced Ada May had also made her sick with the broth she was spoon-fed—punishment for rebelling and voting against her. Deena had learned her lesson. She would follow the group.

She resumed dining with the others and walked with them as usual to class, but the Belles otherwise kept their distance from her, a contagion in their midst, excluding her from everything else: painting fingernails in Prissy's room or joining meandering walks to the stables. They gave her a wide berth, and their talk froze when she entered a room. Deena understood that after a transgression as severe as hers, it would take time to be fully welcomed again.

Then, May arrived with a splash of birdsong. Deena was shocked by the bright spring flowers, the colors seeming to throb with intensity. The sun's rays warmed her, and after so many days spent sick in bed, she felt that despite the Belles' reticence, the world was being rightened.

The centennial and May Queen crowning drew nearer. The Belles had to be careful now. They couldn't risk bruises or scratches or cuts, not when all the eyes of Bellerton would be upon them at the ceremony, Ada May in particular.

They decided, without Deena present, to break curfew a final time before year's end. They would take the horses for a night ride. Deena learned of their plans at supper and accepted the news with both hope and hurt. They hadn't included her in the discussion, but at least she was invited to join in. And although she was nervous about riding for the first time, especially at night, she didn't raise any objections. Things were slowly inching back to normal.

The May air was unusually chilly when they snuck out that night. The evening sky was blank: no guiding moon, no teasing stars. Deena wore a sweater and her coat for warmth, sprinting after the others to the stables, the ripe hay tickling her nose. She sneezed several times in a row, then stood by anxiously while the Belles saddled the horses, the animals brandishing the dirt into shining ruts. Each girl would take her own, and the others would ride pillion. Sheba commanded Beauregard with Fred. Prissy mounted her black-and-white Appaloosa Dixie and let Nell take Dallas. That left Deena to ride Brutus with Ada May.

Brutus's yellow eyes blinked, and his black gums slid across his teeth. Deena backed away, shaking from cold or maybe fear. She was wary of these beasts that were larger and taller than any person, creatures of indecipherable wills.

The Belles stared down impatiently from atop their horses.

"Are you all right?" Fred asked.

"She looks sick," Nell said.

"Don't make us wait all evening." Sheba trotted past her. Beauregard blubbered in agreement.

Deena swallowed, her voice small. "I'm scared."

"I thought you were a champion equestrian," Prissy stated flatly. "At least, that's what my cousin Esther told me about you. She's always been jealous of strong riders. She's not very good."

Deena shoved her hands behind her back. "That wasn't me." Her cheeks grew hot as she struggled to cover her tracks. "I mean, I *did* win those championships, but that was a long time ago. What I meant to say was, I'm scared because I don't know how to ride *these* horses."

As if they sensed her lie, the horses stamped and tugged at their bits, urging the girls onward. She felt as if she was standing on quicksand.

"I'll stay here and keep watch," she offered, though she saw immediately that this was impossible; if she didn't go, none of them would go. Deena wanted Ada May to provide consolation or reprieve but was given nothing. The girl she used to be clawed up her back. Her renewed sense of belonging was slipping away.

"Or maybe—" She hesitated. The Belles leaned forward in anticipation. "Maybe it won't be too hard to learn. Again." She tacked on the last word as a quick afterthought to reassert that she was Deena Williams, former champion equestrian and confident rider.

She trailed the others outside, swallowing large gulps of air. How difficult could riding be? She didn't think they could go far, not at night and without risking getting caught.

Ada May instructed her to place a palm on Brutus's side. "Feel him breathing? See how calm he is."

But he bucked you, Deena didn't say. She inhaled in tandem with Brutus. The warmth of his body steadied her.

She climbed the mounting block and clung like a barnacle to Ada May's back. Her left hand with the nearly healed cut was aching. Ada May crooked her pinky finger and hooked it with Deena's. She whispered, "Belles never tell." It was girlishly conspiratorial until Deena considered how much it suited Bellerton. Maybe Ada May hadn't revealed her secret to the others after all. Deena felt herself relax, just a little.

The horses trotted single file through the pastures, and though the riding was smooth, she held tightly to Ada May, terrified of slipping sideways and tumbling from Brutus's back. At the woods' edge, a figure emerged.

"Someone's there," Deena said.

Prissy marched Dixie fearlessly along the line of trees. "There's no one," she declared.

Deena pressed her cheek to Ada May's cloak, convinced of what she saw. It was then that a decision coursed through the group, the suggestion hovering between them. Shouldn't they take the evening further, claim it as their own?

But did they dare?

The collective response was: *We dare. Yes, we dare it. Let's go into the woods.*

"But it's night." Deena's voice was shrill. She felt the rippling strength of Brutus's muscles, his aching to run wild.

The Belles said: *You are one of us, aren't you? Bound to us, united with us?*

Deena could have chosen then to dismount. But she stayed, riding with the back of the saddle digging into her pelvis as she held tight to Ada May. She wanted that much to prove she belonged.

Then, they were off! Hair whipped their faces and necks. The girls screeched joyfully. The horses crashed through the brush, Deena and Ada May in the lead, Brutus confident beneath Ada May's steady hand and her coos of affection. Gray mist revealed the ground three or four feet at a time. Brutus kicked up clods of dirt and huffed in the unsullied air. Deena buried her face in Ada May's back, dizzied by the ground running far below. He was just a horse, she reminded herself. The solidity of the earth was all the surety he needed.

The woods blurred, and branches clawed at the girls' hair, their coats, their tender peach flesh. Prissy yodeled—half wail, half merry song—a deranged sound that scrambled between the black trunks. Nell whooped jubilantly. Sheba screamed, "Olly olly oxen free!" as she and Fred rode through mist thick as haints, her heels hot irons in Beauregard's side.

Then, Prissy's jubilee twisted into a frightened yip, and Deena craned her head in time to see a tree's greedy fingers batter her face. Deena squeezed Ada May's waist tighter. Shouldn't they slow, check that Prissy wasn't hurt? There was no stopping, her gut said, there was only what lay ahead. When Deena swiveled her head again, Prissy looked fine.

"We should slow down," Deena found the courage to say, but maybe she didn't say it, because Ada May gave no response. The green-stoned ring on her hand winked at Deena.

Without breaking momentum, the girls decided on a spirited game of tag on horseback. Hands flicked outward as their horses crashed side by side through the woods, the girls snarling with glee.

A hand hit Deena's shoulder, and Prissy peeled Dixie away. Nell gnashed her teeth. *Tag, you're it.*

Deena sensed a fracturing that she couldn't name, and beneath her coat, her skin broke with sweat. The ground rolled under Brutus's stomping hooves. Deena thought she heard voices at her back shaping two words: *Get Deena.*

Sheba launched Beauregard forward until he was galloping in pace with Brutus. Fred shoved Deena's shoulder, and Sheba snatched at her hair, her hand snagging loose Deena's ribbon. Deena flung a hand up to catch it, the only real gift she had ever received. Her balance teetered, then righted.

"That's for stealing my room!" Sheba shouted.

Ada May nudged Brutus away—directly into Prissy's path.

Dixie neighed and kicked. He was a powerful, pugnacious horse. He nipped at Brutus's flank, while Prissy clawed at Deena's face. "That's for being a liar!"

Deena cried out, teary with pain.

Nell rode up on the other side and leaned close, her expression mutant-like with fury. "I thought you were my friend!" she yelled. "Friend! And you told everyone my secret!"

Ada May kicked her legs at Brutus's side and he surged forward, galloping over fallen logs and driving them deeper into the unknown. The saddle dug into Deena's thighs. Brutus's nostrils flared. His actions seemed to say, *I know your secrets. I know the sins that you hide.*

Deena wheeled around to take in the others, who were now far behind; their horses were fast, but Brutus was faster.

The earth rose and humped. The trees grew arms. Deena's hair flared behind her, and she squeezed Ada May's cloak, her balance sliding. She righted herself while Ada May reached back to tenderly pat her leg. The reassurance emboldened her, and Deena was swept into laughter. The others couldn't hurt her, not when she had Ada May on her side.

A small clearing opened in the trees, and in that moment Deena's face hovered like a moon: potent, striking. Then, the ground swelled and the clearing evaporated. A branch snagged her hair, grabbed her loose ribbon in its spindly fingertips. Her balance tipped. Deena shrieked, though whether in joy or in pain, the Belles would never know.

◆ ◆ ◆

AND THEN—IT WAS OVER. DEENA LAY CRUMPLED IN THE DIRT, neck snapped at an unnatural angle, spine twisted. Her ribbon dangled from a branch, its long tongue silenced. The Belles circled around. Deena's body lay crooked in the loam like a cleaning woman's rag wrung tight, then left to dry.

Chapter 33

THE BELLES

LATER, the girls would tell themselves that Deena had made the choice to mount the steed. To balance on his back with her fears wrapped in her fists. To ride with them into the dark. And though they coached her on how to stay balanced and how to move in concert with the body of another living thing; though they taught her how to be a passenger, how to navigate in synchronicity with the narrow, twisting woods; though they told her to hold tight to Ada May and not let go; and though they instructed her to watch that her clothes not tangle with a branch—it was her choice to ascend the mounting block and swing her legs astride Brutus's back. It was her choice to lie about who she had been and what she knew—or didn't.

They were only playing a game.

Deena had made her choice.

Chapter 34
MRS. TIBBERT

MORNING arrived unchanged. While the girls slept and the staff went about their duties, the milkman's truck puttered happily along the black ribbon road to stop first at Dr. and Mrs. Tibbert's house before doubling back to where the professors lived, bottles rattling in their cages.

Mrs. Tibbert's ears turned at the truck's rumble. She waited for Edith to bring her grits and orange juice to the table. Though it was only six, the day already tasted wrong, like salt when one had reached for sugar. When the phone rang shortly after ten o'clock, she knew she was about to be proven correct. On the other end was one of the housemothers, wailing: a girl had gone missing.

Mrs. Tibbert shot like a cannonball to South Hall, but the Belles swore they had no idea where Deena could be. She knew they were lying and was furious at them for their ill timing, with the May Queen ceremony and centennial kickoff a week away.

It was after she informed her husband of the situation, then sat stiffly in his office like a caged animal while he telephoned the girl's parents, that good fortune found them at last.

Mr. Williams confessed: His daughter Deena Williams had elected not to attend Bellerton after all, but since he had already paid tuition he saw an opportunity to do a good deed and took pity upon the granddaughter of a former maid, offering to let her go in his daughter's stead. Over the phone wires, Mr. Williams did not apologize, nor did he explain further. In any case, his daughter was in perfect health at home. The college did not need to involve him further in the situation.

Mrs. Tibbert did not believe this was the full story. It was too certain, the polish upon it was too thick. Though what a relief that this prominent man's daughter was safe and sound, and that the missing girl was a maid's daughter—a nobody. The college would have to inform the police, naturally, but a larger scandal had been narrowly avoided. Bellerton could move forward with the centennial celebrations and crown the May Queen unblemished. Tradition was a force that could not be stopped.

As soon as the police opened their investigation, responsibility was lifted from Bellerton's shoulders. A thorough search of the missing girl's room turned up nothing other than that she was a fake and a fraud. When Mrs. Tibbert was questioned, she posited a theory: mightn't such a charlatan simply have fled with the intention of reappearing elsewhere under yet another name?

The college's sanctum had cracked but was not broken. While the white-throated sparrows' high, clear notes rang out, Mrs. Tibbert scrubbed the girl from the school records, taking pleasure in erasing all traces of her and thinking of how Bellerton took care of itself.

The night before the girl went missing, Mrs. Tibbert had watched from her window as four horses and six riders cantered across the pasture and entered the woods. Later, when dawn was approaching and restlessness compelled her to the bedroom window, she saw four horses cross the quad at a solemn cadence. Four horses, five riders with heads bowed. One fewer girl returning than had gone out.

And that's when she knew everything would be fine—better than before—because the Belles did what had needed to be done.

Chapter 35

ADA MAY

A DRAFT skittered across Ada May's skin, waking her; the window in her dorm room was ajar. She rocked her weight uneasily against the sill, not remembering having opened it.

Even with the window now closed, an unnatural cold gripped the room and dug into her bones. Her curlers clacked like teeth. A reflection shimmered in the glass, and she turned unthinkingly toward it.

Deena stood barefoot, the rug discoloring with wet. Ada May wanted to ask, *Why are you here?* but the words that bubbled forth were, "Where are your shoes?"

Deena's fingers curled like birch bark against her coat, and she smelled of damp earth. She opened her hand, and a ribbon snaked down.

Ada May's mind flashed to how she had torn Deena's ribbon from a branch with her gloved hand, then stuffed it into Deena's coat pocket while her broken body lay upon the ground. The necessary thing was done.

It had been a week since then. Tongues across campus wagged with wild speculations, but the Belles kept to themselves, attentive only to the coming May Queen crowning. Deena had not been found. To everyone except the five Belles, she appeared to have simply vanished.

Ada May said, "The trees—the night. It wasn't my fault you had never been riding."

Deena noiselessly trod in place, the rug matted beneath her feet. Her hands clenched, then released; her eyes were twin black holes.

She had suspected from their first meeting that Deena was hiding something: failing to tip the porter, ordering from the Sears catalog. When Ada May had searched Deena's room that fall, the only meaningful thing she'd found was the cracked glass jar. She had dug through its junk contents, searching for the one revelatory item that might tell her who Deena was, but came up empty—except for the glass bead inscribed with the initials LJS. It wasn't enough, but it was a start.

Prissy had planted further seeds of doubt, which Deena fed with her inadequate responses to Prissy's questions. But Ada May needed more evidence and by March she was growing impatient. Mrs. Tibbert refused to give her Deena's file, the old witch, but she managed to take it anyway when the president's secretary wasn't looking. The high school principal's recommendation letter described Deena as a gregarious girl who was popular among her peers. Her grades were listed as rather good—alongside home economics and several science classes, she had taken four years of Latin—and her hobbies were listed as equestrian sports and bridge. None of it resembled Deena. Ada May wrote down the telephone number in the file but thought better of calling it. If she was wrong, word might get back to Mrs. Tibbert.

Then, the final piece clicked into place. As they were leaving class one afternoon shortly before the May Queen nominations, a photograph fluttered from Deena's textbook. Ada May snatched it up before she noticed. Later in her room, she pulled it out and examined the black-and-white image of two people. One was an elderly woman and the other was Deena. She turned it over. Scribbled in pencil on the back: "Lettie + Grandmother."

It told her everything that she had been waiting for.

Ada May knew what it meant to remake oneself. The Delacourt name was her father's. She was descended from women whose identities were subsumed by their husbands, an erasure that became protection. Marriage was its own form of deceit. As were manners, smiles, and pearls. A name could be bought, altered, created. A clever woman could have as many lives as a cat. But what she didn't know was how the girl who passed as Deena Evangeline Williams had wormed into the heart of their home.

"I took your glass jar," Ada May admitted. Her breath was visible in the room's chill, and she rubbed her arms for warmth. "I had to find out the truth."

If Deena had only been honest with them at the start about who she was, instead of tossing off her past so thoroughly, they would have protected her secret. She could have admitted her lies at any point, yet she had refused to come clean. Deena had betrayed their pact by refusing to show her true self.

"You lied to us. We don't even know who you really are." Ada May would forever claim this single truth. "You could be anyone. Anyone at all."

If Deena could slip into Bellerton undetected and conceal it for months, what would prevent others from doing the same? What loomed in the future if anyone could ascend unnoticed? Ada May could not allow dishonor to come to her great-grandmother's ambitions. She had to protect Bellerton's legacy. Preserve her family's heritage. There was no room for forgiveness once the depth of Deena's deceit and betrayal were known.

The creek was wide and deep and muddy. Pure water that had cured ailments in her great-grandmother's time was, in the mid-twentieth century, opaque with silt. The Belles had weighted Deena's pockets and shoes with stones, tied her hair with pebbles. Ada May knotted Deena's velvet ribbon around her neck, a final reminder that she could have been a Belle forever. A body, it occurred to her as the girls moved with solemn purpose, was not such a difficult thing to conceal.

Nell insisted they pray, so they entwined hands while she recited a psalm, though Ada May couldn't name the one. The cold ached in her lungs as they took turns tossing handfuls of dirt onto Deena's body and Nell kept up her litany. Then they heaved her into the murky water. A plume of sediment burbled; she slipped beneath the surface and was gone.

In South Hall, in Ada May's room, the radiator clanged, echoed by a low rumble that resounded from the belly of the building. The water dripping from Deena onto the rug grasped for Ada May's toes. "I knew right away that you didn't belong. You were like a stray cat wandering into our midst. I felt sorry for you at first, but eventually your true colors seeped out. When you betrayed me—when you betrayed the Belles—I knew you could never be one of us."

Ada May felt relief saying aloud the thing she had always known. Nausea danced in her throat, and her knees buckled. Her hands squished the damp rug. Water climbed up her nightgown, tugging at it like tiny pinchers. Her shoulders heaved and she vomited frigid, dirty creek water. She coughed up a strand of moss that was slick as a string of hair.

The first clear notes of morning birdsong drifted inside. Deena wrapped Ada May's hair around her hand, roughly tugging. Ada May saw a flash of scissor blades and recalled the seniors' mutilated doll all those months ago. Her breath caught, but she had decided never to behave like a coward. Her beautiful copper hair dripped from between Deena's fingers like blood.

She bowed her head and waited for the blades to come down.

Chapter 36

THE MAY QUEEN

SUNLIGHT rippled over the quad. The clouds opened to a blue sky, and a hum of anticipation moved with the breeze.

The May Queen watched from the shadows of South Hall as the faculty ambled between rows of chairs, slapping one another's back with congratulations on another year complete. Two photographers scurried like ants, camera bulbs popping. May, she thought, was the season of hope and good things, embodied in her name. May meant promises delivered.

A breeze snapped around her before dying.

The smell of gardenia and lavender filled the foyer. South Hall's air was dense, the thermometer climbing the numbers. The white columns reflected the day's brightness. Bellerton gleamed.

Ada May felt the girls' pride, heard their swelling admiration whenever her chin-length hair sparked like flint in the sunlight. She had told no one about Deena's ghost, claimed only that she was ready for a change. Mrs. Tibbert had slapped her, then drove her to a salon in town to shape the ghastly remains of her copper hair.

Her fingers absently tapped the velvet ribbon circling her throat, snug as a second skin. Her gown rustled. The white satin fabric was stiff, embroidered with delicate lace and glass beading, and the floor-length skirt was girded with tulle, a train pooling at her feet. Her porcelain breasts heaved above the neckline with each inhale.

"You're so beautiful," Nell whispered. Her voice was bound with religious-like awe, and a wreath of green boughs woven with lilies and trillium sat on her head.

Ada May said, "I believe it's almost time."

The alumnae, ice tinkling in their glasses, began to take their seats. Families gathered: fathers in linen and seersucker suits, mothers in crisp cottons. The poet-professor sneezed, his nose damp with allergies and perfumes. President Tibbert dabbed at his forehead, and Mrs. Tibbert sat erect beside him. To an outsider, it might seem that order had been restored.

High in the trees, a blue jay's shrill call pierced the day. Soon, a second blue jay parried with the first. White blossoms drifted to rest on the lawn. Then, the high coronet notes of VMI's brass band rose to fill the quad, and Bellerton's choral society members swayed in their bluebell gowns. Ada May felt a flurry of movement behind her as the Belles readied themselves and the ceremony commenced with the lift of a lone soprano.

Rise up fair one, and come away.

The other sopranos linked their high, floating voices.

Rise up, rise up, and come away.

The altos' low harmonies hovered beneath the melody.

For, lo, the winter is past
The rain is over and gone.
Flowers appear on the earth.

The season of singing is come
And a cooing of doves is heard in the land.

Beyond the gathered crowd, a girl moved in half-shadow, a smudge against the unspoiled day. A flash of annoyance overtook Ada May. Students were supposed to be seated by now, and this girl was refusing to comply. Ada May squinted, hoping for a better look, and the girl stepped into the sunlight. She gasped and the Belles moved closer, checking that she was all right.

The girl was Deena, unmistakable in the thin coat that always left her shivering.

Ada May brushed them off. "I'm fine. Just nerves, that's all."

Then, a second girl snagged her attention, drawing up beside Deena to hold her hand, and together they stood eerily motionless. She was dressed in a black cloak, and her dark curls spilled around her shoulders. Ada May had seen this other girl before. A moment passed as she tried to recall, then the face clicked. It was the girl who had wandered onto the path that day when Brutus bucked and flung her to the ground, injuring her.

On either side of Deena and the mysterious girl, a line of figures flickered into view along the back of the crowd. A chain of girls locked arms, their eyes hollowed and expressions grim. Girls whose lives had ended at Bellerton over the last century.

Ada May's breath caught. What were they doing here, on this day of all days? She rubbed her hands, felt their nakedness. Something was wrong. She flexed her fingers, calculating. The girls at the quad's edge rippled menacingly.

She turned to the others. "My ring. I can't do the ceremony without it."

There was a moment of hesitation, a fluster of anxiety. The ceremony was already underway, and the procession was about to begin.

"Dammit, I'll go," Prissy muttered. She broke from the group and flew upstairs, her satin heels clomping while the others waited breathless with Ada May in the foyer. But Ada May was decided. She would not go forward without the family ring on her finger. She had the idea it would protect her from any harm Deena and the other ghost girls intended.

Prissy returned harried and dropped the ring into Ada May's hand, pearls of sweat dotting her hairline. Ada May brushed her lips to Prissy's cheek in gratitude, then slipped the ring on her finger. She willed the large stone to bring her safety and good fortune.

The procession began, and the Belles jostled past into the sunlight, buoyed by the choral society's harmonies that swelled into a crescendo.

> *The fig tree puts forth her green sprigs*
> *The tender grape vines spread their ripe smell*
> *Fair one, come to us.*
> *Show thy beautiful face.*

One by one, the voices winked out until only the soloist remained, and her final high notes graced the air.

> *Arise, arise, arise! And show thy lovely face.*

The crowd stood in a hush of anticipation. Ada May pulled back her shoulders and lifted her chin. She was about to become part of a history that stretched backward and forward in time, one that would bind her forever to this place. She felt a tremor from the weight of legacy and her fear at the ghosts watching; then, throwing aside every doubt, she emerged into the piercing sunlight. This was her day; this was her crown to take.

She descended onto the platform that had been erected before South Hall and settled onto her wicker throne that was threaded with white gardenias. Her court bowed, then kissed her hand. Ada May anointed them with a brush of her fingers, radiating perfect grace. She felt holy.

Fred and Sheba lifted an embroidered pillow, a crown of white roses nestled upon it. Ada May knelt upon the satin cushion Nell placed before her throne and bowed her head.

"We love you," Sheba said, placing the crown upon Ada May's head. "You are May Queen, today and forever."

And so, she was. The role she was always meant to fill.

She stood, hand raised in greeting to the gathered crowd. Applause erupted. The brass band played.

Ada May took a breath inside the pristine moment, her cheeks pink with joy. Then, at her nod, the VMI cadets hoisted her throne onto their shoulders and carried her away into the startling brightness of the afternoon.

Chapter 37
NELL

June 2002

THE ribbons did it, Nell would later conclude. They began wearing ribbons, vain and foolish things, lingering too long before their mirrors so that they didn't see the danger coming. The ribbons remade them. They shouldn't have stepped so far out of bounds. They shouldn't have thought themselves above the rules. The ribbons had been the start to all that vanity.

When the call came, as she had long feared it might, Nell was pushing a wooden spoon through batter for five cakes, her arms aching with the effort. The cakes were due in the morning for a church fundraiser, a favor to the new pastor, a young man with too many ideas. Nell stayed on because she was sixty-eight and her dead husband—she had left Catholicism after Bellerton—had been the pastor of their Connecticut church for the entirety of their marriage. Plus, the thought of the gossip if she left now was too much.

She dragged the back of her wrist across her forehead, paused from pushing the spoon through sticky dough. The phone jangled. She huffed, annoyed by its intrusion, and let the answering machine pick up. She half-expected her son's voice, but emptiness floated across the static. The caller left no message, so it wasn't her stern and capable daughter either. A telemarketer then. She was right to ignore it.

Nell slid the pans into the oven. She set a timer, then settled into her armchair, a Daphne St. James romance novel unopened in her lap. She wanted to be alone, to do only things that required meeting no one's needs but her own.

She wobbled between reading and napping until the timer clanged, and the cakes sat on the cooling racks. The bowls and measuring cups she washed by hand; the counters she wiped with a blue sponge. She cracked the window over the sink, let the cool air rush in. She swallowed a pill and lay on the couch, the hours long.

She slept, or thought she did, jolted awake by the persistently ringing phone. The pill made her limbs sandbags, and by the time she sat up it had stopped. A minute later, it started again. Nell picked up the receiver just as the answering machine clicked. She waited through the recorded greeting, her own voice strange in her ears, then spoke into the silence that followed the beep. "Hello?"

The phone receiver in Nell's hand grew heavy as she waited for the static on the line to resolve into a voice: Ada May Delacourt, who she hadn't heard from in nearly fifty years, with news that crashed across the decades into Nell's quiet, humble world.

The past always finds you, regardless of how far behind you've left it.

◆ ◆ ◆

No one in her adult life had ever heard of Bellerton, and Nell preferred it that way. She did not reminisce about that place and period set apart from the rest of her life, but after she returned the phone to its cradle and wiped her sweaty hand on her apron, she thought of nothing else.

She settled into her reading chair, propped her feet on the ottoman.

When had Nell known that Deena didn't truly belong? Her mind kept returning to the May Queen election, the evening suspended in the folds of her memory: Ada May glowing, her lips like twin shells. Even all these years later, Nell remembered how she was swept up by that loveliness, Ada May like a beautiful piece of glass. Deena had raised a hand against her when none of the rest dared. That was the first time Nell had an urge to strike Deena, to spit in her face. Who did she think she was? The answer would turn out to be no one. A girl with an unhappy past.

Now that she was no longer young and foolish, could she articulate why the May Queen vote had mattered so much? Or all that silliness with the ribbons? Deena had an unnatural obsession with hers, petting it as one might an expensive fur.

But Nell, too, had coveted her own ribbon. With her pocket money, she bought a length of it. Velvety soft as a cat's ear, she liked how wearing it made her feel—grown-up and pretty. She had penciled her initials underneath, marking it hers. Other girls made similar alterations, laying claim to a thing that they owned. Sheba notched the ends. Prissy stitched hers with a similarly colored thread. Ada May affixed a pin, the brassy color shading into her red hair. Fred borrowed Sheba's lipstick and imprinted hers with a kiss.

But her ribbon, her beautiful ribbon. Nell had lost it during that final journey into the woods. The verdant green blended with the forest, and though they searched, it had vanished into the place where lost objects—and people—went. At losing it, she had sobbed. She should have seen the omen for what it was.

After the incident—when they realized what they had done—she was frantic with fear.

The memory of what happened next was both clear and hazy. She, along with Sheba, Prissy, and Fred, walked up the hill to the president's house, ready to face Mrs. Tibbert and confess what they'd done. She couldn't remember why Ada May had not been invited. The girls were led into the sitting room and tea was brought out, though no one drank it. An unseen clock marked time. The chintz-patterned wallpaper seemed to conceal hidden messages. When Mrs. Tibbert finally showed herself, the tea was cold. The girls had been waiting for nearly an hour.

They told her everything, stumbling over one another to get it all out: the horses, the barn, the ride into the woods. What had happened to Deena. The water, the creek.

"And what would you have me do now?" Mrs. Tibbert asked when they finished.

The four girls looked at each other; this was not the question they had expected. Nell remembered tugging at the collar of her blouse with the feeling that the room was strangling her.

"Bellerton is a special place," Mrs. Tibbert said. She sat back in her chair, tugged her skirt past her knees. "Students, especially anointed ones like yourselves, keep Bellerton's values intact." The hidden clock chimed once. Mrs. Tibbert folded her hands in her lap.

"I'm aware of your evening excursions. I chose not to intervene. Bellerton knows how to right itself. And it did." She leaned forward, her eyes flashing. "I congratulate you on doing what was necessary."

The next thing Nell recalled was Mrs. Tibbert walking them to the door. Her parting words were unequivocal. "We all protect our kind. Like to like, backwards to forwards. We stick with our own. And that's what you did. My Belles."

Ada May was waiting for them when they returned to South Hall. "You're back from your visit with Mrs. Tibbert," she said, though Nell was certain they hadn't told her. "Is everything straightened out now? You understand how things will be?" She was smiling, beautiful and shimmering as ever, but menace crawled beneath her words.

The Belles had escaped the incident unscathed, but were tied for the rest of their lives to one another and to Bellerton.

What had followed was a surprising return to normal. She went back to stealing small trinkets, here and there, but no further punishment came. She had stolen the first time around because the divorce had left her family's finances strained, and she was envious of the others' nice things. She never took from Deena. It was obvious that she also lacked fine goods, and it would have felt wrong.

Now, all these years later, the past had bubbled up. Nell recalled the stories of the girls who had disappeared over the years. How many more secrets would soon come to light? It would take more than one missing girl to tarnish Bellerton's brightness, but maybe the darkness hidden beneath Bellerton's gleam might finally surface at last.

◆ ◆ ◆

THAT NIGHT, AFTER ADA MAY'S CALL, NELL DREAMED SHE WAS back on the Bellerton grounds, and she moved through the campus, attempting to call out a warning to the attending girls. Still dreaming, she returned to her Bellerton room in South Hall, and slipped into the bed. She knew it was a dream, but the room felt real, the furniture arranged exactly as she remembered it. Her hands were balled into fists atop the duvet, and the smell of lavender perfume hung in the air.

Nell was shaken by seeing Bellerton again, even in her sleep. She breathed deeply to calm her beating heart, and slowly she unclenched her fingers, gasping in surprise when two velvet ribbons—hers and Deena's—tumbled out.

Chapter 38

ADA MAY

FOR the rest of her life, Ada May refused to go swimming. She avoided trips to beaches and lakes, and she never used any pool, not even the one in her own backyard. She awoke most nights to the sound of Deena's hushed footsteps outside her door.

Not Deena. Lettie. The girl who betrayed her. The girl who destroyed her family's legacy, undoing everything they had built. A century and a half's worth of educating girls for the world was gone in a heartbeat.

After Peggy found the skull, the rest of Deena's remains were unearthed. Soon, more remains were discovered along the stretch of creek and throughout the woods. Bones upon bones upon bones. There was an investigation into the occurrences at Bellerton over the years, and decades-old missing persons reports resurfaced. Rulings of accidental campus deaths were revisited. Lawsuits against the trustees blossomed. Disgruntled graduates penned op-eds, wrote blogs, spoke to journalists. Students began to transfer to other colleges, first in a trickle and then a flood. A press conference could not staunch the tide until—more than a century and a half after its founding—Bellerton was forced to close.

During it all, Ada May remained silent, wrapped in her private pain, witnessing the decimation of the place that was the crowning glory of her youth, the gem she was meant to pass on to the next generation. The Belles refused to speak to her. They had collectively erased her from their lives.

When Bellerton's permanent closure was finalized, Ada May drove alone from Richmond to visit one final time. Her husband had recently passed; her children had grown and moved away. The campus had been shut down for nearly a year at that point. The land was being sold. Her family would keep the cemetery plot where her ancestors were buried, but the rest of her legacy would be gone.

She arrived a few hours before dusk in the fading days of summer. She parked and strolled to the front quad, remembering the rose beds that had bloomed salmon pink and Southern white in spring, the broad-leafed magnolias, and the azaleas tipped with magenta and coral buds. Bellerton had remained glorious in her memories, a place where young women walked confidently across a sun-dappled quad with books pressed to their chests, the leafy oaks swaying above.

Now the campus was in ruins. The buildings were smaller than she remembered, and the grounds had grown ragged with neglect. Ivy threaded up the brick facades, and weeds sprouted between the cracks in the sidewalk. The overgrown grass ran wild. She climbed South Hall's porch steps, heard the scrabble of small rodents darting about. The paint had worn from the warped boards that had decayed rapidly with no one to manage their upkeep. She tried South Hall's door and was surprised that it opened.

The lights didn't work, but the sun hovered just above the mountaintops and streamed golden into the rooms. Ada May ran her fingers across the wallpaper in the foyer. She tapped her image in the enormous mirror that still hung in the Jackson Drawing Room, named for her great-grandmother, her fingertips streaking through dust. The room had been emptied, the brocade curtains stripped from their rods. A corner of the ceiling was swollen with damp, and the crown molding bubbled and peeled.

Ada May took the stairs to the second floor, where the Belles had lived. The door to every room stood open. Slowly she walked the hall, peering into each one. Furniture was scattered about: a bed here, a dresser there, two desks pushed together. The sun washed the walls with an amber hue that made it feel as if time had stopped.

She saved her old freshman room for last, overwhelmed with nostalgia. She had been so happy here, wrapped in glory days that she believed would never end. Cool air flooded through the open window, and Ada May leaned her weight into the sash, staring out across the grounds. What was she left with but the residue of the past and all that history? Her inheritance, her influence, her power—all lost forever.

She had thought often of Bellerton in her idle moments, especially that feverish spring afternoon when she had been crowned May Queen. The sharp brightness of the blue sky. The brick buildings and covered porches and grand arching trees. She only had to close her eyes to hear the rush of thundered applause and feel the biting heat on her sun-warmed cheeks. The day was like an anointing, and nothing else she experienced in all her years compared to its splendor.

Carefully, Ada May straddled the open window, then swung both feet around to dangle over the side. She estimated she was perhaps thirty feet above the ground, the porch and porticos having long ago been taken down on this side of the building. Not such an easy maneuver in linen pants and wedge sandals, not at her age. She gripped either side of the window frame, nails digging into warped and weathered wood, and looked out over what was left of her family's legacy. Tradition was not so strong a thing after all. She was the end of the line. The last Belle.

Seeing Deena that first day, all those years ago, Ada May had underestimated her. Never in her wildest dreams would she have thought Bellerton able to topple because of one lowly girl gone missing. In all senses of the word, erased. And here she was, facing the same kind of erasure, with nothing left of her legacy.

In the quiet, lonely moments of her life, she wondered what might have been if Deena had voted for her. Perhaps she would have forgiven Deena's deceit and protected her secret. It could have all happened so differently.

Ada May waved at the modest white sign outside the iron gate, took note of the imposing brick wall and the black ribbon road that gaped like a wound. From her memories the pristine white columns rose up, and the solidity of the brick buildings locked into place. The orderly, trimmed paths. The well-tended pasture. The dangerous thicket of woods and the slash of creek.

All of it beautiful, seductive.

All of it a warning.

Ada May belonged to Bellerton. The mountains darkened as the sun dropped behind their peaks. She leaned forward to get a better look at the place she loved more than any other, all of it undone because of that girl.

Then, Ada May let go.

ACKNOWLEDGMENTS

I am deeply appreciative to the many individuals and institutions whose support over the years and throughout this process enabled me to write and publish the book in your hands. I hope it's the first of many.

As a first-generation college graduate and federal Pell Grant recipient, this novel was partially built from my complicated experiences within spaces of learning, especially in higher education. I'm grateful to all my teachers, instructors, and professors along the way, with special acknowledgment to Jan Finkbeiner for her very earliest encouragement, for making space for creativity and play, and for helping me learn about the myriad ways of storytelling; and to Cathryn Hankla and Richard Dillard for putting up with me.

Two books aided in writing this novel, particularly histories and experiences outside my own: *The Education of the Southern Belle: Higher Education and Student Socialization in the Antebellum South* by Christie Anne Farnham, and *From Whence Cometh My Help: The African American Community at Hollins College* by Ethel Morgan Smith. I am gratefully indebted to both writers for these texts.

Thank you to Elizabeth George and the members of the board at the Elizabeth George Foundation for supporting the completion of this novel through a truly life-changing fellowship. Your generosity was a major vote of confidence that arrived at a tender time. Thank you to Sarah Cypher and Alys Dutton for your generous guidance, and to my recommenders without whom I would have never made it through the process: Steve Himmer, Michael Nye, Lisa Page, Lynn Steger Strong, and Cutter Wood.

Thank you to the DC Commission on the Arts and Humanities for annually supporting writers and artists throughout the District to ensure a city where the arts and cultural activities thrive, and for awarding me fellowships that supported the writing of this novel. Special thanks to Kamanzi Kalisa and Kayla Williams. Thank you to the staff and faculty at the Sewanee Writers' Conference, Maurice Carlos Ruffin and Jill McCorkle in particular. Thank you to the program team at Catapult for a scholarship that led to a whirlwind year during which a large part of this novel was written and revised.

Thank you to Michael at the erstwhile Office Depot in Dupont Circle for an end-of-the-day, last-minute print job of my draft in its entirety that was my first time seeing the words on the page; that stack of warm papers made this whole endeavor finally feel real.

My smart and sharp-eyed editor Laura Brown perfectly understood the Belles and Bellerton, and patiently worked with my occasional stubbornness to make the novel shine. This book would be a lesser version of itself without you, and I am so grateful for your enthusiasm and your incisive edits. Natalie Argentina's warm correspondence is always appreciated, as are your skills in keeping the trains moving on time. Thank you Holly Rice-Baturin and Zakiya Jamal for amplifying the Belles' story and continually helping this book find its readers. Annette Sweeney's copyediting prowess is astounding, and I'm grateful your brain thinks in ways mine does not. Tim Hepp, who I knew in the days back when I was a book slinger, and the rest of the tireless S&S salesforce team, thank you for your part in telling the story of Bellerton to a wider readership.

And enormous gratitude to the team at Atria, those I've met and those I haven't, who have touched this book along the way. It takes a village to release a book into the world, and I'm grateful to all of you.

Eternal applause goes to my brilliant, hardworking, and savvy agent Jamie Carr, and the whole team at The Book Group, for seeing potential within a rough pile of pages and leaning into the possibilities. A heartful thank you for taking me on, and for every bit of guidance, editorial feedback, business acumen, and cheerleading you've provided. I'm so lucky to have you in my corner. Thank you for helping me realize this book into existence. We make a great team.

Julianna Haubner provided feedback that lit me on fire in the best possible way. I cannot overstate how much your subsequent generosity and championing of this book set in motion so many things that I was afraid to dream would ever be possible. Thank you for everything.

A huge thank you to librarians at libraries across the country, especially those in my hometown and those in my neighborhood DC Public Library branch. Without libraries, I would not have found the books that fed me, the books that changed me, and the books that shaped me. Beyond just books, libraries are critical institutions whose staff provide resources and services to everyone in the communities they serve, and they deserve our admiration—and our protection. I truly believe that books expanded my empathy and led me to be curious about others and the world at large when I was growing up; they were, in the words of Rudine Sims Bishop, "windows, mirrors, and sliding glass doors." Without access to every kind of book at the library, I would be a different person. Support funding for your local library and librarians' salaries. Vote for library board candidates who understand the necessary role libraries provide. Speak out when these individuals and institutions are facing censorship or dealing with book bans.

Thank you booksellers for uplifting stories every day in your work, often for not much more than minimum wage and galleys. You have a huge role in creating a robust literary culture and providing services to readers and book lovers in cities and towns across the country. This former bookseller salutes you, and I'd love to share coffee with any of you, anytime.

Several people were generous with me or my book in ways that made a difference. Kelly Goodman, aka the horse whisperer, you have my gratitude for your horse read. Any equine or equestrian errors that remain are wholly my own. To the authors who took the time to read my book and write incredibly thoughtful words about it in the form of a blurb, I appreciate you coming to bat for a debut author. Many other authors along the way also generously answered my questions, jumped on phone calls or Zooms, texted reminders to breathe, sent words of encouragement over email, or offered their camaraderie and support. I am so grateful to each of you, especially for your time. None of us have enough of it, and I appreciate that you shared some of yours with me: Kristen L. Berry, Katy Hays, Vera Kurian, Melissa Pace, Joanna Pearson, Katie Runde, Sophie Stava, Abby White, Penny Zang, and Liann Zhang.

To the members of the Writing Group of Awesome, in many different iterations, thanks for sharing space, time, and feedback together. To my writing teachers, workshop classmates, and writing students over the years, both in-person and online, thank you for the opportunity to learn from one another. My appreciation goes out to the editors at various literary journals who I've worked with across the years, and to those who have read and published my work. It's always a labor of love, but being a part of that ecosystem has shaped me and sustained me, and I'm grateful to you all, particularly Steve Himmer and Michael Nye.

Lynn Steger Strong deserves an entire page of acknowledgments. A brilliant writer and a brilliant teacher, you are one of the most genuinely kind people out there. I don't know where I would be if I hadn't been accepted to your novel generator, or where I would be without your ongoing support. A huge, unending thank-you to the cohort of my fellow writers and early readers who were also in Lynn's class: Xian Chiang-Waren, Deena Drewis, Ben Izzo, Sarah Kasbeer, Jean Kawahara, Shari MacDonald Strong, and Peter Mayshle. Special acknowledgment goes to Ben Constantino for his ghost read. And all my love and appreciation to Heart Attach, formerly known as Demon Puppy: Sonia Feldman and Nicole VanderLinden. I'm damn lucky to call you both my friends. Our conversations always nourish me and remind me that, whatever I'm feeling, I'm not in it alone.

Thank you Rita Mortellaro for the donut walks, for having my back with the laptop that one time, and for allowing me to be my best self in your presence. To Kristin Russell, whom I met later in the process of this book but whom I instantly knew I wanted to befriend. You've been a source of joy, support, and grounding in a difficult business. I'm in awe of your strength and wisdom.

My family deserves a huge thank-you for cheering me on, even when they weren't quite sure what the hell I was doing: Tom, Anne, Christian, Courtney, and Thomas. Mom, I'm sorry you can't read this book, but the reason I love books as much as I do is all because of you. Dad, you're a natural born storyteller. I got the gene from you.

To Mike, Melville hater, who encouraged me every step of the way, talked me through every high and low, and who didn't flinch when I said I was writing a novel. Your love and support mean the world to me, and your health insurance is very nice, too.

To Caspar, Pierre, Floyd, and Toby, there's never been a dull moment with you around. Simone, my familiar, I miss you still. You were utterly perfect.

Finally, thank you to the readers who picked up this book. I'm honored and grateful that you chose to spend time with my very bad girls.

ABOUT
the AUTHOR

LACEY N. DUNHAM has received support from the Elizabeth George Foundation, the DC Commission on the Arts and Humanities, the Sewanee Writers' Conference, and Catapult. Her writing has been published in *Ploughshares*, *The Kenyon Review*, *Witness*, and elsewhere. Born and raised on a small family farm, she now lives in Washington, DC. Find out more at laceyndunham.com.

ATRIA BOOKS, an imprint of Simon & Schuster, fosters an open environment where ideas flourish, bestselling authors soar to new heights, and tomorrow's finest voices are discovered and nurtured. Since its launch in 2002, Atria has published hundreds of bestsellers and extraordinary books, which would not have been possible without the invaluable support and expertise of its team and publishing partners. Thank you to the Atria Books colleagues who collaborated on *The Belles*, as well as to the hundreds of professionals in the Simon & Schuster advertising, audio, communications, design, ebook, finance, human resources, legal, marketing, operations, production, sales, supply chain, subsidiary rights, and warehouse departments who help Atria bring great books to light.

EDITORIAL
Laura Brown
Natalie Argentina

JACKET DESIGN
Kelli McAdams
James Iacobelli

MARKETING
Zakiya Jamal

MANAGING EDITORIAL
Paige Lytle
Shelby Pumphrey
Lacee Burr
Sofia Echeverry

PRODUCTION
Annette Pagliaro Sweeney
Vanessa Silverio
Richard Willett
Lexy East

PUBLICITY
Holly Rice-Baturin

PUBLISHING OFFICE
Suzanne Donahue
Abby Velasco

SUBSIDIARY RIGHTS
Nicole Bond
Sara Bowne
Rebecca Justiniano